LOVE, LIFE
AND
ALL THAT JAZZ...

Ahmed Faiyaz grew up in Bangalore and now lives in Dubai. He's a strategist by profession, with a number of years in management consulting behind him. He is the bestselling author of *Scammed* and *Another Chance*. His stories are also featured in the bestselling Urban Shots series.

LOVE, LIFE AND ALL THAT JAZZ...

AHMED FAIYAZ

Published by
Rupa Publications India Pvt. Ltd 2014
7/16, Ansari Road, Daryaganj
New Delhi 110002

Sales Centres:

Allahabad Bengaluru Chennai
Hyderabad Jaipur Kathmandu
Kolkata Mumbai

Copyright © Ahmed Faiyaz 2010

First published in India by Grey Oak Publishers, 2010

All rights reserved.
No part of this publication may be reproduced, transmitted,
or stored in a retrieval system, in any form or by any means,
electronic, mechanical, photocopying, recording or otherwise,
without the prior permission of the publisher.

ISBN: 978-81-291-2993-2

First impression 2014

10 9 8 7 6 5 4 3 2 1

The moral right of the author has been asserted.

Printed by Rakmo Press Pvt. Ltd., New Delhi

This book is sold subject to the condition that it shall not,
by way of trade or otherwise, be lent, resold, hired out, or otherwise circulated,
without the publisher's prior consent, in any form of binding or cover other than
that in which it is published.

Contents

Part 1: Change

1. A Cup of Chai — 3
2. New Beginning and a Night to Remember — 10
3. Adjustments — 17
4. New Lives and Catching Up — 26
5. Choices — 38
6. Memories — 47

Part 2: Together

7. Hope — 59
8. Coming Home — 68
9. Go Goa — 76
10. Strike One… — 88

Part 3: Falling Apart

11. Strike Two… — 97
12. Gloom — 105
13. Distance — 115
14. Loss and Pain — 120
15. Drifting Along — 131
16. Traction — 138
17. Different Directions — 146

Part 4: Another Life

18.	Crossroads	157
19.	Something Else	162
20.	Home, a Different Place…	173
21.	A New Start	184
22.	Someplace Else	194

Part 5: Love and Longing

23.	Lucky Storm	207
24.	Bright Shiny Morning	223
25.	Progress	228
26.	Commitment	232
27.	Standing Up	242
28.	Life is a Mixed Bag	252

Part 6: Living Your Dreams

29.	Bliss	261
30.	In the Skies Above	266
31.	Nostalgia	272

Thank You 285

PART 1
CHANGE

*'Life is what happens to you
while you're busy making other plans.'*
—JOHN LENNON

1
A Cup of Chai

> 'Sooner or later we all discover that the important moments in life are not the advertised ones, not the birthdays, the graduations, the weddings, not the great goals achieved. The real milestones are less prepossessing. They come to the door of memory.'
>
> —SUSAN B. ANTHONY

18 JULY 2003
India Tea Centre, near Churchgate Station, Mumbai

It was 6.30 p.m. Tanveer, dressed in formal trousers, a light blue shirt and a grey tie, struggled his way into the dilapidated old Victorian building that housed the India Tea Centre. He was soaking wet after a short walk from Churchgate Station, having encountered a raging downpour that was considered usual in Mumbai. The sky wore a dark shade of purplish grey, with the setting sun hidden behind the clouds bringing in an air of darkness and gloom, and a storm lurking above. The gusty winds from the Arabian Sea made a whistling sound as they rustled through the branches of the oak tree in the compound outside the India Tea Centre. Tanveer was on time as usual, despite the long train ride and the threatening storm outside and, after a short trip to the restroom to wipe his hair, he took his place at the same table at the far end of the Tea Centre that he and the gang had occupied every other day for the past three years. Removing his tie and undoing his collar button, Tanveer motioned to the waiter to bring him his usual cup of cutting chai. He patiently sat back and awaited the arrival of Tania, Sameer, Vikram and Naina. Tania, Sameer and Vikram were his closest friends from college, with whom he had spent three memorable years. They had completed their Bachelor's in Management Studies just two months ago from the prestigious Sherwood College. Naina was two batches junior to them and she and Vikram had been dating for the past few months. Waiting for his friends and his cup of chai, Tanveer began to think about the interview he had had with Oceania Bank earlier in the day.

The waiter interrupted Tanveer's flow of thoughts, telling him in an apologetic tone, 'Sir, aapki chai.'

Twenty minutes later, Tanveer saw Sameer walk in through the door hand in hand with Tania, who wore a figure-hugging blue dress. He remembered how smitten he had been by Tania when he'd first met her. He was, at that point of time, envious of Sameer who had begun dating Tania. Sameer was not conventionally good-looking but the manner in which he carried himself set him apart from the crowd. He was sophisticated, articulate and well read. All these were qualities that Tanveer wanted to emulate. He thought how naïve he had been in those initial days in Mumbai. Even now, he was awestruck by Tania's stunningly beautiful eyes and her smile. Even though his heart skipped a beat and he averted his gaze from Tania's cheerful look, she put him at ease in her easy-going manner in much the same way as she had three years ago when they had first met. Tanveer rose from his comfortable chair to shake hands with Sam and exchanged a peck on the cheek with Tania. Sam, Vicky and Tanveer had over the past three years become thicker than thieves despite being quite different in their mannerisms, their attitude, family background and their outlook towards life, while Tania had been the centre of their attention for different reasons.

Sameer, with an air of concern, told Tanveer, 'Dude, why don't you come over after Athena and stay at my place for a couple of days? I know your job hunt is on but I leave in five days and it will be good to have you around and make you do my packing. You can even have a good portion of what's being cooked for me. Mum is trying to feed me a little extra, now that I am going away,' he laughed.

Tanveer smiled and remembered the delicious food that Mrs Ahuja had often made for the group. Mr and Mrs Ahuja were among the nicest people one could come across and were extremely fond of Vikram and Tanveer. Tanveer was treated as part of the family and joined them most Sundays for a family lunch. Tanveer had also interned at Mr Ahuja's office during summer and winter breaks and had, during college, taken up little projects every Saturday that earned him some pocket money and gave him experience in finance—his subject of interest. His dream was to become a leading institutional banker some day. The Ahujas were also particularly fond of Tania and it was a given to them that Sameer would marry Tania in the not so distant future. Tania gave him a cynical smile.

'That's mean. You want him around to do your packing! You should be ashamed, using him like this,' she said, looking at Sameer.

'No, he's meticulous and organized. Besides, Mum loves having him around, like she does with you. It takes some focus off me,' Sameer said and continued smiling at her. 'Besides, I could then spend some quality time with you. What say Tani Pie?'

'You're plain evil! That's a great idea, but I still don't know why you have to go away,' said Tania with a gleam in her eyes, being affectionate and feeling sad at the same time.

Sam kissed her long tresses. 'Yes, of course, sweetheart. Without doubt. We've discussed this, right?' he said with a hint of irritation and Tania looked tense. Sameer appeared torn between what he wanted and what he loved, and looked at her with affection. 'We've spoken about this, babe. We'll manage. The UK isn't that far away and it's just two years—they'll fly,' he said.

Tania rested her head on his shoulders, wondering about the two years to come, given that there hadn't been a day in the past three years when they hadn't spoken to each other.

Looking at his watch, Tanveer got restless and asked, 'Where is Vicky? I spoke to him an hour ago and he said he would be here in five minutes. This is typical of him, yaar! I rushed from my interview at Oceania Bank to get here in time.' He signalled to the waiter to get him another cup of chai.

'Chill. Vicky knows we'll head out to the party only after 9 p.m. He'll come accordingly. Hope the interview went well. When will they get back to you?' Sameer asked calmly.

Tania, being accustomed to Vikram's ways, said, looking at her phone, 'Yes, I hope you get the job, Tanveer. Vicky is picking up Naina, who is still getting dressed. Okay, they want us to meet them directly outside Athena in forty-five minutes. So let's leave in ten minutes then.' The boys nodded in the affirmative.

'Yes, I hope I get the job too. They're offering thirty grand a month, and the opportunities to grow are good. I can send back at least half of what I make back home,' Tanveer said with some hope and excitement.

'Spend on yourself too, dude. There are certain things you need in life. Be responsible like you are, but don't neglect yourself,' Sameer advised him in his big-brotherly fashion.

Tania turned towards him. 'Yes, Tanveer. You better eat nicely, get a good place and go buy a decent car. How long will you take the local train?' she asked with concern in her voice.

'True, but my sister needs to get married next year, the younger one, Zoya, goes to college this year. My dad retires from his job with LIC this year too—his pension will barely cover living expenses,' Tanveer replied, looking a little stressed. Tania placed her hand on Tanveer's and gave him a troubled look, knowing that her friend would put his responsibilities above his dreams. That was how deeply rooted he was with his family.

'Vicky and Naina seem to be going steady. Surprisingly, this one has lasted. We don't have a flavour of the week as we did with Vicky in the past. I miss his skirt-chasing stories, dating women and breaking up with them…but it's good to see him settle down with one girl,' Sam said with a grin. Tania, with some concern and an air of doubt, added her point of view, 'Well, I hope she lasts. She is a nice girl. She is so unlike him, she is very focused towards her modelling career. Vicky needs some focus and balance in his life too. He needs to start doing something!'

'Yes, I have been persuading him to join his dad's company,' Tanveer said, repeating the advice he kept giving Vicky from the first day they'd spoken.

'Guys chill, Vicky is a cool dude. He'll sort himself out when the time comes. He's intelligent, I'm sure he'll make it bigger than any of us. He was born with a silver spoon too,' Sameer said. Tania looked affectionately at Sameer. 'But you're the most creative, Sam. It's amazing, the way you come up with ideas and new ways of doing things,' she gushed.

'Yes dude, your advertising campaign submissions last year were amazing. You'll be an ad guru some day,' Tanveer chipped in.

'Don't know about that. My dad really wants me to take over his business. He is facing challenging times with global biggies setting up shop in Mumbai.' His father hoped for him to return and take over Ahuja Financial Advisory Services, an advisory and investment management firm he had built from scratch with a great deal of perseverance twenty-five years ago. Tanveer sat back in his chair and asked, 'I wonder where our careers will take us and what will become of us. Who knows if we will remain the close friends we are now.'

'Time flies na? It seems like yesterday when Vicky and I met you. It was a couple of weeks before Sam took me to Jazz and Blues and sang 'The Way You Look Tonight' to me,' Tania told Tanveer, with her thoughts going back to the old days, and then looked at Sameer.

Tanveer laughed loudly. 'All right, I know he took you there, didn't know he sang to you. Are you going to sing tonight dude?' he asked.

'Oye behave! Tani Pie, introduce him to some girls you know. It's time he went on his first date,' Sameer said with a grin, which had Tania in splits.

They got up to leave for Athena after Sameer settled the bill. Sam walked ahead to get his car out from a parking spot two buildings away, while Tania and Tanveer waited at the portico of the old Tea Centre as the downpour had now reduced to a steady drizzle and the sun had long disappeared across the sea, far behind the monstrous rain clouds. They parked outside at Athena and got out of the car to see Vikram, in cargos and a T-shirt that read 'FCUK WAR', striding across from the opposite side of the street with Naina, who was in a black dress, in tow. She had her hair let loose about her shoulders and looked stunning. Sameer walked a step forward to embrace them.

'Hey, Naina, you're looking great,' he said and looked at Vikram with a sarcastic grin, 'An extended noon nap huh, Vicky? Why didn't you make it for a game of tennis yesterday?' Vikram in his cool, devil-may-care tone and demeanour said, 'Sorry dude, Mum sent me to pick up some relatives at the airport and after that I took Naina shopping. Let's play for sure tomorrow. You leave in a few days anyway. You must be busy packing, na?' Sameer nodded. Naina said a warm 'hi' to everyone while Vikram patted Tania's cheek affectionately and moved to talk to Tanveer, saying to him in a hushed tone, 'Dude, don't worry. I have you covered tonight, no thanks needed, and don't say anything about paying me back.'

Tanveer gave him a thankful nod but felt a bit embarrassed at having Vicky or Sam cover for him every time they went out for dinner or to party. 'Dude, I keep telling you it's time for you to bag a lady and not carry a ladies' bag,' Vicky said with a broad grin, at which everyone laughed.

'It's Tania's, yaar! She asked me to hold it for a minute while she adjusted her hair,' Tanveer replied, looking flabbergasted and turned to move towards Tania, quickly giving her back her clutch. Tanveer, remembering how early he got to the Tea Centre, looked at Vicky and said, 'Yaar, you mentioned one hour back that you were getting here in five minutes and you walk in here late as usual.' Vikram laughed defensively and put on an innocent smile, 'Really? No dude, I meant you get there in five minutes and I will see you at Athena directly,' he said, winking at Sameer.

'Sure! I'm sure that's what you meant,' Tanveer said sarcastically. Tanveer and Sameer walked in with Naina who told them excitedly about her advertisement shoot for an ice cream brand earlier that morning, while Tania and Vicky followed a few steps behind, discussing the plans for a surprise farewell party at Vicky's Alibaug cottage for Sameer before he went away.

∽

2
New Beginning and a Night to Remember

'Life...is not simply a series of exciting new ventures. The future is not always a whole new ball game. There tends to be unfinished business. One trails all sorts of things around with one, things that simply won't be got rid of.'

—ANITA BROOKNER

1 August 2003
Said School of Business, Oxford University, UK

It was Sameer's first day at the university. It was a warm and pleasant day at Oxford but Sameer was feeling extremely homesick. He felt butterflies in the pit of his stomach. He had been finding it difficult adjusting to the food and doing his own laundry. For the past six days while settling into his room and campus life, he had been talking to Tania and his mum three times a day. His dad had called him to wish him luck the night before and had told him to keep faith—that he would get used to it. One saving grace was his roommate, Samar. He was an Indian but had been born and raised in Australia. Samar and he walked towards the cafeteria. Samar asked, 'So how did you like the first day? What do you think of the professors and our batch mates?' Reflecting on his day so far, Sameer said, 'Well, the professors seem good; I look forward to class. With the batch mates, I don't know. Most of them are so many years older than us and with such different backgrounds. I guess it will take time for people to open up. I look forward to networking though. We have two years to make friends and build a network don't we?'

'You're right on that, mate! Many of these people are over thirty years old. We've got make an effort. Well, there is Kim, the girl from our class,' Samar replied, waving out to her. Kim and Simone, who was her roommate and was doing a communications course at Oxford, walked up to them and exchanged introductions with Samar and Sameer.

'Why don't you girls join us for a beer? We'll walk you back to your dorm after that. I could really use a drink,' Samar said. The girls agreed and the four of them headed to a pub nearby for a drink. Sameer got a call. It was Tania at the other end, 'Hey Sam, how was your first day at school? Hope you had a good one.'

'Well, not bad. Just going down for a drink with my roommate and a few others from class. It's a mixed bunch, people from different places who have done different things. Most of them are older than us. But I will get used to it. It's a matter of time. We have assignments already, do you believe that?' Sameer replied and asked, 'How was your day? Did you get started on your first project?' They spoke for a while before hanging up as the four of them entered a pub. 'You have a good start at work. I won't be able to come online for a couple of days. We have these assignments already and my team wants to meet every evening to get them done. By the time I get done it will be midnight for you. I'll give you a buzz after class tomorrow though. Goodnight,' Sameer said.

'It's okay, we'll manage. We'll talk tomorrow, good night,' Tania said and hung up. She thought, *it's not okay, I don't know how we are going to make this work.* She told herself, *I need to relax. I'm just too used to having him around all the time. We'll get used to it.*

'Was that your girlfriend, mate?' Samar asked him, to which Sameer nodded. Samar continued, 'Good luck managing the long distance. It won't be easy, mate. Cheers to your long-distance relationship.'

'Well, it is difficult. I broke up before I came here. It gets difficult managing expectations. Being in different places can drive you apart, but hope it works for you,' Simone added.

'Thanks. Tania is a sweetheart. We've been through a lot in our relationship. It's been three years. I'll do what I can to make it work. She is very understanding too,' Sameer said with hope. After two beers with his new acquaintances he decided to leave and go back to his room.

'I'll see you later, people, it was nice catching up. I need to go and rest. It's been a long day,' he said walking out of the pub after hearing, 'Cheers, take care, mate!' from the girls and, 'I'll be back in an hour,' from Samar. He walked towards their residence accommodation with a desolate look on his face, battling the piercing cold breeze. He looked at the purplish glow in the sky and watched a stream of people walk to and from the lane leading to the underground station, realizing that the English summer was cooler than the winter back home in Mumbai. Alone for the first time, he remembered the night before he left Mumbai to embark upon his new journey in life.

SEVEN DAYS EARLIER... 24 JULY 2003
Tania's home, Cuffe Parade

Sameer and Tania walked into Tania's room and he pulled her close with a mischievous grin while his gaze met hers. He took off his shoes and his sweatshirt while Tania looked at him invitingly.

He put his arms around her and helped her undress before he took her in for a warm shower together.

'I love you so much, this feels so good,' he told her. He moved her hair to one side and kissed her at the nape of her neck and her warm bare back at which she exclaimed 'Mmm...' ecstatically. Sameer realized how long it could be till they made love again. Tania smiled coyly at him and splashed water on his face. Her initial shyness about being in this situation with Sameer had almost gone. They wiped each other dry after the warm bath and Sameer carried her to the bed where he made love to her passionately.

'I have waited so long to let you make me feel this,' she told him softly while he kissed her again. 'It's been worth the wait, sweetheart,' he said with an intense gaze and added, 'After this, I'm only going to miss you more. It's going to make it harder for us being apart.'

Tania sighed and clung on to him, realizing that he would be thousands of miles away from her at the same time the next day. She felt pangs of loss and sadness. The person who had grown to be the closest to her and with whom she was waiting to spend the rest of her life was moving so far away from her. For her, a world beyond him did not exist. They had managed to spend the past three hours together without anyone disturbing them. They made up after the argument they'd had as Sameer had been too busy to spend time with Tania till that evening, having to meet relatives and wind up his shopping. He'd met her at the Louis Pierre store in Crawford Market and they had come to Tania's place together. Sameer meanwhile playfully ran his fingers through her beautiful tresses and had mixed feelings about flying out the next evening. On one hand, he was sad and worried about a life away from his parents, his younger brother Rajveer whom he adored, Vikram and the gang and, most importantly, Tania. Tania was his first love. He remembered the intimacy they had shared four nights ago after they had spent time with friends at Athena, and the dip in the sea and the long walk with her on the beach in Alibaug two nights ago, after his farewell party. Sameer and Tania lay in a tiny bed ideally suited to Tania's small frame with their thoughts far away, oblivious to the world outside them. He wondered how he would make the long distance work and about other guys being attracted to Tania. He would miss the way he felt when she smiled at him, when she kissed him softly on his lips while putting her arms around him, her voice, her soft skin and the look in her eyes when she spoke to him. At the same time, Sameer was excited and was looking forward to his life in Oxford and the MBA programme he was enrolled in. He looked forward to meeting and interacting with people from over forty different nations, attending seminars and conclaves where business leaders would speak, and the opportunity to acquire knowledge and hone his skills.

Tania's parents were out for a movie—one which she had planned for and had persuaded them to go to. The Mishras were an easy-going, open-minded couple who understood Tania's wish to spend time with alone Sameer before he left. Sameer and Tania's thoughts were interrupted by Sameer's phone ringing. It was 8.10 p.m. and Vikram had called to say that Naina and he would be picking them up in twenty minutes for a quick dinner. Tanveer had decided not to join them and would instead come to Sameer's place early the next day to help him pack. They got dressed slowly and went down together with Tania's hand in Sameer's and a smile on their faces. The four of them headed for a relaxed dinner at Blue Sea, a popular restaurant near the beach, known for its seafood and great ambience. That night was exceptionally good as there was a clear sky and some gentle breeze—which wasn't a frequent occurrence in the month of July. The rain gods spared Sameer on his last night for a long time to come in Mumbai. The two couples spent some intimate moments and shared a few laughs about the old times. They sipped wine and conversed about the life ahead of them, their plans, things people they knew were doing and how life after college was so different. After dinner, Vikram dropped Tania off at her place. The four of them spoke little during the drive back, being a little drunk and sleepy. Sameer walked her to her porch and gave her a long goodnight kiss while Vikram used the time to flirt with Naina in the car. Tania had tears in her eyes. 'I'll see you tomorrow morning. Please get some sleep,' she said and gave him a tight squeeze.

'Hey, take it easy on yourself. I'll call you when I get home, okay?' Sameer said, running his fingers through her long tresses. Tania nodded and walked towards the door, turning around to look at him again while he stood there smiling at her and waved goodnight. A few minutes later, Vicky dropped Sameer outside his building and with a yawn said, 'Sam, I'll see you tomorrow morning…oops, tomorrow afternoon, I can't wake up that early. I will come with you to the airport. What time do we leave tomorrow?' Sameer leaned against the rear window. 'Come as early as you can. Tanveer and Tania should be there by 10 o'clock. Try and come by lunch time at least. We leave at 4 p.m. for the airport. The flight is at 6.30. I'll give you a wake-up call,' he said and pulled away from the window with a weary smile. Naina got out of the car. She was dolled up as usual, wearing a tight red dress and an intoxicating fragrance. She gave Sameer a hug and stood on her toes to give him a peck on his cheek.

'Goodbye, wise guy. Will miss hanging out with you. Let's chat online whenever you can. Sorry I have my shoot and can't make it tomorrow, but good luck with Oxford and living in the UK. Stay the same,' she said sweetly. Sameer gave her a hug, thanking her, and walked away saying a difficult goodbye to Naina, after which Vicky and she drove away. Sameer wasn't really close to Naina, but her words now and Tania's tears a while back made him realize that he really was going away. Come tomorrow, his life would be completely different from what it had been for twenty-two years.

∽

3
Adjustments

'Wanting to be someone else is a waste of the person you are.'
—KURT COBAIN

2 August 2003
Oceania Bank—Corporate Banking Division, Flora Fountain, Fort, Mumbai

Tanveer was through most of his first day at work. It was past 7 p.m., but he was unsure about when he could go home. He had walked in cheerfully that morning and had spent the first couple of hours filling up forms for human resources. No sooner had he been assigned a desk, a short grim-looking guy with a walrus moustache had walked up to him and told him, 'I am Vinod and you will be working on my team. Remember not to wear dark shirts with cream coloured trousers next time. This is a bank, not an advertising agency. Wear light shirts with dark trousers and shave properly every day.'

Tanveer had nodded along, hanging on to every word. He realized that it was important to get his appearance right. Vinod added, 'Now come with me. You need to sit today and read the manuals and policies we have on lending processes and criteria for lending. I want all of this to be read today. I will ask you questions tomorrow. Also, don't think you can leave at 6 p.m. You will stay and work for as long as you are expected to. That's the way we work.'

Tanveer followed him to his cubicle and said, 'Yes, Vinod, sure, Vinod,' to every instruction that was given to him.

Vinod Agarwal, Tanveer's boss, was an up and coming star at Oceania Bank where he managed a portfolio of over fifty crore rupees in credit and had generated handsome returns for the bank. He was not intelligent or analytical as one perceived most bankers to be, but he made that up with his selling skills, suave personality—and his ability to get someone else to do the work and take the credit for it. Tanveer had spent the whole day reading elaborately drafted manuals and standard operating procedures for lending transactions. He had almost fallen asleep a couple of times but had forced himself to stay awake by having a few more cups of coffee in the pantry. He also met a few other employees who had recently joined and managed to bond with a few of them. None of them had anything nice to say about Vinod and pitied Tanveer for being assigned to his team. Vinod walked towards him while he was going through the last few pages of the manual.

'So, you're almost done, huh? All right, now here are the financial statements of three companies. Tell me, what is the maximum exposure the bank could take in lending to them in light of their financial position? Get it done quickly. You have one hour,' he said firmly.

Tanveer read the financial statements carefully and marked out key facts and figures. He then used the appropriate step-by-step processes in light of the information and, making reasonable assumptions along the way, came up with solutions. He took his recommendation to Vinod in forty-five minutes. Vinod was dumbfounded seeing that Tanveer had managed to work through the documents and come up with solutions. 'All right, leave for today. For the next one month you will be doing stock checks in companies where we have lent against the finished goods inventory. Prepare for a lot of travel and time under the sun,' he said grudgingly.

'No problem, Vinod. I might just need a day off at the end of the month as it is my sister's engagement. Please do oblige,' Tanveer said meekly. Vinod laughed at him and, with a sadistic grin, said, 'Day off? It's your first day here, man. I don't think you will be getting any leave. Forget about it. Here, people are happy if they can attend their own wedding. Anyway, off you go. See you tomorrow. Also boss, spend less time socializing in the pantry. There is enough work to do. When you don't have anything, tell me. I have a lot lined up.'

'Yes, okay Vinod. Thanks and goodnight,' Tanveer said submissively and went to pack up. He walked to the station feeling low and got on the train thinking about how different life was back in college with friends. He had to go and look for a new place to stay close to work as Andheri was too far. Tanveer got a call from his parents as he was walking towards the stairs of his building.

'Our prayers have been answered with you getting the job you wanted. Can you please send us twenty thousand when you get your first salary? We have to arrange for your sister's engagement. These things are your responsibility now,' his mother said to him.

'Don't worry, Ammi, I will send what you need. I do not need so much money anyway. Please make the arrangements from your side,' Tanveer replied.

'Achcha beta, that's good. You also know that Zoya has to start college in a couple of months. You will need to support her. We have done what we could for you, now it's your responsibility towards your sister,' his mother explained carefully. A little irritated at having such a conversation on that day, he said, 'Don't worry, I'm here. You don't have to keep reminding me. Let me at least get my first salary, Ammi!' After a short conversation with his sisters he hung up and took the stairs up to his room with a heavy head. He walked into his room at 10.30 feeling completely exhausted. He got into bed and wondered what his friends might be doing right now. He remembered the last time they met, one week back, the day Sameer left for London.

One week back... 24 July 2003
Sameer's home, Juhu, Mumbai

Sameer woke up on a bright and sunny day and dragged his feet to the restroom to get ready for the puja at home. He was to fly out to London later that night. A number of relatives and family friends were to join them for the puja and stay on for breakfast. He overheard a lot of hustle and bustle at home with Rajveer and his mum packing a suitcase filled with thermal wear, a raincoat, necessary medicines, boxes of sweets and namkeen, which Sameer's grandmother had sent him, and a whole lot of other knick knacks which his mother felt her precious son could not do without. Tania and her parents joined them for the puja as well. After completing the necessary rituals, obtaining the blessings of his elders and exchanging a few pleasantries, Sameer snuck away with Tania in tow on the pretext of packing. Rajveer's offer to join in to help them was bluntly rejected by him with a wave of the hand and a wry grin in the direction of his sibling.

Tania and Sameer spent an hour undisturbed, packing very little but using the precious time to hold each other and pack in some long passionate kisses. Sameer was intoxicated by the scent of her hair and the mild perfume she was wearing and could not get his hands off her, while she kissed him with hungry passion and ran her fingers around his neck and the back of his head. He wondered how he could bear to stay away from her. Tania cried a little and lay in his arms for a while. Soon, there was a knock on the door and they were joined by Mrs Ahuja who looked restless and agitated. She was upset with thoughts of her son leaving home and with the worry of having so much packing to complete. She chastened Sameer meekly about his habit of leaving things till the last minute. His dad walked in with a pouch containing his passport, foreign exchange currency and other important university documents. With a sense of urgency, he approached Sameer.

'Please put these in the knapsack you're carrying as hand baggage. Also, please call your airline and check whether your flight is on time,' he said. Mr Ahuja had sold a piece of land he owned in Noida to fund the tuition fees for Sameer's MBA. The land had been bought twenty years ago with the intention of building a dream home and moving there. But after twenty-five years in Mumbai, the Ahujas were too used to life in the Maximum City to want to settle down anywhere else. Even if they did want to move, Rajveer would never let them, as he was a true-blue Mumbai boy who also played for the city's under twenty-one cricket team. Rajveer came in, followed by Tanveer, which drew away some attention from Sameer. Tanveer exchanged handshakes with the boys. Mrs Ahuja got upset with him for not having come for a Sunday lunch two weeks in a row. Tania giggled in the background, watching him make excuses.

'Loser, you didn't show up for dinner last night. Where were you, man?' Sameer asked him.

'Sorry yaar, I got held up. The landlord whose place I stay at had to be rushed to the hospital. He slipped on the wet floor and hurt his hip. His wife was helpless and worried, so I had to accompany them to the hospital,' Tanveer said.

'It's okay, I hope he gets better. It's good you got here early.

Packing will get done quickly now.'

'Yes, let's finish quickly. We can enjoy a family lunch then,' Rajveer added.

Tanveer had lied to them about not making it for dinner the previous night. He had, in the past, made similar excuses to exclude himself from plans to go out with the group. The truth was that he could afford very little of these additional expenses and barely scraped through with what was sent to him as his monthly allowance. He also felt embarrassed with Vicky or Sameer covering for him so often.

Sameer remembered Rajveer's gift from the night before. 'Hey, thanks a lot, Chotu! It was very thoughtful of you. I really like the pullover and the pen,' he said.

Tania patted Rajveer's back and added, 'You're a good kid, Chotu. Look after your folks while Sameer is away. Where's the CD? Let me put on some music. We could listen and enjoy it while we pack.'

They turned on the music and Sameer and Tania took a break from packing and spent some alone time in Sameer's balcony. Rajveer and Tanveer carried on packing, while Rajveer animatedly explained to Tanveer his knock of sixty-two runs, which had helped his team win a match against Baroda the week before. Tanveer listened on eagerly. He loved cricket and had represented his school at tournaments. At one stage, he wanted to become a cricketer but circumstances ensured otherwise. He had family responsibilities and couldn't risk his future on a career which had no guarantees. He wished his parents were like the Ahujas. Tanveer's thoughts were interrupted by Vicky who strolled into the room casually in an old T-shirt and a pair of khaki shorts. He handed Sameer a nicely wrapped gift on behalf of Naina, Tanveer and himself, and a nice little card which Naina had written for him. Sameer, after a manly hug, thanked him and ripped open the wrapping paper. The gift was a dozen of his favourite graphic novels—*V for Vendetta, Watchmen, Daredevil, From Hell, The League of Extraordinary Gentlemen* and a few *Batman* comic books. Some of these were from Vicky's collection—classic editions which Sam had borrowed from him a few times. Their fondness for graphic novels and comic books was something they had always bonded over. Sameer could not believe Vikram was giving him his much treasured collection.

Vikram explained nonchalantly while putting his arms around Tania, 'Dude, I'm sure they will be put to better use by you, being away from all of us. They could use a change of scene after spending many years in a box in my wardrobe. I'm sure you'll treasure them like I have over the years.'

'I'm sure these classic editions are worth a lot of moolah,' Tanveer added appreciatively.

Vikram said mischievously, lying back on Sam's bed, 'Yes, I am sure if had given them to you, I could expect to see them auctioned on easybay.com in a few hours. But don't worry. Tomorrow if you go somewhere I'll give you my *Playboy* collection, it will be of use to you.'

Tania looked at Tanveer and laughed a little, which made him uncomfortable. Tania pulled out her gift for Sam and handed it to him. While he was unwrapping it, she said, 'Shut up, Vicky. You can't resist having a go at poor Tanveer! Did you book tickets for *Love Actually* for tomorrow evening? Tanveer is coming too.'

'Yes, I sent Shyamlal to Adlabs to pick them up yesterday. It's the 7.30 p.m. show. Naina can't make it earlier than that. She has a shoot tomorrow,' Vikram responded with a yawn.

Tanveer continued packing and struggled to close a suitcase with Rajveer while Sam pulled out a Benetton sweatshirt, a pair of formal shoes and a framed picture of both of them taken a few months ago from the box. Sam, overwhelmed with emotion, drew her close and gave her a kiss, running his index finger down her cheek to her chin. 'Thanks. I'll wear the shoes and the sweatshirt every possible day I can and our picture will be next to me always,' he said. Vicky, who was bored with the mushiness around him, laid his eyes on his favourite target, Tanveer.

'Do you want to do an ad for Axe? I could arrange an audition for you. Naina is doing this ad next week and they are still looking for the lead guy for the TV commercial,' he said, suppressing a grin and trying to sound serious and business like. Tanveer dropped the pairs of socks he was beginning to pack and asked, 'Sure, I would love to. But why would they take me? Why don't you give it a shot? You're the stud.'

'Nope, they are on the lookout for an ordinary-looking chap who becomes a babe magnet after using Axe. I thought you would fit the bill perfectly,' Vicky said, trying to sound convincing.

'Well, I don't mind giving it a shot. Please put in a word, dude. How much do you think they'll pay?' Tanveer asked with hope of getting the part.

Tania interrupted, with Sam and Vicky laughing in the background and exchanging a high five, 'Shut up guys! Tanveer, don't you get it? These two have made an ass of you so many times.'

Tanveer, like a child who was being scolded for not doing his homework, said, 'Yes, Tani. You're right. Guys, you're not going to pull a fast one on me this time.'

Vicky tried to entice him. 'Dude, I am serious. You so fit the part. Think and tell me. Imagine seeing yourself on TV and on hoardings all over the city. You will be famous.'

Tania, with her finger pointed at Tanveer, said, 'You focus on getting your bank job,' and looking at Vicky added, 'Vicky ya, stop trying to get him into these scams!'

Bharat and Jitin walked in and exchanged pleasantries with the rest. Bharat was Sameer's closest friend from school and had just returned after finishing his graduation at Boston University. Jitin, a theatre actor, was another friend from school who lived in the building. His family and Sameer's had close ties and their fathers were business associates and had been close friends for years. The group had animated discussions about their school and college days, life after college, career aspirations, films and, of course, music. Bharat and Jitin had got Sameer a hardbound copy of *Jonathan Livingston Seagull* with illustrations. Tania raved about the book, having read it many times over. She was an avid reader or a bookworm, as Vicky called her back in school.

Their conversation was interrupted by Sameer's mum calling them for lunch, saying that the rest of them were already at the table waiting for them. Mrs Ahuja had made aloo parathas, chicken biryani and her special mango chutney. A scrumptious family lunch was enjoyed by all of them while jokes were traded. Tanveer, Sam and Tania were the target of all jokes instigated by Vicky and supported ably by Mr Ahuja, a man known for his humorous anecdotes, impersonations and fun-loving nature. The rest of them joined the two mischief-makers in taking digs at the hapless couple. Sameer was the centre of attention and they also needled Tanveer about the women, or the lack of them, in his life. Bharat and Jitin excused themselves after a couple of helpings of the mouth-watering chocolate mousse. Bharat was to join Mr Ahuja's office as a management intern and was keen to learn the ropes from Anil Uncle. The boys started taking down Sam's four suitcases to Vicky's and Mr Ahuja's cars downstairs. Sam took Tania's hand in one hand, with his knapsack in the other, and walked over to take a final look at his room. He remembered his school days, when his mother would cajole him to wake up each morning to go to school. He felt tears welling up in his eyes and walked into his parents' room and gave them a long tight embrace. He let his mother shed a few tears this time.

4
New Lives and Catching Up

'If you can spend a perfectly useless afternoon in a perfectly useless manner, you have learned how to live.'

—LIN YUTANG

23 DECEMBER 2003
Sea View Cafe, Marine Drive, Mumbai

It was the most pleasant time to be in Mumbai, with the temperature at twenty-four degrees and calm winds blowing by. It had been six months since Sam had left the shores of Mumbai for his MBA. Tanveer and Tania sat in the outside seating area of the café, enjoying the gentle breeze. They watched the sun go down across the sea while the sky was illuminated by a beautiful orange and purple glow. They spent a few quiet moments and listened to the sound of the waves as they slowly brushed against the rocks across the promenade a few metres away from them. Tanveer now worked close to eighty hours a week at a cramped desk, facilitating loans and credit facilities to small and medium-sized enterprises. He had learned a great deal in the past few months and had been absorbed in the pressures of the new job. His aim was to impress his boss by completing impossible tasks within set deadlines. He stayed on Peddar Road as a paying guest with a Parsi widow and her daughter, the commuting distance from work being fifteen minutes. Tania and he were meeting after three months. They were busy during the weekdays and spent most of the weekends in bed, recuperating from their busy and stressful lives.

'I hope you're settling in well at work. How is your boss treating you now?' Tania asked Tanveer with concern.

'The work is good. It is a great learning experience. But my boss is a pain, Tani. He makes it his business to give me a hard time. One day, I am going to give it back to him,' Tanveer said with a hint of frustration in his voice. 'That guy treats me like his slave!'

Vinod, his boss, preferred to work with staff who did as they were told, no questions asked. He found Tanveer's direct questions, his proven ability to analyse and interpret data efficiently and his easy-going nature, which had helped build and foster relationships within the bank and outside, a threat to his position. His aim was to frustrate Tanveer to a point where he would leave of his own accord. Tania looked at him with concern while sipping on her vanilla cappuccino. After a few moments of silence, she said, 'It is okay, relax. Don't let him get to you. He wants to frustrate you. Don't let him win, ignore the guy.'

'It isn't easy, Tania. He's sending me for a factory inspection to Pimpri on a Sunday for an inventory count. This can be done on a weekday too, right?' Tanveer said with anguish in his voice. Tania sympathetically put her hand on his folded arm.

'Chill. This too shall pass. How are things coming along with your sister's wedding in February? Preparations must be on at home, she must be busy shopping, right?' she asked with interest. She was keen to attend his sister's wedding.

Tanveer lightened up. 'She's quite excited yes. Preparations are on in full swing. Vicky, Naina and you have to come,' he said, then looked upset again and added, 'That moron Vinod has approved only three days of leave for me. The wedding is turning out to be a very expensive affair. My parents are inviting three hundred guests. They are buying a lot of gold and diamond jewellery, a motorcycle for the groom and gifts for his family. I am spending all of what I have saved till now for her wedding.'

'Phew, some things never change! Anyway, Vicky, Naina and I will be there,' she said. He decided to change the topic, feeling that he might be depressing Tania. 'By the way, how is Sameer?' he asked.

'Sameer is all right. He hardly finds time to talk to me. He is very busy with his assignments. As you can see, he isn't coming home for the Christmas break since he is on a short internship with some advertising firm in London,' Tania said with a frown.

Vicky in his usual carefree spirit joined them with Naina, who was dressed in the same colour as he was, in tow. 'Now someone's been colour coordinating,' Tania said cheerfully.

'Not really, but yes we've been getting dressed together,' Vicky said with a mock grin and winked at Tanveer who looked embarrassed. He could never be as open about relationships as Vicky was. Naina cut him off with a friendly whack on his arm, 'Ssshhh, Vicky, you're the limit!'

'How are things at your dad's office? You're the only one among us with a plush cabin and an easy job,' Tania asked teasingly.

Naina, with a grin, said, 'He barely spends time there. Wakes up late and comes to college to hang out with me every day. He goes to office after 4 p.m. and heads to his gym from there.'

'Thanks, love, for sharing my timetable. But I do get some work done. In any case, there are enough people there to work. I wouldn't want to take away anyone's job. What say, loser?' Vicky retorted cheekily.

'Absolutely boss, you're ensuring employment in the country. India needs more people like you,' Tanveer said with mock sarcasm.

'Right you are. How's that khadoos boss of yours? Have he

and you traded punches yet?' Vicky asked Tanveer while Naina and Tania had their own conversation about Tania's progress as an interior decorator—she had completed her first independent assignment of decorating the new home of a young Bollywood starlet, Anjili Vimani. The girls gossiped about the lives of the rich and famous and their sometimes weird ways. Naina was awed by showbiz and had plans to launch a career in the movies or on television after she finished college.

'I would love to be in Bollywood, but song, dance and melodrama seem a bit over the top for me. Don't think I can pull it off,' Naina said with some doubt in her voice.

'Why? Of course you can. Tanveer thinks you look like Basanti. He's seen *Sholay* some thirty times,' Vikram said with a grin, looking at Tanveer. Tanveer almost jumped out of his seat.

'No, I didn't say that. Though you do look like Zeenat Amaan in *Qurbani*. You should try and do crossover films,' he said and added with a grin, 'I am dealing with Vineyard Pictures who have signed Vinay Bose and Ritu Roy for three such films.'

Tania laughed quietly—she had missed Tanveer's spontaneous unsolicited advice to people—while Naina sat there wondering what to make of his comments and thanked him for the compliment. She initially had not liked Tanveer much and had found his comments to be weird and intrusive, but she had warmed up to him considerably on getting to know him better through Vicky.

Vikram, sipping his cold coffee, looked at Tanveer. 'How is that cute Parsi girl you're living in with? How are you progressing with her?' he asked, holding back from pulling his leg.

'Tania, did he tell you about this girl?' Naina asked and added with a smile, 'You should meet her some time. She's really sweet—Tanveer's secret girlfriend.' Looking at Tanveer she said, 'By the way, Tanaz and I went to the same school, though we were never in the same class.'

He had first met Tanaz in the elevator up to the apartment he was moving into and remembered her cheerful 'hi' to him, and how beautiful she had looked in her pink pyjamas and a white top. His hand had touched hers as they had reached out to press the same button in the elevator. Tanveer had pulled his hand away and said, 'Sorry, I didn't mean to touch you,' to which she had smiled shyly with a twinkle in her eyes. She had struck him like a thunderbolt and he remembered muttering something which sounded like, 'Hi, I'm Tanveer and have just moved into this building,' at which she had giggled.

On reaching Mrs Rustomjee's apartment, they had realized that they lived in the same place and laughed about it. Tanveer was the new paying guest who had just moved in. They had a long conversation at the dining table where Tanaz asked him a lot of questions while he sat there chatting with her animatedly, smitten by her. She had offered to drop him to office the next day on the way to her college on her Scooty. They quickly became fast friends and enjoyed spending time with each other. Tanveer, from day one, thought of her as more than a friend, but for some time at least, he did not let it show. She found him to be funny and intelligent while he considered her to be a goddess.

Tanveer blushed and lowered his eyes while Tania, whom he once had a crush on, had a gleam in her eyes. 'Tanveer and Tanaz, living in together? When did all this happen?' she asked, giving Tanveer a puzzled look. *Tanveer didn't open up to women easily,* she thought.

'No Tania, it is not like that. She is my landlady's daughter. We're not dating. She's a nice girl and she studies in Xavier's. Her mother already looks at me with a lot of suspicion when Tanaz speaks to me,' he said.

'Go for it dude, marry her. You can live rent-free then. When the old lady bumps off, the place is yours to keep,' Vikram said, giving him a wink.

Naina interrupted, looking at Tanveer, 'Your girl is quite a sweetheart. She is very simple and easy-going as far as I know her. She also teaches slum kids with her friends every other evening. I'm sure she'll take good care of you,' she laughed.

'Naina and I walk into this *Spiderman* movie and we see our friend sharing a tub of popcorn, sitting like a lord with this cute girl. I meet him every other week for chai and he tells me nothing,' Vicky said, looking at Tania. 'I took a picture on my phone and sent it to Sam too. He likes the girl, dude. He says he will call and congratulate you,' he added, looking at Tanveer with a smirk. T

Tania took Vicky's phone to see the picture of Tanaz while Tanveer sat there wondering what to say to get the focus off him. Tanveer was really fond of Tanaz. They liked to hang out, watch movies, take long walks and go for a cup of coffee now and then. Tanaz also managed to parcel in whatever she cooked for Tanveer, who loved her cooking, without her mother getting wind of it. He was unsure whether he was in love with her, but did want to spend any time he got with her. Mrs Rustomjee held Tanveer in deep suspicion while, at times, Tanveer found Tanaz's comfort level and fondness for him a little too hot to handle. He kept her at bay, knowing religious and cultural differences would make it difficult for things to work out. The irritated look on Mrs Rustomjee's face whenever Tanveer spoke to Tanaz in her presence confirmed his insecurities.

Tanaz had a small but curvy frame. She had hazel eyes, long dark brown hair and the sweetest smile. *Quite like Tania's smile and frame. She is so fragile!* Tanveer often thought. He felt that a girl like her would end up with someone with a personality like Sameer or Vicky. He, in fact, had felt jealous and insecure when she merrily spoke to Vicky at the cinema and kept turning back to smile at him when he threw popcorn from a couple of rows behind on Tanveer.

While Tanveer was lost in his thoughts, Tania raised an eyebrow after seeing Tanaz's picture. Vicky continued his salvo, 'Dude, you looked cool riding off into the sunset behind Tanaz on her Scooty,' while the girls looked at Tanveer and laughed. He leaned towards Tanveer while the girls chatted about Tanaz, 'Take Sam's car or mine and take her for a nice dinner. Play it smooth, dude.'

'Relax dude, she's just a friend. We hardly meet or go out, as her mother is very strict. The movie was a one-off thing.'

The truth was that Tanaz's company was an antidote to the bullshit he had to deal with at work. Being away from his family—and now his friends, too, whom he met occasionally—Tanaz's presence was the sunshine in his life amidst the dark clouds of a demanding job, responsibilities towards his kin and living on a tight budget.

Vicky and Naina chatted about their plans of going out to party that night and tried to coax Tanveer to get Tanaz to join in. Tania sat back sipping her coffee and thought about Sameer a lot. She imagined how it would be if he was here and sitting with his arms around her. She wondered how they were so into each other once and now spoke just for a few minutes every day and chatted online for a while on the weekends.

Vicky settled the bill and all of them rose to walk towards his car and drive over to Jimmy's Bar and Grill for dinner. Tania realized that there were so many times when she wanted to call and share something she had experienced or how a certain job had gone but could not as they were in different time zones and Sameer was either sleeping or in the classroom or library through most of her waking hours. This definitely was a night she wished Sameer was around. She remembered the day he had left Mumbai she saw him off at the airport.

SIX MONTHS AGO... 24 JULY 2003
Chhatrapati Shivaji International Airport, Andheri, Mumbai

Sameer's parents, Tania and Sameer reached the Chhatrapati Shivaji Airport after a short drive during which his mother repeatedly advised Sam to keep himself warm, pray, eat well and call home regularly, while Sameer responded cheerfully that he would do all of this and requested them to stay in good health. Tania had a quiet ride at the back of the car with her head on Sam's shoulders and a look of helplessness and sorrow on her face. She tried camouflaging it by smiling every now and then. They reached in time for Sam to check in while Vicky, Rajveer and Tanveer waited outside with Sam's luggage. They had reached a few minutes earlier in Vicky's car, having left a little before them. Sameer, after spending a couple of minutes with each of them, requested Vicky and Tanveer to take care of Tania and drop in on his parents now and then. He requested Tanveer to, in fact, move to his place and stay in his room, which would be unoccupied for a while.

Tanveer said, to everyone's surprise, 'I got the job at Oceania Bank this morning and I have to start work in a week.' This was met with a cheer and pats on his back from everyone. Sam, with concern, told his kid brother, 'Chotu, practise well, study too and take care of Mum. Argue less with Dad. He means well.' Rajveer nodded to the man he revered.

'Yes, Bhaiyya. You take care and come back soon. I will email you regularly. Please keep messaging me too. All the best!' he said, embracing him.

'Don't worry about things, dude. I am here if there is anything. Keep in touch with Tani. She's really going to be in the dumps without you,' said Vicky, slapping his back and added, 'Come back soon. Will miss beating you on the tennis and basketball court.'

'Yeah, right! Let's see about that. I am going to try and practise there. Hang on to Naina, man. You have a good thing going with her. Start with something on the work front soon,' Sam said with a grin and, turning to Tanveer, added, 'You better get a good thing going too. Now that you have the job, remember what we discussed.'

'Thanks, dude. You've been a great friend. Keep in touch,' Tanveer said in a sad voice, choking with emotion, unable to say anything more.

Sam moved over to his parents and found his mum crying on his dad's shoulders. He gave them another hug, promising to call them every day, telling his mother he would miss her a lot and requesting her to take it easy. He thanked his dad for making his dream to study in London a reality. 'Anytime, any thing for you, beta,' his dad said with profound affection, patting his back. Sameer felt ashamed for leaving his parents and his loved ones. It was the first time he had seen tears in his father's eyes. His father added emotionally, 'We will wait for the day you decide to come back.'

'Yes, Dad,' Sameer mumbled and looked at Tania who was waiting patiently to say her goodbye. He felt guilty, seeing the pain in his parents' eyes watching him leave home. He took Tania's hand and they walked for a short distance away from the rest of them. Sameer planted a quick kiss on her forehead and told her sincerely, 'I love you. Will miss you the most every day. I would have kissed your sweet lips if my mum and dad weren't around.'

She smiled a bit and, ruffling his hair, said, 'I would too! On your trip back home, lover boy.'

'I will be back soon. There are summer breaks, winter breaks and two years will fly by, trust me,' he said, looking into her eyes with intensity. Tania nodded with a faraway look and smiled bravely. He moved to touch his parents' feet, shook hands with the boys and hugged his mother once more. He then took Tania's hand and put a two-carat diamond ring on her finger as a sign of his commitment and walked reluctantly towards the departure gate with his luggage. She covered her mouth with her hand and more tears rolled down her cheeks. She ran up to him and gave him a hug, burying her now wet cheeks into his chest.

Once inside, and after checking in, he turned around and waved goodbye, half wanting to come back and forget about his MBA at Oxford. He saw his mother crying uncontrollably, flanked by his dad and Rajveer on either side, consoling her. He saw Tanveer and Vicky huddle around Tania and the three of them wave out to him. He half wished to turn back and go home with his parents, have dinner with them, go out with Tania and have her soft, beautiful, scented hair in his face while he kissed her. This, it struck him, was not going to happen for a while. He walked ahead, dragging his feet with a heavy heart. It was threatening to pour outside and Sameer walked through departure gate eleven to board his Union Jack Airways flight UJA428 to London. He boarded the flight which was half empty and was greeted icily by an air hostess with a fake smile. He fell asleep shortly after the flight took off, before spending a few moments looking out of the window, remembering love and life so far in Mumbai.

Tania had a quiet drive back with Vicky who tried to cheer her up. He complimented her on how her new ring made her glow radiantly and how much time Sam, Naina and he had spent a few days back looking for the right ring for her. On reaching her home, he walked her back to her porch and gave her a hug before reminding her to be ready on time for the movie the next day.

'Why don't you join me and Naina for dinner at Café Churchill tonight? It will be fun. Naina won't mind,' he said.

'No, it's fine. Thanks for asking. You guys go ahead. I had an early start today and I am really tired. I have to go with Mum to see a client tomorrow for an office she has to design. I am learning the ropes from her, remember?' Tania said unconvincingly.

Vikram did not remember but said, 'Yes, that's great. Hope you enjoy it and it keeps you busy. You're okay, right? If you want, I'll cancel dinner. No big deal. We can sit and chat on your roof.'

'I'll be okay! You go ahead have fun tonight. See you tomorrow. Thanks for picking up the shoes for Sam,' she said, sounding exhausted.

'No worries. Rest and sleep well. See you at 7 o'clock tomorrow,' he said before driving away.

Tania walked back inside where she saw her parents in the living room. After talking with them for a few minutes she went to her room and crashed on her bed with no energy to change. She woke up, hearing her phone ring. She picked it up to hear Sameer say, 'Hey, I landed a few minutes ago. Remember that I love you. I am going to miss you loads. Can't wait to see you again.' She smiled and she spoke to him cheerfully, feeling reassured about her relationship.

Today, on a train heading towards Oxford…

Samar and Kim, sitting next to Sameer, were absorbed in each other and oblivious to the world around them. Sameer missed Tania and wished he could ride down the tube with her for a play, walk down to Trafalgar Square and cuddle with her to keep them both warm in his tiny room at Oxford. *Wishful thinking,* he sighed and began reading a copy of the *Financial Times* he had picked up outside the station—but his mind was far away, imagining Tania in his arms, remembering the scent of her hair, her long tresses and her innocent eyes. He wished he could go and spend a few days with her back home. He realized that he had to prioritize on his studies. He was in the bottom half of the class and found statistics and management information systems particularly difficult. He was also at a disadvantage as he had no work experience prior to coming to business school. It was a really competitive environment in their batch. So he had to work extra hard on the assignments and also network a lot outside the course hours to ensure that he was building the right relationships that would help him find a job. He got a message from Tania telling him about the evening she had spent with the gang and where they went to party. She mentioned how much she missed not having him with his arms around her on the dance floor that night.

'I'm sure Tanveer with his funny moves would have kept your spirits high,' he messaged.

'That he did, he is so damn funny! I can't wait to meet Tanaz!' she replied.

He went through mood swings when he got depressed, missing his family, Tania and his friends back home. Though now the days were more bearable, with him coping better in class and keeping company with Samar and Kim, who were fun to hang out with.

~

5
Choices

'Throw your dreams into space like a kite, and you do not know what it will bring back, a new life, a new friend, a new love, a new country.'

—ANAIS NIN

15 June 2004
Tania's home, Cuffe Parade, Mumbai

Tania woke up on a pleasant sunny day and turned on her laptop. It was Sameer's birthday and they spent an hour chatting on Skype. She chatted away, feeling extremely happy and realized it had been a while since they had spoken for so long. She had so much to share with him about her demanding but thriving interior decorations business, things at home, the books she was reading and the complete update on Tanveer's sister's wedding, which they had gone to Sholapur for. She mentioned to Sameer that Tanveer's parents didn't particularly like her or Naina as they came across as too liberated and independent. Though his family had remained civil with all of them, they seemed to prefer a distance from the 'forward' girls. His sisters, however, were in awe of both her and Naina and took a few tips on beauty, fashion and men—tips which she and Naina were ready to share. Vicky, however, was loved by all and played to the gallery.

'Vicky is hard not to like,' Tania said to Sam and added that he had made an extra effort to keep in touch since Sameer had left almost a year ago. He would often come over for a late night cup of coffee and chit chat on her balcony.

'So what are your plans for the rest of the day? Are you heading out to someplace with the gang?' Sameer asked her thoughtfully.

'No, I don't have plans to meet them today,' Tania cheerfully replied and added, 'Ankur wants to go buy some DVDs in the evening. I may have dinner with him too, but I have not decided yet.'

'Who is Ankur? How do you know him? Wow, it's my birthday and you're going for dinner with some other guy? Doesn't make me feel very nice, does it?' Sameer said, feeling insecure.

'He's working with me on the restaurant we are designing. I told you about him moments ago. He moved here recently from Kolkata after his divorce. He's a really nice guy and we get along well,' Tania said with some hesitation and concluded in an irritable tone, 'In any case, you aren't here to go to dinner with, so why taunt me?' She immediately regretted saying this to him. She knew it was as tough for him as it was for her.

'So it doesn't mean you go out with someone else! Look Tani, I am not comfortable with you dining with random guys! I don't do that here. I don't take random women out here for a drink or dinner,' he said in a sharp voice, getting agitated at the other end.

'Look, you have your assignments and priorities, right? You are too busy to come home for even a few days and, besides, he's a friend and not a random guy. He knows that I am committed to you. You cannot tell me what to do and what not to!' Tania cut him off. 'I need space, Sameer, and maybe you shouldn't hold back from going for dinner or a drink with a friend. I have no issues. I trust you, but I am not sure if it is the same for you,' she added.

'Anyway, your choice. You're a free woman. I do trust you, but I don't trust other guys with you! Got to go, I have an assignment to finish after which I am heading out with Samar, Kim and some others to celebrate my birthday or whatever is left of it. You have fun, chat later,' Sameer said in a tone of defeat. He felt low after the conversation they'd just had.

'You have fun too. Have a great day, bye,' Tania said calmly and hung up. She got upset with herself for a while for having fought with Sameer on his birthday. She called him back an hour later and he picked up immediately. 'Sorry about what I said earlier. This long distance makes it hard for me, but you have to trust me, Sam! Ankur means nothing to me. You're the most important person in my life,' she explained to him in her sweetest voice.

'It's all right. I love you. I understand what you are going through. I'm sorry too. I know how difficult being far away from each other is,' he calmly stated. 'I didn't want to tell you earlier as it would have made you upset, but I am not going to be able to come down during the summer break either as I am doing an internship with Jaguar Motors and will be assisting their product team during the launch of XJ19, their new convertible.'

'What? Come on, Sameer it has been a year, honey. You're joking with me, right? You almost had me for a moment. Now tell me the truth,' she said. She was starting to lose patience with him.

'I just did. I am sorry. I know this will be hard to deal with, but I'm coming this December for sure. Most of the course and placements will finish by then. This time I will be getting just a week's break after the assignment and I was thinking of seeing a bit of Europe since I am here. Samar and Kim will be taking this trip too and there could be a couple of other people...' Tania paced up and down in her room. 'Well, you make all your plans and then tell me. If I was told a month ago, I could have been there too, right?' she told him with some disappointment. She wished for him to come for a short trip, knowing how long it had been and how difficult it was for her.

'Sorry, but all of this happened in the last couple of days. You know how important it is to focus on my career. This is such a big assignment! It will help me a great deal as I will not have any work experience on my résumé apart from this assignment and the one I did in winter. Recruiters, whether here or in India, will make decisions based on how these projects turn out and the recommendations I get,' Sam said earnestly.

'Well, this is all sensible and practical for you, but think about me. It is so stressful managing a long-distance relationship. There is so much pressure. We hardly talk!' Tania replied. There was silence for a moment. Calming down, she said to him in a conciliatory tone, 'Okay, forget it. What choice do we have? It's your birthday. Go have fun. But if you don't fly into Mumbai the day after your term ends in December, you'll be dead meat, Mr Ahuja!'

'Yes, ma'am. I promise. And hey, I've ordered this book on Amazon for you. I know you will love it. I read it last week,' he said, sounding relieved that he had been able to communicate his not coming down to her and the fact that she was taking it well. He had ordered a copy of Khalid Hosseni's *Kite Runner* for her.

'Thanks, but why the trouble? I could have picked it up here. I hope you get your birthday gift and you like it. Off for a shower, bye,' she said sweetly.

'I'm sure I will. Whatever you send will be special. Enjoy the shower. Imagine I am with you, like the day before I left,' he reminded her with repressed glee.

'Shut up. Stop being a brat and go now,' she said, managing to smile. They flirted for a minute or two before Sam hung up. Tania called Ankur after a while and called off the plan to go DVD shopping. She felt bad feigning some family commitment and said that she would see him at work the next day. It was tough being alone for Ankur, who had come out of a short but tumultuous marriage and a messy divorce. Tania felt extremely low and spent most of the day in bed reading or watching television. She asked Vicky to come by later for a coffee after he'd dropped Naina off after dinner. She felt lonely and wanted to be with a friend. She was in low spirits about Sameer not coming down for summer but did not want to hold it against him. Sameer kept texting her through the day, which lightened up her mood a little. Ankur called her a few hours later.

'Hey, you sounded really low earlier. Hope everything is fine. I just picked up the DVDs and I'm quite bored. I'm in your neighbourhood, actually. Do you want to go for a short drive? We could go get some ice cream or a coffee.' Tania hesitated for a while. 'Yeah sure, come over. I'll be ready in ten minutes. We can go for a drive and pick up something to eat. I haven't had lunch or dinner. I'll see you in a bit,' she said.

'Great, see you in ten. Let's go and get you something to eat,' Ankur said, thinking, *yes*! Ankur was attracted to Tania and tried to spend as much time with her as possible. He found Tania beautiful and dignified while being intelligent and hard-working as well. He often made a pass at her by getting her flowers and pastries at work and going along to do things she wanted to do. He had, in a sense, taken the space Sameer had ceded—he accompanied her for her once-in-a-while shopping binges and had started coming over to her place for lunch or dinner on weekends. Tania, over a paneer wrap, told him how upset she was about Sameer not being able to come down and how occupied he was with his priorities. Ankur sympathized with her but also felt good. Friction between Sameer and Tania was exactly what would help him get what he wanted.

'Let's head back, Ankur. Vicky is coming over in an hour.

Thanks for this. I feel better after talking to you,' Tania said and gave him a friendly hug.

Vicky's home, Colaba

Vicky woke up to the phone ringing. It was Naina at the other end and he lazily got out of bed while talking with her. He had begun to spend more time in his father's office learning the ropes, and met Naina only late at evenings and over the weekend. She, too, had begun spending time with a group of friends from her class during the day, his juniors whom he did not relate to. He gave Sameer a quick call, wishing his buddy on his birthday and passed on Tanveer's wishes too, since he did not have an international calling facility on his phone. He was the next to hear of Sam not coming down that summer.

'I would love to join in on your Europe trip. Sounds like fun. But Naina heads for the Miss India contest that time. She is one among the twenty selected and I've got to be there for her,' he said.

'Wow, that's great! Hope she wins. I'll call her in a few weeks and wish her. I got a text message from her this morning. Glad to see you guys have lasted a year,' Sameer replied.

'Thirteen months, dude. All of it has been great too. Hope we continue to make it work.'

'Yes, hope so too. When you started off, it didn't seem it would last, but you seem to have pulled it off. Bravo! How's Tanveer doing? Is he taking care of himself?' asked Sam.

'Same old Tanveer, his work sucks, his dad is ailing, his boss is an asshole, and he saves most of his money and sends it home. He eats street food and takes the local when he has to go out. He just cribs about it and does nothing to change his life,' Vicky replied dejectedly and added, 'Tanaz seems to like him. The five of us partied together last week, Tania must've told you. We all like her but our boy is too scared to make his move and take things forward. There are walls in his head.'

'That sucks. But he's the only one who can do anything about it. Anyway, I'm off for a drink. I will buzz you later,' Sam said and dropped a thank you text message to Tanveer before leaving his room.

Vicky sipped his orange juice, stopping to read about an alleged affair between his father and a Bollywood star beyond her expiry date in *Mid-day*. *She's damn hot,* thought Vicky. He was used to this by now. His parents lived under one roof but had separate lives. His father was a big shot in business circles and had many affairs with Bollywood starlets and ramp models. His mother was a socialite who ran an art gallery to stay busy and in the limelight, and had her own share of dalliances with much younger men, though she kept things more discreet. At anniversaries, birthdays, festivals and family dos, his parents put up a united front and painted a pretty picture of marital bliss. Vicky did not have anything against his parents for the lives they led, but did not like the media sensationalizing their private lives. He went in for a shower in a grim state of mind, thinking that he did not want to lead the life that his parents did. He thought about the altercation he had last night at the nightclub where Naina and he were together. He got out of the shower feeling relieved that Naina was okay now. Her temper had cooled off and she had called him first thing in the morning and had spoken sweetly, as if nothing had happened last night.

Last Night at Ice Bar...

A middle-aged flabby guy walked up to Naina while Vicky and she were enjoying some intimacy. 'Hi, you're from the 'Freeze It Juice' advertisement, aren't you?' he asked, to which Naina nodded.

He continued, 'I am Anil Khosla from B.S. Plugs and Bearings. We need a model for a swimsuit shoot for our annual calendar. You are beautiful and you would be ideal for this shoot. If you're interested, we could talk over a drink.' He tried to take Naina's arm and turned to Vicky and said, 'If you don't mind, please excuse us, man.' Vicky trained his gaze at him with a grimace.

'Look, thanks for the offer, but I am with a friend. Please give me your business card and I will call you later,' Naina replied with little enthusiasm.

'Sure, here you go, dear. Maybe we could chat over dinner tomorrow night. Why don't you come over to the Beach Palace Hotel tomorrow night? The money will be good—whatever you ask,' Khosla replied, handing her a card and looking at her suggestively.

Naina tried to put him off politely and said, 'Sorry, I don't work like that,' but Vicky cut her off and grabbed his collar.

'Hey, you talk to my girl with respect, man. Who the fuck do you think you are? You sleazy old bastard, you think everyone is on sale, right?' he said, rolling up his sleeves, ready to swing a punch.

Khosla looked exasperated and wanted to get out of the situation. A bouncer who knew Vicky stepped in. 'Is there a problem, Mr Khanna?' he asked firmly. Vicky loosened his grip and told the bouncer, 'Don't worry, Desmond,' and continued looking at Khosla with a grimace. 'You bother Naina again and I'll knock your teeth out, samjha? Now get the fuck out of here.'

Khosla walked away shamefaced, muttering a 'sorry' to Naina. Vicky watched him leave the lounge with a couple of his associates. Naina looked upset and pushed her drink away.

'You didn't have to create a scene did you? I know how to handle such people. This isn't college, Vicky, it is the real world! You can't threaten people like you did with Ankit in college because he was bothering me. These people can be dangerous. They can have links to some sleazy politicians or the underworld. I'm so put off now, you spoilt my mood!' she said.

'I did? Come on, you expect me to stand around when that crass guy talks to you like that? It was vulgar, the way he kept looking at you. It made me feel sick. I can't stand around and ignore these people, Naina. I know you are a model and there are some assholes out there, but there are things I cannot take. He cannot disrespect you with me around. No one can,' he replied, feeling that he had done the right thing. *No one can misbehave with her while I'm around*, he thought.

'Drop me home. I don't feel like staying here any more! You made me feel like a slut, with the "people aren't for sale" business,' Naina said, standing up to leave.

Vicky took her arm. 'Okay, I am sorry, Naina. It gets difficult for me when people behave with you badly. I am just being protective. You know what he was suggesting,' he said.

'I don't need protection, Vicky. I am a big girl! I know what I am doing and can take care of myself. You scare me, getting aggressive like that. Now drop me home or I'll take a cab,' she said firmly.

Vicky paid the bill and followed her out. They didn't speak till Vicky dropped her home. He came home and ordered flowers with a 'sorry' card, which was to reach her the next morning.

~

6
Memories

'Pause, you who read this, and think for a moment of the long chain of iron or gold, of thorns or flowers, that would never have bound you, but for the formation of the first link on one memorable day.'

—CHARLES DICKENS, *Great Expectations*

15 JUNE 2004
Tanveer's PG Accommodation (Tanaz's home), Peddar Road

Tanveer woke up to read a message from Sameer thanking him for his wishes and asking after his dad's health. He had returned from a client visit in Mangalore last night. His thoughts went back to home, thinking about his mother's call the night before about his father being hospitalized again for a dialysis. Tanveer had applied for a personal loan from the bank to meet the mounting medical expenses for both his parents who had health complications. His room was sparse and comprised an old bed, plastic chairs, an old table and a little sofa set provided by Mrs Rustomjee. He missed the old carefree days with his friends and wished he could meet them more often. He received another message from his boss, Vinod, ordering him to have the proposal for Allied Industries' shipping credit completed and sent to him by

9 a.m. the next morning. He began to feel depressed as he realized that he would need to put in close to five hours that evening to complete it. His phone buzzed just then. It was Vikram at the other end. 'Hey dude, how are you holding up? How was your trip to Mangalore?' he asked.

'It was fine. I am really tired, man. Thankfully, I got twelve hours of sleep last night and am feeling a bit better. My dad is in the hospital—it's his kidney again,' he said, sounding worried.

'That's bad. Let me know if there is anything I can do,' said Vicky with concern.

'Thanks, dude. That's okay. I already owe you fifty grand. I have it covered this time.'

'Forget your hisaab-kitaab, man. No big deal. Anyway, let's go to Tania's tonight for a cup of coffee. She's been in the dumps with Sam deciding to stay back in the UK for summer. He has some internship coming up. I'll pick you up at 9 p.m.?' Vikram asked him.

'It will be good to meet, but sorry, yaar. I have a lot of office work to finish. I have an early start tomorrow too. You go ahead,' Tanveer said contemplatively. Work came before anything else for him these days. He knew that it was up to him to lift his family out of the struggles they were facing. His younger sister, who was quite bright herself, was studying engineering in Pune and Tanveer had to support and insulate her from the family problems. He was glad that his other sister, though married, was around to provide emotional support to his parents. Moving them to Mumbai was something he could not afford, given how expensive it was to live there. Besides, they had a nice, palatial bungalow in Sholapur, which made things comfortable for them.

Vicky headed down the stairs towards his garage. 'Oh, I wish you could come. It's been a while. Anyway, I'm off. I have a family lunch in a few minutes. We'll talk soon,' he said and hung up quickly after hearing an 'okay' from Tanveer.

Tanveer sat on his bed for a while in his old track pants and his faded T-shirt and realized he needed to do some shopping. Tanaz walked in, opening the door with her sunshine smile. Looking at her made him forget any and every problem or challenge he was facing.

'Hey wise guy, hope you slept well last night? Now eat this,' she said with a smile. She had a plate with four warm pancakes with maple syrup and sugar sprinkled over them. 'Thanks,' he replied, taking the plate from her and focusing his eyes on the pancakes. He ate ravenously, enjoying every bite, realizing how hungry he was, having skipped dinner the night before as he had been too tired to go and sit in someplace and order. Tanaz sat next to him, putting one palm on his knee and began reading the newspaper. She was in a floral dress that showed off her beautiful legs and smelt like a fresh daisy. Her presence distracted Tanveer who was fascinated by her.

With difficulty, he turned his gaze back to the pancakes and asked, 'Did you make these, Peaches? They are yum.' Then he added, 'They are heavenly. Like you.'

Tanaz blushed and said with a glitter in her eyes, 'Yes, I made them especially for you. I realized you did not eat last night. I'm glad you like them.' She loved his pet name for her—Peaches. She found it funny and adorable at the same time and remembered the awkwardness with which Tanveer had called her 'Peaches' the first time many months ago. He had grown to occupy a very special place in her heart. She found him kind, honest and responsible towards his family and friends. She had never heard him bitch about other people or demean anyone. However, she did feel that Tanveer had a traditional mind-set and an inferiority complex. She wondered why, given that he was way smarter than many guys in college who had a lot of money and little intelligence or sophistication. With some excitement she said, 'Hey, here's a picture of your friend Vicky's dad with Sumana, the girl who acted in *Aur Pyaar Hai*,' and added, 'Here's another one of Naina. I didn't know she'd been finalized as a Miss India contestant. It's a picture of all the contestants.'

Tanveer moved closer to her and, for a moment, he was blinded by the fragrance she was wearing. He stuck his head into the newspaper. 'Naina looks beautiful, and I really hope she wins. Do you know they first met because of me?'

Tanaz smiled at him. 'No, I didn't know. Tell me how?' she said. For a smile like that, he could do anything. He began his story which took place on a pleasant and noisy day in Sherwood College.

14 JANUARY 2003

'The college festival "Welcome 2003" was on, with youngsters from all the colleges in Mumbai thronging to the festival to have fun and meet new people. There was a fashion show as well in which Tania, Vicky and Sam walked the ramp and I was the volunteer in charge to ensure things went on smoothly for this event, which was to take place in the evening. All those participating were practising their walk on the ramp, guided by Tom Pereira, a former model and choreographer in the fashion industry, who was an alumnus of Sherwood College. Rajiv Kapoor, the upcoming Bollywood actor, was to be the star attraction for the night and he was to walk the ramp in support of his alma mater. The college had arranged for security to assist me as the campus was packed with girls from all the nearby colleges who had come to get a glimpse of the star. Vicky, who was practising walking down the ramp with Rajiv, caught a glimpse of this stunning girl with a beautiful smile standing behind the barricade and watching them as they walked. During the break, he called out to me. Quietly indicating towards the girl, he said that she was his mother's friend's daughter from New York and that she wanted to have a picture taken with Rajiv Kapoor. He requested me to organize this for her. He gave me a camera he had in his bag and moved away to the enclosure where Rajiv Kapoor and the rest were taking a breather. I felt awkward, initially, with the unusual request and I did not know Naina was a first year student from our college. I called Naina out from the crowd and let her move into the enclosed area from behind the barricade, which was met with jeers from the crowd. Naina, not knowing why she was singled out, walked meekly towards me. Apparently, she knew I was the topper in college and had won many inter-collegiate debates and quizzes.

'So, you're a big Rajiv Kapoor fan and you want a picture with him, huh? Go sit there and I'll click. Don't worry, a lot of girls want a picture with him. Mention not," I told her with a smile.

Naina had this confused look, not knowing why I said that, and responded with worry, hearing the cheers and jeers behind her, "No, I don't want a picture with Rajiv Kapoor."

Hearing this, I got confused and, while wondering how to deal with this faux pas, I made it worse by mumbling, "Okay, so why don't you take a picture with me? Come, smile." I beckoned to her to stand next to me.

Naina felt she was being ragged by the nerd in college. "No, no. I don't want to click pictures with you," she pleaded. She could hear some of her batch mates calling out her name. Though undoubtedly beautiful, she didn't want this attention from a kurta-clad senior in college.

Coming to her rescue, Vicky interrupted us, "Hey, I am Vikram Khanna. Tanveer just has a little crush on you, don't mind him," and told me, while I stood there feeling stumped, "Dude, don't rag juniors, man. Even the ones you have a crush on."

I just nodded along, feeling like a bakra, and started sweating.

Naina smiled. "I'm Naina, first year BMS. You walk confidently on the ramp. Even better than Rajiv Kapoor," she said, enjoying the attention from the most wanted hunk in college.

Vicky made his play. "Do you want to walk the ramp with me? There is a slight change. Rajiv wants to walk solo at the end. These narcissist Bollywood types! You're tall and, of course, beautiful. And besides, I would rather walk with you than anyone else here," he said charmingly, looking in her eyes. She said, with a shrug of her shoulders, "Okay. I have walked the ramp back in school for a fashion show. It should be fun."

Vicky led her back to where the other participants were and they began organizing an outfit for her. With the help of the security guards, I spent hours controlling the boisterous women who were hurling abuses and jeering at me and wanted to be let through the barricades like Naina whom they believed had been let in by me unfairly.'

15 JUNE 2004
Tanveer's PG Accommodation (Tanaz's home), Peddar Road

Tanaz rolled her head back and laughed till there were tears in her eyes. She found stories of Tanveer's group back in college extremely hilarious, with Tanveer usually being the butt of all jokes. His awkwardness in these situations and at times, his small town mind-set and innocence was extremely funny and, at one level, adorable to her. Tanveer was the only man she was close to. She did not really know her father, who had passed away a few years back, too well as her parents had a bitter separation when she was a child. Her father had taken a mistress and had lived in Pune till his demise two years ago. Tanaz didn't hold anything against her father. She believed it was his right to get out of a difficult marriage and her mother had prevented his overtures towards maintaining a relationship with Tanaz. He, however, left her the apartment and a generous trust fund that would pay for her education.

Tanveer smiled sheepishly. 'It took Naina three to four months to actually start speaking to me. She thought of me as some madman pulling her out of a crowd to click snaps with her. Not just that, Sameer and Vicky kept taking my case about it,' he said, shaking his head. Tanaz laughed some more, throwing a cushion at him and asking him to stop and go for his shower. Her mother was going to be out all day at her brother's place, and they could spend some time together.

'I have at least five hours of office-related work this evening and that's why I'm not heading to Tania's place at night for a coffee. But we could go out now if you want,' Tanveer said eagerly.

'Well, yes. We have a few hours before you start working. Let's go shop a little for you and grab a quick bite at Moshe's. Come on now, don't be a lazy ass. We will be back by 3 o'clock and then you'll have enough time to work. Momma is going to be back at night and there's no way she will she let me go. Get ready fast. I have to go teach the kids later in the evening,' Tanaz said in a tone of urgency. Tanveer got up from his slumber and patted her head with affection. Her long brown tresses and her soft skin felt so smooth. *She is so delicate,* he realized.

'All right, Peaches. Give me fifteen minutes and I will be ready,' he said.

'Right on,' Tanaz said, adding, 'Wear the blue shirt I have pulled out,' before she walked out of his room with a smile.

26 AUGUST 2004
Tania's home, Cuffe Parade, Mumbai

Tania returned from a tired day at the office after putting through a number of changes in the design she had made to best suit her client's requirements. She remembered how lazy she had been in college, when Sameer helped her to complete her assignments even when they worked separately. Her thoughts drifted back to over two years ago as she changed into her nightdress and got into bed with a book.

Tania had called Sameer and had told him about her anxiety about the costing exam the next day. 'I am going to flunk! I know nothing about anything in this textbook.' She had studied very little and did not understand most of the illustrations in the textbook, which she had opened for only the second time all year. Sameer had stopped studying and had come over to her place with his books. He'd spent the whole evening teaching her and working out the problems with her, giving her confidence for the exam the next day.

She smiled to herself, remembering that she had scored three marks more than Sameer in the exam—something Vicky and she had often teased him about for a while, back in college. She also remembered her birthday two years ago, when Sameer had taken her to Vicky's beach house in Alibaug straight from college. He had arranged a candlelight dinner on the beach and had spent the whole day pampering her with orchids and Hershey's Kisses. He'd spent an hour telling her all the things he would like to do with her if they were marooned on an island together. She remembered how clichéd it sounded, but had blushed nevertheless on hearing the things he had said. They drove back that night after taking a speedboat back from Alibaug, and Sameer had placed a small piece of paper in her palm. It was a sonnet he had written for her, called *You*. He'd kissed her goodnight, saying, 'The most beautiful thing I have seen in my life is the smile on your face right now.'

She smiled to herself again, thinking how deep his feelings for her were and how romantic that birthday had been. She sent Sameer a text message, 'Hey honey, hope you had a great day and hope your market research assignment is going well. I just got back! It's been a tiring day, don't ask. I'm lying in bed and reading, what's up with you?'

'Hey, enjoy your book. I am really busy with the assignment. I guess it is going to keep me up all night. Everyone on the team has a different view on our solutions. Chat later, good night,' Sameer replied.

She heard her phone ring. It was Ankur at the other end. 'Hey, I have two tickets to the Rolling Stones gig tomorrow. It will be fun. Front row seats. Are you on?' he asked.

She thought for a moment, worrying about how Sameer would react, then said in a tired voice, 'Okay, sure. Sounds like fun. We'll talk about it at work. Goodnight.' She lay back reading, wondering for a moment if it was a good idea going with Ankur. Sameer was quite sensitive to her spending so much time with him. She realized that Sameer was too busy with his assignments these days to be bothered about it. There was no reason why she could not go out and have a nice time. As far as she was concerned, Ankur was just a friend, though she realized that Ankur possibly had feelings for her. But she had kept a respectable distance and had given him only so much space in her life.

The next day...

'Thanks, I had a great time tonight,' Tania gushed as they drove towards her place after the concert. She looked sexy in a grey tube top and a cream skirt which showed off her legs. Ankur smiled at her and tried to be charming. He decided to make a move once they reached her place.

'All right, goodnight, Ankur. See you tomorrow,' she said, unlocking the door to get out. He put his hand across and stopped her from getting out by placing his hand on hers. She looked at him with confusion, when he leaned in to kiss her.

'Stop! What are you doing? I hope I haven't sent out the wrong vibes, Ankur! I love Sameer and I'm in a committed relationship,' she said, carefully trying not to show her annoyance.

'Sorry, I don't know what came over me. Guess I got led away by the music and the way you look tonight. Please don't feel bad. I feel like an idiot. See you tomorrow, Tania,' he said, trying to clear the air.

'Okay… I just hope you understand. We work together and I like hanging out with you. Goodnight,' she said with a look of worry and confusion on her face. Ankur flashed a smile before he drove away. *This is tough*, he thought. He went back home and sent her a text message apologizing again for getting carried away.

∽

PART 2

TOGETHER

'Sometimes the heart sees what is invisible to the eye.'
—H. Jackson Brown, Jr.

7
Hope

'The grand essentials of happiness are: something to do, someone to love, and something to hope for.'

—ALLAN K. CHALMERS

14 OCTOBER 2004
Tania's home, Cuffe Parade, Mumbai, and in a classroom, Said School of Business, Oxford University

Tania woke up with a broad smile and yawned lazily. It was her twenty-third birthday and she had a nicely wrapped gift lying next to her. It was from Sameer and had a little card on it saying, 'Hey beautiful, open me up.' She opened the gift wrapper with a grin to reveal a sexy black cocktail dress. She heard her phone ring at the same time. It was Ankur on the other end, and he had called to wish her and ask her to meet him for dinner. Tania cheerfully agreed and hung up to receive calls from Vicky, Naina and her other friends. She took a long lazy shower, enjoyed a scrumptious breakfast with her mum and dad who teased her about her little gift from London. They suggested that Sameer and she should start planning their wedding when he came down in December, at which Tania blushed. Discussing her plans to settle down with Sameer made her extremely happy. She felt that they had been through the worst, having survived the long distance for over a year. Though they had gone from talking every day to now speaking only two or three times a week, she felt that their relationship had stabilized over time and Sameer seemed to be less possessive and more understanding about her friendship with Ankur than he used to be.

While her thoughts went back to him, he was sitting in his classroom at Oxford and looking out of the window far into the distance, enjoying the lush green scenery that surrounded the university. The weather was wonderful, being a pleasant sunny day, and Sam was thoroughly enjoying the English summer. He had been up in Scotland with his friends for the weekend and was thinking about how beautiful the place had been. His thoughts and attention were far removed from the entrepreneurial finance lecture in class. This was his only other elective in finance apart from acquisitions and restructuring. He had taken up four electives in marketing—branding and communications, customer insights, retailing and media strategies for a networked world— and one in strategy—strategy for a dynamic environment. He had changed track considerably from his initial intention of specializing in finance. His dad was a little disappointed but Sam realized that in this one life it was better to do what your heart was in. He realized quite early that it wasn't in the field of finance, which did not hold his attention. He thought about getting a job in London and eventually buying a place in the English countryside. He dreamt about Tania and himself living there, of cycling with her in the woods. He felt, *life is so peaceful, public transportation is great, better traffic situation, cleaner streets and cleaner air.* Though he missed Mumbai at one level, he felt that he could build a future in the UK. He had, of late, begun to think of the many problems India faced and how difficult life was back home with the poverty, poor infrastructure and corruption one came across every day. A smile came to his face when he imagined Tania being in London with him—*We could go for plays and take trips to Paris,* he thought. He wanted to take her to Bordeaux, France, where they could go wine tasting and tour the best vineyards in the world. He felt his parents would eventually be okay with his decision to stay back in the UK for a while if he found a good job, and his dad would understand his need to find his own path and make his own future. It was something his father had done almost three decades ago. He was yet to speak to his parents or Tania about his plans and the thoughts running through his head.

He got a text message from her while in class, thanking him for the dress and saying that it fit perfectly. He messaged her with a grin, 'Of course, love, no one knows your size better than me! I wish I was around to help you put it on and take it off… sigh…' His Nokia E95 beeped again. It was a picture Tania had clicked and sent of her in the dress. He felt rushes of passion and longing. *Femme fatale,* he told himself. His thoughts were homeward bound now. He could not wait to get back home in December.

Khanna Group, 18th Floor, Phoenix Towers, Lower Parel

Vikram was in his office and was looking at pictures from the Miss India pageant, which Naina had participated in the month before. She had won the 'Miss Beautiful Hair' and 'Miss Beautiful Smile' and had also won the poll by 'Smart Cellular' for 'My Miss India', with over forty thousand people voting for her. It is unfortunate that she couldn't make it past the last five, but Naina sure got noticed, he told himself. She was the new face of Naturale, the leading brand for beauty and skin products.

While Naina found herself getting extremely busy and finding popularity and fame, Vicky was confused as manufacturing auto components and industrial tools held little appeal for him. He, however, kept himself busy on the finance side of the business and, with valuable advice from Tanveer, he managed to refinance the company's debt and reduce interest costs by thirty-five per cent. Cash flow had improved with his new receivables management initiative. He was thankful to Tanveer who had spent considerable hours after work to help him design these processes. His father and uncle were extremely proud of him and Vikram had begun to emerge as a budding star in business circles. *Times* had been printing pictures of Naina and him together, given his good looks and lineage and her new-kid-on-the-block profile. Being featured in tabloids and on page three was something he did not like and he often avoided the photographers while Naina smiled cheerfully for the cameras. It had been eighteen months since they had started going out—a lifetime by his standards. His snazzy new phone rang while thoughts of Naina were clouding his mind. It was Naina on the other end.

'Hey Vicky, sorry I have to cancel out on dinner. I am the last minute addition to the Berlin Fashion Week. I will be walking for Niharika Roy who is showcasing her collection,' she said.

'Wow, fabulous news, baby! When do you leave? I'll drive you to the airport,' he responded cheerfully.

'I need to leave in a couple of hours for the airport! I got to get home and pack and try outfits too. God, everything is happening at the last minute,' Naina said with urgency in her voice.

'Don't worry. You go ahead. I'll leave office in a bit and see you at your place in a while,' he said coolly. He was unfazed by the demands of time. He thought for a moment and called the travel desk in his office. Vicky booked two first class tickets to Frankfurt and then on to Berlin on Lufthansa. He called Naina back and gave her the good news. He had booked a suite at the Adlon Kempinski for a couple of nights for both of them.

'After the fashion show tomorrow night, we could stay another day and see a bit of the beautiful parks, museums, historical monuments and the swanky cafés of Berlin. Besides, Berlin has fabulous night clubs and bars. Without the prying eyes of our tabloid reporters, it'll be fun letting loose where no one recognizes us,' he explained.

'Super! Sounds like fun. Go home, pack now and come over to my place. We'll leave from there and I'll get my economy class ticket cancelled,' Naina added with a smile. Vikram wrapped up for the day for the unplanned trip to Berlin. He had also been to Milan, Madrid and Paris with her in the past one year.

Oceania Bank—Corporate Banking Division, Flora Fountain, Fort, Mumbai

Tanveer sat at his desk, swamped with three deals he was working on at the same time. He had grown in stature within his department for striking profitable deals and getting the bank into arrangements that generated handsome returns. His relationship with Vinod Agarwal remained strained as Tanveer had grown to threaten his position.

Vinod approached his desk and told him sternly, 'I do not like the manner in which this proposal is put together. Saale behenchod, do your work seriously!'

Tanveer held back his resentment. 'Yaar, please talk with respect! There is no need to be abusive. I'll have it done "your way" in a while and bring it to you,' he replied calmly.

'Have it done in thirty minutes, chutiya, and leave it on my desk. Don't fool around. You're not paid to daydream here, samjha?' he muttered gruffly before walking away.

Tanveer held himself back, thinking about the interest-free loan he had taken from the bank, his responsibility towards his parents and Tanaz's smiling face. This always gave him a sense of calm and peace. He smiled. *A wonderful girl like Tanaz is something an asshole like Vinod will never have.* While working on the proposal he was summoned to Shekhar Gupta's cabin. Shekhar had been at the bank for ten years and was the VP—Corporate Banking and Institutional Credit for South Asia. Tanveer walked to his cabin with apprehension. He normally interacted with Shekhar only via email. He wondered if Vinod had filled his ears with something about the proposal. He hoped not as, in his opinion, he had done a competent job. He walked in, knocking meekly. Shekhar Gupta was a shrewd guy and focused all his energy on building and fostering relationships with big industrial groups.

'Tanveer, come in!' he said with a broad smile. Tanveer thought, *the guy is being nice before he fires me.* Shekhar asked him about his parents and sisters, how he liked his job and where he was staying. Tanveer, in his nervous state of mind, gave monosyllabic answers to everything.

Shekhar told him with a broad grin, 'I am very impressed with you. Yesterday, Vikram Khanna from Khanna Industries called about the impressive job you had done for them. These guys are big customers of ours now and you managed to channel all of their debt and credit facilities to our Bank. It's huge for us! Great going, Tanveer! I am pleased with your performance.'

Tanveer looked relieved and smiled.

'I know the manner in which Vinod treats you. See, this isn't really his fault entirely. It's the culture of this business. He once was a bright young lad like you and he is good at what he does,' he explained carefully.

'Yes, Shekhar,' Tanveer said cheerfully, happy to hear good things said about him.

'Well, I am going to ask him to take it easy with you. I want you to lead your team when he is away next month on his wedding leave. I am giving you a raise from this month. Keep up the good work,' he said with his wide smile and added, 'Take the week off. You work too hard. Go see your parents. They have been sick, right? I don't want to see you in office this weekend and all of next week. Clear?'

'Yes, Shekhar. Thanks a lot for everything. Have a nice day,' Tanveer said with a smile of relief, nodding at him and almost bowing with reverence as he left the room. Shekhar walked him to the door, patting his back and giving him an encouraging handshake.

Tanveer felt like he was walking on clouds. He went back to his desk and gave Tanaz a call, which she answered in her cheerful voice, 'Hey, how come you're calling me in the middle of the day?'

'Can I take you for *Rang de Basanti* and dinner at The Bayview this evening, please?' Tanveer asked in a charming voice.

'That sounds nice. I know there's good news. Don't tell me now. I will hear it from you in person. I will pick you up at 6 o'clock from your office. I'll book tickets. I'm near Inox right now. Let's go back home separately, though,' she said with caution. She, at a certain level, enjoyed the hide-and-seek manner in which she and Tanveer spent time together, without her mother having a clue about their blooming relationship.

'Yes, Peaches,' Tanveer replied cheerfully. The next day, he planned to take a bus to Sholapur. *Ammi and Abu will be pleasantly surprised. I must do some shopping for the family.* His elder sister had a baby on the way. He called the younger one, Zoya, in Pune and asked her to come home for the weekend as well. It would be a welcome occasion for their parents. He wanted to come back by the following Friday as it was Tanaz's birthday on Saturday. He was planning to buy her something nice and take her to a nice but affordable place. He planned to get Tania's help on the gift and Vicky's help on where to go. Vinod gave him dirty looks the rest of the day but did not say anything.

Tanveer and Tanaz enjoy a relaxed dinner at The Bayview. Tanveer realized that he had not been able to sit back and relax without worrying about his work and family for a long time. The last time he had done so was back in college. He missed those days and his friends—but Tanaz, in a short cream kurta and grey jeans, with her hair held up by a clip, more than made up for his friends not being there. He moved closer to her and removed the clip from her hair. *She looks like an angel when she lets her hair loose.* He drew her close and kissed her softly on the cheek while she smiled at him dreamily. She had grown to love Tanveer. She remembered her first thoughts of him—he was cute and funny to her back then, till she had begun to get to know him for the person he was. She wondered whether both of them would have the courage to make it work. From the rooftop of the restaurant, Tanveer looked far into the distance watching the waves tumble against the rocks and the moon emerge from behind dark clouds. The night felt exceptionally romantic with Tanaz by his side and the soulful ballads that were playing in the background. *You've come a long way baby,* he told himself. He wished that his friends could see him there. He wondered what they were doing right now. It struck him that it was Tania's birthday. He called and wished her, letting her know that Tanaz and he were having dinner at The Bayview. Tanaz also wished her while gazing at Tanveer ardently and hoping that their love would last.

Sameer's room, Oxford University

Sameer was lying in bed contemplating his future career choices and thought about the advertising case study solution he had to present the next day. He listened to 'Imagine' by John Lennon on his iPod and his thoughts drifted to falling asleep with Tania next to him. He remembered the day they had first met in college. He could still remember what she wore that morning, over four years ago. She looked like a breath of fresh air in her light blue top and her pair of faded, low waist Levi's jeans. He hadn't been able to take his gaze away from her. He had walked up to her in class and had asked if the seat next to her was taken. On hearing a shy but conscious 'no', he sat next to her for the rest of the day. His mind had been far away from the lectures that went on, captivated as he was by her beauty and innocence. He had asked her for her phone number, which she wrote in his notebook shyly and looked away from him, blushing and seeing if her friend in the seat behind her (who turned out to be Vicky) had noticed. They had spoken for over an hour on the phone that day. He had flirted with her a lot.

Smiling to himself, he drifted off to sleep.

Sizzlers and Steaks, Kala Ghoda, Mumbai

Tania had her birthday dinner with Ankur and a couple of other friends. She felt a bit low that Sameer was not there and the fact that Tanveer and Vicky could not make it either, for different reasons. Ankur drove her back home.

'Hey, cheer up! It's your birthday, champ. At least it still is, for another forty-five minutes. You look stunning tonight, by the way,' he said to her.

'Thanks, Ankur. It was sweet of you to convince me to go ahead with the dinner plan. I'm okay, really. I am very excited about Sameer coming back, just counting the days now,' she said before smiling at him innocently. Ankur thought, *I wonder how Sameer's name comes up in every conversation.*

'That's nice. I'm happy for you, Tania,' he said cheerfully, thinking, *I have to play this smooth.*

~

8
Coming Home

'Live as if you were to die tomorrow. Learn as if you were to live forever.'

—MAHATMA GANDHI

18 DECEMBER 2004
Oxford University

Sameer got ready in a rush. He had a flight to Mumbai in the next three hours. He rushed down with his two suitcases and his laptop bag. He had a couple of assignments to finish over the period of the winter break. He decided to finish both of them on his flight to Mumbai. It was a dark, chilly and gloomy winter morning but Sam was far from gloomy. This was one of his happiest days in the UK. He hailed a taxi and requested the driver to take him to the tube station. He had to take a train to Liverpool and then switch to the Heathrow Express which would get him to the newly opened Terminal Five in twenty-five minutes. On the train, he began reading George Orwell's famed novel *1984*. His phone rang. It was his mother, calling to check whether he had woken up on time and whether he would make it to the airport to catch his flight. He reassured her that he would be home soon. Hanging up, he sent Tania a text message that read, 'A few more hours before I kiss your sweet lips,' to which he got an immediate response, 'Can't wait! See you soon, hugs and xx.'

Tania and Ankur's Office, Prabhadevi, Mumbai

Tania was at work, with her thoughts far away from the place she was decorating. Ankur and she were now working on a project to decorate the test cricketer, Vikrant Dighe's home in Lokhandwala. Tania gracefully asked Ankur, 'Hey, can you please take over some things in a couple of hours? I need to head to the parlour in some time. Sameer comes in tonight.' Her mind was adrift from work that day.

'Sure, guess I won't be seeing you around for a while. You will be busy with him, of course,' Ankur replied with some hesitation and implicit sarcasm.

'No, I am committed to finishing this project. I will try and complete my bit before the twenty-fifth. We leave for Goa then. I'm really looking forward to that. I get back after a week of sun, sand and the sea,' Tania said innocently and asked, 'Are you going back home?'

'I will be here, working on this project. I can't afford a holiday at this stage. Vikrant wants the place ready in three weeks,' Ankur added with a touch of professionalism. 'Don't worry, Tania. I will cover for you on this one.' He'd been bending backwards to be nice to her since his failed attempt to kiss her months ago.

'Thanks,' she replied with repressed glee. She moved towards him and gave him a peck on the cheek which brought a smile to his face. Ankur was not happy with the news of Sameer coming down and Tania going away on a holiday with him. He wished that Sameer Ahuja did not exist. Tania spoke a lot about him which depressed Ankur. *Thoughts of Sameer and her commitment to him hold her back from moving things forward with me.* Ankur decided to play the waiting game. *In most cases these college relationships come to nothing,* he told himself. He had begun to see cracks in Tania and Sameer's relationship over the past few months. Sameer seemed to talk more about his fascination with London and the prospects there, based on what Tania told him, while Tania loved her work and Mumbai, and couldn't think about moving away. It was a classic case of two people wanting different things in life. *If the relationship falls apart, Tania is mine to keep,* he thought.

Vikram's home, Colaba

Vikram woke up with a hangover. It was 12.30 on a pleasant day. He decided it was too late to go to office and it would be okay to take a day off. He had had a late night with Naina. They had enjoyed a romantic dinner and they both had had a lot to drink. Naina was sleeping soundly next to him. He kissed her on her cheek and realized how beautiful she looked sleeping in just his old sweatshirt. He lay back in bed, cuddling with her and woke her up with a kiss. Naina and he had broken up a few weeks ago, soon after they had got back from Berlin. They had been having trouble for some time, with Vicky getting very possessive and protective and undercurrents of tension had been growing in their relationship. Vicky often told Naina that she was surrounded by people who were too flaky and self-obsessed and were focused on building an image of themselves rather than being who they were. He'd read one mischievous article the week before, about how father and son had both dated women who were contestants for Miss India and had represented 'Sparkling Essences' as the face of the brand. That made Vikram sick. Naina's agent, however, felt that it would be detrimental to her career to have the baggage of a boyfriend and wanted her to end the relationship. She had Naina quote a single status to the glossies. Vicky, who had read this statement by her in different places, did not like it. This had led to a bitter fight and a break up. Unlike his parents, he was who he was and did not want to present a different face to the public eye. Besides, he did not want his name thrown around in the papers and glossies, nor did he want to be the subject of speculation.

However, the night before, Vicky had picked her up from the MTV studio where she had been shooting for *What's Hot*, her first show as a VJ. She was pleased to see him standing there, dressed in a suit, waiting for her with a bunch of lilies in his hand. He felt that he had possibly over-reacted and wanted to make an effort to bridge their differences. He realized that he really loved her and knew that she felt the same about him. She packed up and left with him for dinner where they enjoyed the ambience and music and talked things out. Vicky wanted her back and wanted to put the whole tabloid report row behind them. She wanted him back too, but wondered if he could cope with the media attention that she was getting—which would only increase in the future. They, however, made up and decided to give their relationship another chance. *The trip to Goa will be a nice break and a welcome relief from the public glare in Mumbai,* both of them believed.

Vicky went downstairs and made a cup of coffee for her. *Last night felt so good,* Naina thought, biting her lower lip a little. Vicky came back in a short while and after placing the cup on her bedside table began planting kisses on her bare knees and thighs and they rolled back into bed after her cup of coffee for another round of sensual love-making. After they finished, Naina told him in a tired voice while lying with his arms wrapped around her, 'I am going to Singapore for three days to shoot a segment on *Star & Style* with VJ Ranveer. They are sending us to a different location every month. It is quite exciting!'

'That's great! I will book our tickets today and the room too,'

Vicky said cheerfully. Naina sat up and told him seriously in a cautious tone, 'No, please don't come. It's different with fashion shows—the guys at MTV don't like it. They feel I am not focused enough.' Hearing that, Vicky looked dejected. 'But Goa is coming up in a week. That should be fun,' she added with a sparkle in her eye, to which Vicky leaned forward and kissed her lips, easing her back into bed, and they lay there for a while lost in each other's arms.

Oceania Bank—Corporate Banking Division, Flora Fountain, Fort, Mumbai

Tanveer was busy filling in the fields in the loan processing and authorization system while talking on the phone with the Credit Control Manager. He had to get an important deal signed today. He had been invited to dinner that night by Sameer's parents but he would not be able to make it given his deadline. He planned to go and meet Sameer the next night instead, as he realized he would have to put in another late night. He felt he was being pushed to the wall by Vinod who wanted him to make up for the time off in Goa by making him work extra hard now. Mrs Rustomjee had raised a hullabaloo when she saw Tanveer talking to Tanaz in hushed whispers a few days back.

She'd told him angrily, 'Stop doing khusar-pusar with my daughter you fellow. I see you trying to speak to her again and I will pack your bags and throw you out. I will get another fellow tomorrow. Go to your room, Tanaz.' *She had a rough exterior,* he thought. She had made toast for him the next morning and smiled at him cheerfully. *She had her mood swings,* he realized. He would pick up pastries now and then for her and Tanaz and would, at times, get her medicine too if she requested. Mrs Rustomjee, on the other hand, felt secure with a man in the house and would get Tanveer's laundry done and often instructed him to eat with them.

'Useless, good-for-nothing fellow,' she often called him. The dinners were difficult with him sitting opposite Tanaz, pretending not to know her. The previous night, she had run her toes up his leg with her mother next to her, while smiling at him innocently and requesting him to pass the chapattis. She would often slip into his room for a goodnight kiss after her mother had gone to bed. With her college being close to his office, she met him for lunch at Fort whenever he was free. Vinod had seen them once, having a quiet lunch at Darshan, the south Indian restaurant across the street. Tanveer was apprehensive about the look Vinod had given him. Back in office, he had walked up to Tanveer with a sly grin.

'Fooling around with young girls, eh chutiya? I see that college girl dropping you to office. Don't meet girlfriends in office hours, huh? This is an office, college nahin hai!' Vinod had said, with some contempt.

'Who I eat with or how I come to work shouldn't concern you,' Tanveer had replied, walking away, with irritation in his voice. He had begun giving it back to Vinod.

Chhatrapati Shivaji International Terminal, Mumbai

Later that night, a jetlagged and sleepy Sameer walked out of the bustling and noisy arrival terminal. His eyes looked for familiar faces among the many hundreds who stood there with misspelt placards for people they were supposed to receive. A few sweaty cab drivers and travel agents heckled him, checking if he wanted a taxi or a room to stay in the city.

'First class room sir, with AC, attached bathroom, good view, breakfast, just ten minutes' drive from the airport. Only two thousand rupees a night, sir. Bar also is available. How many days you stay in India, sir?' a travel agent pestered him.

'No thanks. Don't worry, man, I don't need a room,' he said, walking away from the agent. He felt a tap on his shoulder and turned around to receive a welcome kiss and a tight hug from Tania who was wearing a slim V-necked black top and blue jeans. He saw Vicky standing in the background with a grin and, with his arms around Tania, walked over to say hi to him. Tania had convinced his parents to stay back home, saying that she and Vicky would pick him up and bring him home in a while. Mr Ahuja did not mind that—he felt tired at the end of the day and did not want to navigate through the peak hour traffic jams of Mumbai. Work for him had been stressful and tiring of late.

Sam noticed that Tania had grown a little leaner than she used to be and was looking extremely beautiful. She sat back looking at him, thinking, *he looks great in shorter hair and those glasses look good on him.* He thought, *she has done something with her hair and has grown it a bit longer, making her look dreamy. He likes me to keep it long,* she remembered, smiling to herself while Sameer ran his fingers through her long tresses like the old times and talked to Vicky excitedly about his MBA course, life at Oxford, the *Play Station* games he had picked up and Naina's new start with MTV.

They soon reached Sameer's place. His mother opened the door to give her son a teary embrace. His dad, looking tired, also hugged him with a smile. His brother walked in a few minutes later to give him a high five. They sat around the dinner table enjoying a delicious meal and a few laughs. Vicky, in his usual spirit, entertained them with jokes about certain prominent businessmen and their ways. Sameer walked out with Vicky and Tania after dinner to see them off downstairs. While Vicky walked down to the basement to bring his car from where it was parked, Sameer gave her a long passionate kiss and wrapped his arms around her for a brief moment. 'Boy, you can't believe how much I've missed you! Twenty months! We are survivors,' he said, to which she nodded dreamily.

He sat for a while with his mum and Rajveer, while his dad had retired for the night. He spoke to them about college and how he'd been enjoying it and heard from them stories about neighbours, family friends, relatives, Rajveer's season with the cricket team and how his dad's business was doing. He went to his room and collapsed in his bed soon afterwards. The excitement of being back home had kept him up longer than he should have. He was jetlagged and did not have the energy to change. He felt some restlessness about things back home—something was different and he felt something bad was waiting to happen. He put those thoughts out of his head, remembering the touch of Tania's lips, before falling into a deep sleep.

~

9
Go Goa

'When one is in love, one always begins by deceiving one's self, and one always ends by deceiving others. That is what the world calls a romance.'

—OSCAR WILDE, *The Picture of Dorian Gray*

24 DECEMBER 2004
Domestic Airport, Santa Cruz, Mumbai

The group of friends was dropped off by Vicky's driver and Rajveer at Santa Cruz's Terminal B on a pleasant windy day to take their Indus Air flight to Goa. Tania and Sameer, dressed casually, strutted in together, with Sameer carrying their duffel bags. Naina was dressed in a short white skirt and Aviator sunglasses while Vicky, in an old T-shirt and cargo shorts, yawned away, waiting to get on to the departing aircraft to catch up on lost sleep. Tanaz and Tanveer held hands like a newly married couple. Tanaz had managed to come on this trip, with Tania and Naina convincing Mrs Rustomjee that she was going with them on an all-girls bonding trip. Tanaz stood with Tanveer in her floral printed skirt that displayed her much admired curves. Tanveer grinned sportingly and traded barbs with Sam and Vicky who teased him about the silk cream shirt he was wearing, which had palm trees printed on it. It was something he had picked up after work the previous evening. Vicky teased him as the boys walked to the security check enclosure at the airport, 'Remove the price tag from the garments you buy. Did you shop on the way to the airport, dude?' while Sameer pulled off the price tag from the collar of Tanveer's shirt.

Goa...

The flight to Goa took off on time and reached Goa within forty-five minutes. The girls had a long conversation on the flight, discussing tans, swimwear and the things they planned on doing. The guys, who were fast asleep, were woken up from their slumber to disembark from the flight with their respective partners and the rest of the passengers. They entered the tiny, over-crowded old arrival terminal and headed downstairs to pick up their luggage. The group walked out to find representatives of the resort waiting for them with a misspelt placard in the name of Vikram Khanna. They soon boarded the minibus with their baggage and commenced on a breezy drive through the narrow roads of sunny Goa towards the Taj Holiday Spa which was located at the southern tip of the state, an hour's drive from the airport. Naina began to apply her Sunsave SPF 30 suntan on her arms and legs. She did not want to get tanned as she was negotiating on getting a *Star & Style* cover shoot the next week.

They reached the picturesque resort in one hour, with Sam complaining that it took less time to fly to Goa from Mumbai than it took to get from the airport to the resort. He added a few words of praise for the trains and roads of London and the wonderful infrastructure the UK had. Tanveer was hardly listening to him and was taking in the sun and the breath-taking view around him as they drove past the scenic coast. This was a welcome change for him, getting away from the traffic, routine and the abusive boss in Mumbai. The group was welcomed at the resort with glasses of refreshing lemonade and was escorted to buggies waiting for them downstairs which were to drive them to their cottages. They had three cottages booked, with a view of the sea from their balconies, courtesy Vikram and Naina, while Sameer and Tania had taken care of the air tickets for everyone. Vicky and Naina took the cottage in the middle, flanked by the one on the right which was taken by Sameer and Tania, and the one on the left, taken by Tanaz and Tanveer. The couples decided to relax for a while and meet in an hour at Vikram's cottage where they could order for and have lunch together. In the evening, after lunch and an afternoon siesta, the group walked down to the beach for a bit of sun and sand.

They divided themselves up into teams where Vicky, Tanaz and Tania beat Sam, Tanveer and Naina at a game of volleyball. Sam and Tania lay back after the game, enjoying being around each other at the private beach. Most people around them were British or Russian and seemed to enjoy the sun, sand and the sea, getting away from the freezing temperatures back in their countries. Sam rubbed some suntan on Tania's bare back after untying the knot on her bikini. She looked angel-like in her peach bikini. They caught up on their time away from each other and then enjoyed a few hours of reading. Tania was engrossed with *On Beauty* by Zadie Smith while Sam was eagerly flipping pages of *Kafka on the Shore*. Vicky, wearing just a pair of shorts, showed off his chiselled frame and took Naina, who looked seductive in her little red swimsuit, into the water where they splashed at each other and enjoyed getting wet. It was a refreshing relief from the scorching sun. Tanaz, in white shorts and a short top, took a long walk with Tanveer on the beach, which stretched for a few miles. They spoke about their dreams, hopes, desires and what they wanted from life, stopping on the way to play a little bit with a bunch of cute toddlers. Tanaz loved little children.

'Your kids will look cuter than this, but then you can't say—what if they end up looking like me?' he said, to which she blushed and walked on with her hand in his. They all converged back at the spot where Tania and Sameer were lying down and quietly watched the beautiful sunset together. Vicky began to pull Tanveer's leg as usual. 'Ask those hot women if they want to take a picture with me. If not, ask them to take one with you,' at which they all laughed.

Later, after a shower and a change of clothes, they headed to the shack on the beach for a seafood dinner in the wonderful ambience created partly by nature and partly through the ingenuity of the resort's management. They were entertained by a talented Goan in a Mexican hat who serenaded the women with his guitar and his deep voice. Sameer sat back, enjoying the music and looked passionately at Tania whose eyes glowed with love and longing for him. *Boy, she is mesmerizing,* he felt, while Tanveer was in seventh heaven enjoying the music and the attention Tanaz gave him. He even managed to sneak in an awkward kiss with her. Vicky took Naina by her hand and walked away further down the beach. After the two of them got back, they walked back to their rooms to retire after a long but fun-filled day. Naina and Vicky kissed passionately and held on to each other. *Naina is something else,* Vicky thought and knew that he couldn't get enough of her. He, however, did not like the way in which men at the beach stared at her. *She is the centre of attention for all the guys at the resort,* he realized. He hated the public attention she got and wanted both of them to be left alone.

'I might come back to Goa for a shoot next week for *Star & Style*. It will be my first cover shoot and, imagine, in a swimsuit! I'm a bit apprehensive, but I think I'll do okay,' she said, sounding excited and asked, 'I'll do okay, na, Vicky?' Vicky pulled away his arm from around her and sat up.

'Do you have to do it? I would prefer you didn't, baby. I hate the way people kept looking at you on the beach. Guys will drool over your pictures, making you their pin-up girl. I don't like the idea of you doing this shoot,' he said in all seriousness, circling her bare navel with his index finger.

'You're such a chauvinist, yeah! You have to make everything I do seem vulgar. Can you please relax? Think about how this helps my career. This is good for me. Let's not argue. We haven't come here to do that. Anyway, I'm tired now and need to sleep. Goodnight,' she replied, pushing his hand away.

'I just want you to think about it. I don't want you to do things that you and I will look back at and feel embarrassed about. Please consider what I have just said,' he said gently and kissed her on her forehead, trying not to upset her.

'I won't feel embarrassed! I wonder what happened to the easy-going guy you once were. You helped me get started, you supported me through all the auditions, shoots, fashion shows and encouraged me through the Miss India contest. You've become so possessive now!' She looked at him with irritation, but seeing him not reacting she calmed down. 'I'll think about it though. You should also consider being supportive. Goodnight now,' she said, ruffling his hair and kissing him softly on his lips.

'Goodnight,' Vicky mumbled, managing a faint smile, and walked out of the chalet, towards the beach, to sit down for a while and clear his head. Sameer called him. 'Hey, do you want to chat for a bit? If you aren't busy, that is,' he said.

'Yes, sure. We can talk, dude. What's up? I'm just walking towards the beach,' Vicky replied.

'All right, I'll come there then. Let's meet at the same place we were sitting at in the evening. Tania has gone over to the business centre for a while to check her work emails. Tanveer is also joining us as Tanaz has gone with her too,' Sameer said while walking out and shutting the door behind him.

'Cool, I'll see you in a bit,' Vicky said. He sat on a chair by the sea listening to waves tumble against the rocks. The sea was rougher than it had been all evening. He took out a cigarette and lit up. Sameer walked up with Tanveer behind him. Sameer saw Vicky looking lost, watching the waves, with a raised brow.

'Dude, there is a good opportunity to buy gold now and sell it in six months. The prices have dropped a lot and I'm sure they'll rise soon, looking at past trends. Do you want to invest, guys?' Tanveer asked them.

'You know, when we grow up we stop taking pleasure in little things. As kids we used to love star gazing, watching the birds chirp, collecting sea shells and running into the sea. Now we have little time to appreciate the beauty of nature around us. Our lives today are complicated and are filled with a lot of irrelevant bullshit. We lose who we are and spend night and day in mundane jobs doing things we don't believe in and losing ourselves in the bargain to earn more money,' Vicky said, gazing intensely at Tanveer. 'We join the rat race and indulge in diamonds and platinum, condos and sports cars which marketers say will make our lives happier and more fulfilling. It's a vicious circle of consumerism, guys,' he added.

'That's deep, haven't heard something like that from you! What's up, bro? You look off colour, all okay with Naina?' Sam asked Vicky with concern, while Tanveer thought about what Vicky had just said.

'Actually not, man. She wants to do some revealing cover shoot for a magazine. I'm not comfortable with it. She does what Smita Ganguly, her agent, thinks is right for her career,' Vicky said, looking frustrated.

'That's bad, yaar, I wouldn't let Tanaz do these revealing shoots or wear revealing clothes. It is improper and indecent. You are too liberal, man! The bikini she wore today was shocking. You should have seen the way that group of college kids was checking her out,' Tanveer said, voicing his opinion.

'Dude, chill, Vicky and Naina are from a different world than you are. He cannot dictate terms to her. I don't feel even you should tell Tanaz what to wear. Let her wear what she likes. Forget this small town mentality, man! The world has changed today,' Sameer said firmly to Tanveer and added, 'Vicky, relax, dude. Don't be so condescending. Enjoy the holiday. Don't let these things affect you. Naina is a nice girl and, even if it is a revealing shoot, she is just doing her job. At the end of the day, she is with you.'

'True, but it is difficult really! I love her so much and expect the world to look at her and respect her in a certain way. Anyway, I've told her to reconsider and hope she does. You tell me, what's up?' he asked Sameer. Sameer sat down opposite him and signalled to Tanveer to sit as well.

'I have been offered a job with Smith and Robinson in London. It's a leading marketing consulting firm—exactly what I want to do. The money and growth opportunities are good too. The thing is, Tania and my parents want me to come back after the course,' he said and added, 'My mum and dad I can convince, but Tania? I don't know. It's a tough one. The long distance is tough. We've had these rows quite often, especially over this Ankur guy she is close too. I don't know how she will take it. I don't want to lose her, man. I want things to work out between us. Maybe she can move there and work as well. You know both of us very well. What do you guys think?' he asked with a look of concern.

'Talk to her openly, dude. I don't see why not. Maybe she'll be willing to move and you guys could stay together. Long distance could drive you apart, dude. Maybe you should come back more frequently than you have done so far. But I think you should take the job. It will help you gain experience in what you really want to do. It sounds great, congrats!' Vicky said cheerfully, feeling happy for him.

Sameer turned his gaze to Tanveer who said, 'I know you guys think I have a traditional outlook but it is difficult, yaar. I feel you should come back, Sameer! Tania spends a lot of time with this Ankur. We don't know who he is as we are busy with our lives and seldom meet. You guys could drift apart because of him—and you say you've been having problems too. There are many opportunities with similar firms in India.' He added contemplatively, 'Besides you do not need the money like I do. What Tania and you have is too special to screw up. Think about it.'

Sameer's phone rang. It was Tania. 'Hey love, I just got done. Where are you?' she asked.

'We guys are down at the beach. Same spot where we spent the evening,' he replied.

'Okay, we'll walk up. Tanaz and I will be there in ten minutes,' she said before hanging up.

'The girls will be here in ten minutes. I'll speak to Tania later. I feel that, with some convincing and reassurance, she'll be okay. I'll keep in mind what you guys are saying. I don't want to spoil her mood tonight,' Sameer said, looking at the boys for reassurance.

'True, but talk it out with her,' Vicky said, looking up at the stars after taking a long drag. He told Tanveer, 'Tanaz sure loves you buddy. Hope you know where you're going with her. She's a great girl, but you know your family situation and hers. Keep that in mind.'

Elsewhere in Taj Holiday Spa, Varca Beach, Goa

The girls were walking up towards the beach. 'Tanveer said he was going over to chat with Sameer about something important. Vicky was going down to the beach too. Are you thinking what I am thinking? What would Sam call the guys to discuss at this time which is so important?' Tanaz asked Tania teasingly.

'I don't know. These guys have their guy things to talk about. Sameer never lets me in on what he talks with the boys. Despite being close to all three of them in college, they had a lot going on which I wasn't a part of, you know,' Tania said jovially, pushing strands of hair behind her ears.

'Sameer could propose to you, that's what I think. Vicky and Naina aren't quite there yet though they have gone steady for a while. Sameer and Vicky have planned the entire trip. There could be something special in store. I'm pretty excited for you!' Tanaz said.

Tania blushed, 'Well, I don't know. You never know with these guys. They might even be meeting to discuss something trivial like their *Play Station* games or graphic novels or even Scarlett Johansson,' she said, smiling to herself. The thought of Sameer proposing marriage started to play on her mind.

'Well, it is an ideal setting—the beach, this resort, all of us here. Hypothetically, if he does, what will your answer be?' Tanaz asked teasingly. Tania wrapped herself with her arms and looked up at the clear moonlit sky.

'Well, if he does, it will be a yes. Sameer and I are happy despite these last eighteen difficult months. I feel we can hold back a year or two till we get married. It will be nice getting engaged though,' she said dreamily and Tanaz hugged her. They got to where the boys were sitting.

'Let's go, big boy, time to sleep,' Tania said, putting her arms around Sameer and smiling sweetly.

'Yes, let's go,' Sameer said and rose to walk back, thinking, *she looks like a dream, look at her smile*. They were followed by Tanveer and Tanaz a few steps behind, along with Vicky who looked at Tanveer with a smirk and said, 'Good luck, loser,' before heading towards his room.

The same night… Tanaz and Tanveer's cottage

Tanaz invited Tanveer into bed with her. She was wearing a pair of tiny shorts and a tight old T-shirt that showed off her curves and her cute navel. Tanveer got into bed and let Tanaz undress herself, smiling shyly. She was embarrassed as Tanveer gaped at her naked body with wonder. She tried to wrap a sheet around herself and he stopped her by taking her hand into his and drew her close. He ran his fingers all over her, telling her how much he had wanted her from the day he set his eyes on her eighteen months ago. He grabbed her arm, not wanting to let her go and grazed his fingers all over her back. His nose brushed against hers and he kissed her softly on her lips. He made her lie down gently and entered her slowly. This was the moment of his life.

He woke up the next morning and saw Tanaz sleeping next to him with a sheet wrapped over her luscious body. It was like a dream to him, with Tanaz lying next to him while he ran his fingers through her tresses and kissed her forehead, at which she woke up with a smile. *This is it,* thought Tanveer. This was the woman he loved and would never let go. He thanked her awkwardly for giving herself to him and trusting him and almost began a sermon on love and trust, when she leaned over on top of him and, putting her delicate fingers on his lips, smilingly told him, 'Shut up, my sweet loser.' He loved the way she called him 'loser' affectionately.

The next morning…
Taj Holiday Spa, Varca Beach, Goa

Vicky woke up, deciding not to broach the topic of Naina's cover shoot over the next few days. He ordered breakfast for her and served it to her in bed. They spent intimate moments together and made love, putting aside their differences.

Sameer wanted to discuss his future plans with Tania, but seeing the mood she was in he decided to put it off for later. He decided to make the most of the moment and enjoy spending time with her—he wished to make up for the last eighteen months he had been away.

Tanveer ended up getting into a fight with Tanaz over her decision to wear a two-piece swimsuit. Tanaz refused to go with him to the pool and stayed back in her room all afternoon. Watching the other two couples play Frisbee and splash around in the pool, Tanveer moped around alone and realized his folly. He made it up to her by sending flowers, a sorry note and a new stringy two-piece swimsuit he picked up from the beach shop at the resort for her to wear to the pool in the evening. The note said, 'This will look better on my Peaches. Waiting for you in the pool, all alone and missing you.' Tanaz soon joined him, looking seductive, which brought a smile to his face. Sameer and Vicky had a good laugh over his change of opinion about 'indecent attire' and told him it was a wise decision.

'Take a picture and send it to your ammi for approval,' Vicky told him, which brought a worried look to Tanveer's face. He was scared of his mother. The group spent the next seven days having a blast in Goa. All of them went for a relaxing couples' massage. The girls did yoga in the morning and enjoyed moments of intimacy with their men, midnight dips in the sea and late night walks on the private beach. Every other night, they went over to the bar at the hotel for a drink where an old Goan couple and their band played old hits by Tracy Chapman, Fiona Apple, Eric Clapton and others to much cheering from the crowd. During the afternoons, they met at one of the chalets and played Pictionary or chess after lunch. Sam and Tania also managed to play table tennis for an hour every day, while Tanaz defeated Vicky for five days in a row at the snooker table over a game of pool. Vicky took his losses with a sporting grin while Tanveer and Naina sat on the sidelines cheering Tanaz on. They also went paragliding, rented bikes and rode out to the carnival, and went to the beautiful beaches in South Goa and other attractive tourist spots such as the flea market and the old cathedral. On New Year's Eve, they headed to a cruise ship where they gambled all evening. While they played for fun, all of them came away losing money, except Vicky who tripled his money in net takings. After dinner, they drove down to a private party on a beach near their resort to bring in the New Year. The couples let their hair down and partied hard and were among the last few people around when the DJ played the last house anthem before calling it a night. At 4 a.m., they drove back in the rented car to their resort and headed back to their respective rooms for a much needed snooze.

∼

10
Strike One...

'The beginning of love is to let those we love be perfectly themselves, and not to twist them to fit our own image. Otherwise we love only the reflection of ourselves we find in them.'

—THOMAS MERTON

1 JANUARY 2005
Taj Holiday Spa, Varca Beach, Goa

Tania woke up to see Sameer already up and drinking a glass of orange juice. They were to take a flight back to Mumbai that night. She looked at him with passion, thinking about the night before. *Last night was steamy, better than any other time.* She got out of bed and lazily walked to him in her baby blue pyjamas and a matching sleeveless top and sat on his lap giving him a nice warm kiss and a dreamy look saying, 'Happy New Year, love, I don't want to go back. I want to stay here for a few more days with you.' Smiling at her with intensity in his eyes he said, 'That's the way I would like it too, but what do we do? Go freshen up, Tania. I'll order your breakfast.' *Maybe I should talk to her. It isn't right of me to hold things back*, he thought. She went in for a shower and was back after a short while, wiping her hair and smelling like a daisy.

He drew her onto his lap again and kissed her again. He made her sit down before him and told her in an earnest voice, 'Tania, there is something important that I have to say to you.'

Tania felt butterflies in the pit of her stomach. 'Tell me,' she said with a shy smile on her face, anticipating that Sameer might ask her to marry him.

'I have been offered a job with Smith and Robinson. They are a leading marketing and branding agency in the UK. You name it and these guys have done work for them. They are a part of the global marketing and advertising conglomerate—the WIP Group. They are offering me a salary of forty-eight thousand pounds per annum,' Sam said with contained enthusiasm.

'That's great. What do you plan to tell them?' she said, hiding the disappointment in her voice.

'Tell them yes, of course! I invested so much in this course only to be able to see this day, Tania,' he said in a matter-of-fact way.

Tania felt disappointment and anger rising from within her. 'You were supposed to come back, Sam! Do your parents know about this? You know how tough it has been for them and me while you have been away. What about your dad's business? Does he have to keep struggling on his own? Think of all of us before you decide,' she said, starting to get emotional.

Sam felt guilty but defended his decision, 'Look, my dad can sell the business. Multinationals will want access to the quality of his staff and clientele. His set-up has a good reputation. Mum will learn to manage; it isn't forever. She could come and visit me in London. Besides, I could come home during the winter break. Maybe you can move there too. We could stay together and you could work for an interior decorator in London.'

'Sam, this isn't right! Now you're taking decisions for everyone! Ask your mum and dad what they want. As for me, I work for myself here. I am running my own company with Ankur and we are doing really well. I do not want to throw it all away and move. I wouldn't be allowed to just go and live with you,' she said and added, 'I'm going to be twenty-four in a few months. My parents want me to get married in a year or two. They are under a lot of pressure from the family.'

'Do not get agitated. We'll work it out. I'm not going to stay there forever. It's a couple of years at the most. They'll fly by. You can at least come over and visit, now that you're doing well and making money. Take a month's break and come and stay with me. We can work it out, really,' he tried convincing her.

She replied, getting upset, 'I don't know, Sameer. You promised to come back after two years and now, when the time has come, you talk about staying there for another two years. I don't get it!'

'What do you not get, Tania? This is crazy, get real! My parents have spent over forty lakh rupees on my course. It makes sense for me to gain some good experience while recovering this investment. We have to look at it practically. Look at it from my perspective too,' he said, raising his voice.

'That's what I've done for the past two years, Sameer! I have looked at things from your perspective and I have been pretty miserable. Look at Vicky and Naina, or even Tanaz and Tanveer. They spend quality time with each other. They make each other happy. They don't argue on the phone like we do,' she said, looking jaded.

The argument was interrupted by a knock on the door. Tanaz sashayed into their room followed by Tanveer. Tanaz and Tanveer greeted them warmly and Tanaz challenged Sam to a game of snooker as her favourite opponent, Vicky, was sleeping. Tanaz and Sameer decided to go and play, while Tanveer, who was tired, decided to stay back with Tania who said she wanted to finish *On Beauty*. Tania was disturbed by Sameer's decision and wondered how he had decided all this without taking into account and considering what she wanted and where she wanted to be. She held back her tears and went to the restroom and broke down. Tanveer, who was sitting in their room and reading the newspaper, heard her sobbing loudly and knocked on the door. Tania opened the door and cried in his arms, telling him about the argument. She told Tanveer about Sam's decision to stay in London, which saddened him as well, but he tried to placate her, saying that things would be okay. He felt that the Sameer he knew was not like this and that he had made the wrong decision.

Their conversation was interrupted by Naina, who walked in wearing a short black skirt and a smirk on her face. 'Guess what? I'm coming back to Goa next week to shoot for *Star & Style's* cover for February. This is huge for me, great for my career!' she told them with a broad smile.

'This is great news! It is pretty exciting,' Tania said, getting up to hug her.

While Tanveer said a feeble congrats, he thought, *wow, I hang out and holiday with the most desired women in the country. It's been a long ride from Sholapur to this.* He wondered about the envy with which his school friends back home would look at him if they knew who his friends were. He also thought, *thank God, Tanaz doesn't model or want to be featured in a men's magazine. I would never be okay with that.* He did not want people drooling over her pictures. The girls chatted about what she would be wearing, who would be shooting the cover, her stylist and the like when Vikram walked in looking drowsy.

'Happy new year, buddies!' he mumbled and put his arm around Naina. He kissed her and asked what the excitement was all about. Naina turned to face him and gave him a sloppy kiss on his cheek, ruffled his hair and told him excitedly, 'I am going to be shooting for the cover of *Star & Style*! Imagine, Naina Jaiswal in a swimsuit on the cover. It's going to propel me to the next level.' *I hope he understands*, she wished. Vicky looked at her with disappointment and looked away.

'Well, I better go take a shower,' he said, unable to camouflage the expression on his face. Looking at his reaction, Naina got upset and followed him back to their cottage. 'Why did you have to walk out like that?' she asked.

'What next level do you want to be propelled to? Come on, you do not have to do this! You're better than that. You are on MTV, people love your show. You do not have to flaunt yourself for a men's magazine! You did not bother to check if I was okay with it before saying yes,' Vikram responded, looking irritated.

'You're incorrigible! This is my job—deal with it. I've told you not to interfere with my work decisions. I think we agreed on this before we got back together. This is my decision and I did consider what you told me,' Naina said, feeling enraged.

'Why on earth, Naina? I could get my mum or dad to talk to people they know and get you some movie auditions. You don't have to get there by being a pin-up girl,' he said.

'Vicky, stop it. This is enough! I think I'm done discussing this. This is who I am. I am a model and a VJ. I have a television career and doing the cover shoot helps me sustain the position I am in. I don't want to do song and dance movies and I sure don't need auditions arranged! If you aren't comfortable with what I do, we should end this. We keep having the same issues!' she said firmly, looking in his eyes with despair.

'I am not comfortable! If you go ahead and do this shoot, I'm not sure as to where this would lead us. It drives me crazy to watch the way guys drool at you,' he said.

'You're making me feel vulgar and cheap. This is it, Vicky, we are through! I've had enough. I can't deal with this pressure any more,' she broke down, sitting on the bed. Vicky stood there and watched her cry with disbelief. A part of him wanted to wrap his arms around her and say sorry, but he stormed out in anger shutting the door behind him.

Naina came back to Tania's room and said that Vicky and she had had a huge row and that they had ended their relationship. Tanveer walked down to the beach where Vicky was having a drink to have a word with him. Tanaz and Sameer returned after their game to hear from Tania what had happened while they were away. Sameer left for the beach immediately to speak to Vicky and placate him. Vicky hung out with the guys and Tanaz in the pool and later at the beach, while Naina sobbed most of the afternoon and ate a sandwich in her room with Tania for company.

The group drove back to the airport in silence, with Sameer and Tanveer trying to crack jokes at each other to lighten things up. They took the nearly full Indus Air flight back to Mumbai. Tania sat in what was Vicky's seat with Naina, while Vicky sat a few rows behind with Sameer. Sameer and Tania tried to talk sense into both of them to sort things out with little luck.

Tanaz, exhausted from the trip, fell asleep with her head on Tanveer's shoulder in the last row of the aircraft. Tanveer wondered what was going to become of them. Vicky and Naina were breaking up after close to two years of being in a relationship where they saw each other every day. Sameer and Tania had problems of their own and wanted different things in life that were pulling them in different directions. He wanted to go and see his parents the next weekend and tell them about Tanaz. Mrs Rustomjee was a different story and would need a lot more convincing, but he felt he could bring his parents around to accepting her.

Tania was unable to reason with Naina on her break up with Vicky. Though she was angry and upset over the row with Sameer, she felt it is best to let sleeping dogs lie for the moment. She wanted to take time and think, especially since they'd had a nice time in

Goa. She did not want to end up having a huge argument with Sameer in the heat of the moment and end up the way Vicky and Naina had.

Sameer realized that he should handle things with Tania with a cool head. He did not want to say things on the spur of the moment and regret them later. It did make him realize that he'd made a commitment to her—that he'd come back after his course. He felt that life had changed and taking the job in London made sense given all that he had put in to do an MBA in the UK.

He took the car from Rajveer at the airport and drove Naina and Tania home, while Vicky's car took Tanaz, Tanveer and Vicky back home. After dropping Naina off, he drove Tania home and talked to her about books and movies. He walked her to the door and put his arms around her neck. 'Wear that sexy black dress I sent you from London and, yes, also those boots that I got this time. Shall I pick you up at 8 p.m.? Go get some sleep now,' he said.

'Not tonight, Sameer. I am really tired. I'm depressed seeing Vicky and Naina break up and I'm really not in the mood to go out. I need some time to think,' she said, sounding distant, and turned around to walk away. She held back from kissing him goodbye as she was still upset with him.

PART 3

FALLING APART

*'If the things we believe are different than the things we do,
there can be no true happiness.'*
—Dana Telford

11
Strike Two...

'But I, being poor, have only my dreams; I have spread my dreams under your feet; Tread softly because you tread on my dreams.'

—WILLIAM BUTLER YEATS

4 JANUARY 2005
Sameer's home, Juhu, Mumbai

Sameer was getting ready to go back to the UK. Tania and he had just gotten back from a quiet lunch at Out of the Blue. *She seems to be better now than in the past few days,* he realized. Sameer and she had spoken only twice over the past three days and they hadn't brought up the discussion they'd had in Goa. Sameer did notice that something was amiss and she did appear to be aloof and distant while at lunch, despite his attempts to cheer her up. Sameer took Tania to his room and sat down next to her, taking her hand in his. *She looks breath-taking,* he thought watching her look at him with confusion in her eyes. Once again he realized how fortunate he was to have Tania in his life. He squeezed her hand and looked at her with warmth and affection.

'See, we've spent two years apart. It could be two more years at the most. You can come visit and I will come more often, promise.

Trust me. Getting this experience is good for me. Once I am a little more settled, we can discuss marriage. That's what I want eventually too.'

'I trust you,' she said weakly, with a pleading look in her eye. 'But I am not sure if this is working out. I am not asking or pressurizing you to marry me. But please understand that I'm a girl, my folks are worried. Everyone knows about us, there is so much pressure for me,' she added.

'I don't know why these people cannot leave your parents alone! We still have a couple of years in my opinion. Look at me. I'm committed to you, right? Just give me a bit of time and think about moving there as well. If you want, I could speak to your dad,' he said, lying down in her lap.

'You know he won't agree! You are aware of the society we live in and the kind of talk that will go around if I come away. That's really what's holding me back. The work is not more important than you, Sammy!' She looked troubled and torn between two worlds. 'I know,' he said. He took her in his arms and kissed her. He felt the same about her as he had before he'd left for London.

They heard a knock on the door. Vikram walked in, looking downbeat and with a three-day stubble. He looked heartbroken and appeared to be taking the split up with Naina quite badly. His calls to Naina over the past few days had gone unanswered and unreturned. Tania and Sameer tried to cheer him up but failed.

'I may be seeing you soon. I have been contemplating doing a ten-month intensive Master's course in Entrepreneurship Management at the London School of Business. The course starts in a few months. Earlier I thought, forget it, as being away from Naina would be a bitch, but I guess I'll take the change of scene,' he said and added, 'Love is a bitch really.'

Sameer patted his back. 'Doing this will be a great value addition for you. Tanveer is also doing his MBA from IIM-A through a distance learning programme. It will give you a fresh perspective and being in a new place with a diverse culture and meeting new people is always good,' he said wisely. Tania put her arms around him. It was the first time she had to console him about a break up. In the past she had often had to console the girls he dated in school and broke up with.

'Cheer up, Vicky, take it easy. It wasn't meant to be. Let's go over to Hard Rock Café after we drop Sameer to the airport.' Vicky looked up and smiled at her with a glum face.

'Sure, that should help getting things out of my system. So far, I'm not able to get over it,' he said and turned to Sameer, 'So your folks know about you taking this job and staying on in the UK? How have they taken it? Your mum must be upset, dude.'

'I spoke to them a couple of days back. They are okay. They are not particularly happy but you know how supportive they are. Mum will be okay, she has my dad and Rajveer to look after, plus her charity work keeps her busy,' Sam replied guiltily, shifting his gaze to Tania to see her reaction.

'That's great. We'll party our hearts out when I get there, man. I can't wait to get away from this place. Everything here sucks. Is Tanveer coming today?' Vicky asked.

'No, dude, he's busy at work. I met him for lunch yesterday. He is going to Sholapur this weekend to talk to his parents about Tanaz. It is a big step for him,' Sameer said with a smile.

'All right, yes. Good for him! I hope he talks about Tanaz instead of cribbing about the traffic and pollution in Mumbai and his chutiya boss,' Vicky said with his vintage tone when it came to Tanveer. They laughed about the scene involving the British girls at the beach. Vicky had convinced them to pretend that they knew Tanveer from Mumbai, which got him into some trouble with Tanaz until Vicky explained to everyone that he had pulled a fast one.

Three days later. 7 January 2005
Sholapur, Maharashtra

Tanveer left for Sholapur for a couple of days after putting in a weekend and late hours to compensate for the time off from work. He walked into his parents' home after a jerky bus ride. He was greeted by his parents—Ibrahim and Sameena Patel—who were delighted to see him. After resting for a while, he took them out for lunch in their battered old Maruti 800. He was hoping to buy the new Alto for his father on receiving his bonus in April. *I have done well this year and should get a nice bonus,* he thought. They also visited his sister Sitara and he spent a couple of hours playing with her toddler. She was to bring him and come over to their parents' home the next day for lunch before Tanveer left for Mumbai. On the way to Sholapur he had spoken to the younger sister Zoya about his relationship with Tanaz. During his conversation with her, he had told her excitedly, 'She is really special, I can't let her go.' She had said she would stand by him but convincing Ammi and Abu would be a huge challenge. Having felt uneasy and nervous all day, Tanveer finally decided to broach the subject with his parents.

'Uh, I have something to discuss with both of you.' His mother stopped eating and his father looked at him, trying to read what he wanted to say. Tanveer looked uneasy and fidgety. 'There is this Parsi girl, a friend of mine—Tanaz. We really like each other and I want to marry her,' he stuttered with little confidence. His mother looked at him angrily and Ibrahim got up and walked away from the table with his dinner half eaten.

'Who do you think you are to go and marry some girl from another community? Do you have any respect for your father or your family? Who will marry your sister?' Sameena responded with rage.

'I love her, Ammi, and want to settle down with her. You don't understand the feelings we have for each other,' Tanveer said, mustering a timid response, pushing a photograph of Tanaz in a salwar-kurta he had clicked a few days back across the table. His mother angrily continued her tirade. 'That's not the way we do things in our family. Your grandfather and your father have not taken such rash decisions and broken tradition and religion for you to do it. No son of mine will go and marry a non-Muslim. Do you hear? Is that why we gave birth to you? Why did I have to live to see this day?' she asked angrily, pointing her finger at him.

'Tanaz is the only girl I want to marry, Ammi. It is either her or no one else. I cannot look at anyone else in the way I see her! She is the one I love,' he said, standing up and folding his arms with some courage.

Sameena, with a tone of finality in her voice, said, 'Go and do what you want. Why don't you kill me and your father before you leave tomorrow? We do not want to live to see such a day. If you have any feelings at all for us, you will think about our feelings. What about your religion? What will the society we have lived in for fifty years say about us?'

She banged her hand against her chest before breaking down. His father rushed into the room and put his arms around her. 'It's those scoundrels you associate with who have ruined you. That industrialist Khanna's son is your role model. That other boy, Sameer, who studies in London, is teaching you the wrong things in life. You want to be like those loafers who have no morals. You have forgotten where you come from and your culture,' Ibrahim added with distaste.

'Yes, you will call Vicky names after he paid for your kidney transplant and spent nights in the hospital a few months back. Where was your son-in-law who was showered with all your provident fund money and my savings? Where were all those morally and religiously upright people you proudly associate with?

Sameer's dad came to see you in Mumbai Hospital. How often did the men you worked with for thirty years come to visit their friend? It's a spineless society you live in,' Tanveer said, raising his voice, leaving his father speechless, and turned to walk away.

'Look at the way he talks to his father. Be ashamed of yourself. If you want to see your mother living, don't take this step,' his mother shouted at him, collapsing on a chair and trembling. She got hysterical and it appeared like her blood pressure was shooting up. Ibrahim gave her some medicine while Tanveer sat next to her, holding her hand. The next day, after his sister and nephew left, he decided to leave too. He did not want to spend any more time with his parents.

'I will think about it,' he told his mother before leaving.

Tanveer thought about Tanaz and his parents on his trip back to Mumbai. Tanaz and Zoya kept sending him text messages but he did not reply to any of them. Vicky and Tania also tried calling him. They were having coffee together at Mocha and wanted to check on him to see what happened. He told them things were not good and his parents had taken it extremely badly. He explained with anguish their firm opposition to his relationship with Tanaz and that his mother was in bad shape. He thought about the life his parents had given him, and the struggles they had faced as a family. His father used to ride a moped through much of his life, coming home drenched when it rained while his mother walked great distances and stood for hours at ration stores to buy provisions. The two of them had cut corners and suppressed their needs and desires to give him and his sisters a comfortable childhood and education. He could not recollect a time when his father had taken his mother out for a dinner or a movie. They could not afford to.

He reached home late in a troubled state of mind. Tanaz opened the door for him and he could not get his eyes to meet hers. She was in her baby pink pyjamas and looked worriedly at him. Tanveer walked in with a solemn look on his face and told her in a grave voice with tears in his eyes, 'My parents are very upset. Let us sit and talk over breakfast tomorrow morning. I am not sure if I have the courage to take this forward any more.'

He walked away to his room with an air of defeat and disillusionment. He put his head down on the pillow and went to sleep after a while, wishing he had been born as someone else. He woke up after a couple of hours and lay in bed thinking.

Tanaz stayed in her room with her quilt wrapped around her and cried for a long time. She also tearfully called Tania and told her what Tanveer had said. Tania promised to speak to him the next day. Deep down, Tania knew that it was very difficult for Tanveer to take a decision that would go against his parent's wishes.

The next morning…
At a restaurant, near Flora Fountain, Mumbai

Tanaz walked into Deepak's with red eyes from crying all night and a worried look on her face. Tanveer was already waiting for her and ordered a cup of tea for her. He explained the discussion with his parents in Sholapur.

'So what do you want to do? Can you not give it time and convince them?' she asked him nervously.

'I'm sorry, Tanaz. I'm very sorry for everything. It is my fault and I should have known how my parents would react before taking forward our relationship. I hate myself now, considering what we did in Goa and my promise to never leave you.' He had tears in his eyes and looked away.

'It's very easy to say sorry and walk away now. I've given myself to you, Tanveer. I trusted you! Why can't you stand up and do what you believe in? I'm willing to do it from my side. How could you say and do all those things when you can't take your own decisions?' Tanaz was angry and felt let down.

'My mother has taken it very badly and my dad anyway has a lot of health problems. I am not that strong Tanaz. I am very sorry. I owe my parents everything. I cannot do this,' he concluded as he turned his gaze away from her and stared at his plate of idlis.

In a fit of anger and helplessness, she slapped him hard on his face and broke down. They noticed the waiters and people at the other tables staring at them with interest. It was entertaining for them to watch the drama in somebody else's life. Tanveer placed his hand on hers while she looked like she wanted to get up and leave. They sat there and cried for a while, holding each other's hand, while people walking in and out looked at them. People sitting at the tables near them started to lose interest in the crying couple. Tanaz rose after thirty minutes and walked out of the restaurant, leaving him behind.

Tanveer paid the bill and walked out of the restaurant. He took a taxi and headed to the Worli seaface. It was a place Tanaz and he often went over to on weekends. He sat at the promenade and thought about how his life had come crashing down just as he felt things were falling into place and his dreams were coming true. He remembered the first time he met Tanaz, their first kiss, the first time he took her out for dinner. The first time they slept together in Goa.

He looked around him to see couples sitting by the rocks, sharing moments of intimacy. People moved about at a rushed pace, too busy to take in the calm breeze at the seaface. A woman shouted at her toddler to stay close to her and away from the promenade. Dogs battled over leftovers at an overflowing dustbin nearby. Urchins offered him fake sunglasses and wrist watches at throwaway prices before he decided to get up and leave.

12
Gloom

'I find hope in the darkest of days, and focus in the brightest. I do not judge the universe.'

—DALAI LAMA

2 JUNE 2005
Hill Road, Bandra, Mumbai

Tania had just finished a pitch to decorate the famous actress Niharika Chopra's villa in Delhi. Ankur and she walked out of the actress's building in Bandra and walked towards Ankur's car. Tania decided to wait outside Niharika's building and requested Ankur to bring his car from a spot he had parked at a few streets away. She dialled Sameer's number to give him the good news. He picked up and spoke in a hushed tone, 'Hey, I am busy working on my branding case study due in a while. I will call you later, bye,' and hung up.

Tania looked downcast and felt put off, not able to share the news of her big win with him, and stood there with a frown, waiting for Ankur. She removed her blazer and put on her Aviator sunglasses. It was a hot and humid day in Mumbai with the monsoon setting in. Across the street, she saw a few of people sipping colas at a small convenience store and kids from a slum nearby running around barefoot playing with tyres and sticks, oblivious to the traffic around them. A teenager with a baby begged her for something to eat. She claimed the baby and she had not eaten for two days. Tania quickly took out a fifty-rupee note and handed it to her. She was soon surrounded by two other girls asking her for money.

She quickly got into the car with Ankur, who took her out for lunch at Olive to celebrate their latest success before their next meeting in a couple of hours. *It will be great to spend alone time with Tania in Delhi*, Ankur thought. *I wonder what Mr Sameer will have to say about that. He should just leave her alone. After all, I am here to look after sweet Tania.* He smiled to himself while getting out of the car and giving the key to the valet parking attendant. In his opinion, after the Goa trip, Tania had drawn closer to him and further away from Sameer. Just as he had expected.

Radio Chilli's Office, Media Zone Towers, Lower Parel, Mumbai

Tanaz waited at Radio Chilli's swanky office, watching with awe the pace at which people rushed in and out of the office. She was there for an interview for the position of an RJ on their morning show. The station needed a new voice to connect with their young audience on the morning show—*Good Morning Oye!* This was her first ever job interview. Her friends felt that with her voice and her cheerful personality there was no one better for the job than her. She was extremely nervous and sat fidgeting with her file of certificates. She wondered what the outcome of the interview would be. She wanted to call Tanveer and talk to him about her nervousness and anxiety, but she could not get herself to call him. They had spoken very little for the last five months. She had initially avoided him after the break up and Tanveer could barely look at her any more. She felt he hated her now and all her attempts to talk to or reason with him had failed. He would leave home early in the morning and return after 11 p.m. on most days. He kept to himself and rarely came out of the room. He also began getting his own copy of the *Mumbai Times,* not wanting to request Tanaz for her copy every day. Even her mother wondered what had happened to the awkward comical character he normally was. Wondering if he was going through some personal crisis, she had, in fact, become more motherly towards him. She often insisted that he join them for lunch and dinner on weekends, which was very difficult for Tanaz and Tanveer.

Tanaz waited for her interview, thinking that it was extremely difficult to move past that relationship. She had been emotionally shattered after their break up and she had even missed college for a few days. She spent a lot of time thinking about what could have been. She remembered bunking classes to meet him for lunch, the times when Tanveer came by to her college and took her out for a coffee or ice cream. She remembered their long walks on the beach in Goa and a smile came to her face.

The secretary to the station head called out her name and asked her to go in for her interview. Half an hour later, she walked out of his cabin with a big smile. She had got the job. She was to do a morning show to start with, and would need to work four hours a day. She was to go on training from the next week and would go on air after a month. She could not contain herself and sent Tanveer a text message giving him the good news.

'Congrats. I am happy for you. You'll do really well as an RJ,' he replied.

Oceania Bank—Corporate Banking Division, Flora Fountain, Fort, Mumbai

Tanveer was at his desk, clouded by his feelings for Tanaz and memories of their time together. He wanted to take her out to a nice place and treat her like his princess. He realized that Tanaz was not going to be with him. *She is too good for a small town, old school character like me*, he thought, chastening himself for not having enough courage. *A real man would fight for his love*, he told himself. He found it difficult to live with his decision and he felt how tough the past few months had been. He continued to be in low spirits since the break up. He spent most of the weekends reading in coffee shops or watching movies with his office friends to avoid being anywhere near Tanaz.

On her birthday a week ago, he had walked up to her and wished her very formally. He felt terribly guilty for how much his behaviour was hurting her. *I have to move out of Mrs Rustomjee's apartment. This emotional turmoil for Tanaz has to end. As long as I am around it will be difficult for her.* At work, every morning, he looked at advertisements for places to rent nearby. They were too expensive at this stage, given the commitments he had. He was also looking out for a new job. He did not enjoy coming in to work any more and having to deal with people like Vinod. These days, he was giving it back to Vinod in good measure and there were heated exchanges between them on many occasions. Last week, they'd had a big disagreement over the paperwork for a lending transaction.

'You understand what I've said, na? Work during the weekend if you have to, but get it done. I want this to go through by Sunday. Mr Sharma from Speedway Engine Oils is getting edgy. It's been on my desk all week,' Vinod had said.

'Well, you should have given it to me earlier in the week if it is that important. You cannot pile up work and expect me to do it on a weekend. I'm sorry. I will start working on it on Monday when I get in and you can expect this to go through earliest by Wednesday,' Tanveer had replied.

'Dekh boss, don't dictate terms here. Do what is given to you. I had other priorities during the week and this is a priority now. We have limited staff as you know. Jaldi salta de, argue mat kar!'

'Please recruit some staff then, Vinod. I work twelve hours a day and I have worked the last three weekends. I cannot do it any more. If you have a problem, talk to the big boss and I will too.' Tanveer had looked frustrated and had turned away to pack his bag and leave for the day.

Vinod had looked at him with irritation. 'Achcha, because you are appreciated by him and got a big bonus, you're acting smart. Wait till your next appraisal. We'll pick this up there and address it.'

'Do what you want, Vinod. I do my work in the interest of the bank and that shows in what I have achieved. I don't work here to please you and cover for your inefficiencies. I would be happy to discuss this with HR as well. Goodbye,' Tanveer had said, walking away, leaving Vinod stunned.

He was applying for jobs in Delhi and Bangalore, and was talking to head-hunters to find him a job in Singapore or the Middle East. He wondered if Sameer could circulate his CV and try to get him a job in London. *There is potential to earn more outside India,* he thought. *Without Tanaz, nothing here feels good any more.*

Vikram and he met sometimes and chatted about their respective break ups. Vicky was also in the same position as him and both of them got drunk and called Naina and Tanaz at 3 a.m. over the weekend to apologise for what they had done. Their calls went unanswered. Tanveer sent Tanaz a sorry message the next morning for calling her late and requested her to forget why he had called. Without Tanaz, the rose-tinted glasses were off and all he could see was the negative side of everything around him. He, however, kept working relentlessly, wanting to earn more and create a better life for himself. *What was better? Where is earning more money going to take me*? He had begun to realize that what was most important in his life had been pushed out of it by his own doing.

Vikram's home, Colaba

Vikram was getting home after completing some bank formalities. He was to leave Mumbai in fifteen days for his course at LSB in London. He was quite excited about moving out of Mumbai for a while. All he did was sit and watch Naina's show on MTV and also watch as many re-runs of it as possible. He felt she looked absolutely stunning on the cover of *Star & Style* the previous month. Looking at it made him angry but he also yearned to be with her. He had gone to three different newspaper vendors near his home as well as Crossword and purchased every copy of *Star & Style* they had that month. *A futile exercise,* he thought in hindsight. Her pictures were splashed online.

'She is going to be on next month's *TV Stars*,' Tania had casually told him. He wanted to leave the city before that issue came out. He was preoccupied with winding up work in his father's office and preparing to leave. A number of women in his social circle were trying to make a play for him but he decided to keep a safe distance from them and women in general for a while. Zoya Sehgal, an aspiring model who worked out with him at Tony's Gym, had been inviting him for coffee and milkshakes, which he had been politely refusing. Ruchika Roy, a classmate from school who worked in a PR firm, met Tanveer and him at Hawaiian Shack a week ago.

'Wow, she's beautiful and seems intelligent and fun to hang out with. She also seems to have an eye for you,' Tanveer had told him while looking at Ruchika dance with her group of friends, with her gaze still set on Vicky.

'Yeah, man, but I move to London in a few days. Why complicate my life more than it already is. I want to stay away from these women for a while,' he said, looking dishevelled with his unshaven beard. He asked for another tequila shot.

'I would go for the kill and enjoy the dalliances. These flings could help you get over Naina. This love-shuv doesn't get you anywhere, yaar,' Tanveer said, smiling in Ruchika's direction.

Vicky looked at him with disbelief and a frown came to his face. 'What's happened to you, dude? In close to five years I saw you only with one girl. You were a steady ship, man. You're in a state of shock over your break up. Have another glass of whisky and go get some sleep. You have bloodshot eyes,' Vicky said.

Tanveer stared at his glass and looked confused and upset. Vicky looked at him. *Love is tough.* Thinking about Naina made him feel depressed. He had tried calling her many times but his calls went unanswered. Naina sent a request through Tania requesting him to leave her alone, which made him feel low and unwanted. He sat down for lunch with his sister and thought about the conversation with Tanveer over lunch the day before, a week after they had met for a drink.

'Dude, don't be stupid. Do what your heart tells you to do. Don't leave Tanaz like this. You cannot live your life the way the society expects you to. They have different rules for different people.' Tanveer had looked disturbed and helpless.

'You live in a different society from my parents. I will be blamed and cursed all my life if anything were to happen to them. It's not so easy.' Vicky was losing his patience with him.

'Neither is what you've done with Tanaz. Why did you go down the road and do what you did in Goa with her? You gave her hopes and dreams and now you step back because your parents won't be okay. What will you be okay with? Following the path someone has predetermined for you? Crushing your dreams and pretending to be happy? Let's face facts, dude—you do a lot for your parents. It shouldn't hurt if you end up with a woman of your choice.'

Tanveer had not seemed completely convinced by his advice. He had toed the line too long to stop doing it now. Vicky was surprised by the intensity of his voice when he spoke to Tanveer. *But Tanaz is a very nice girl and Tanveer is making a horrible mistake,* he felt.

Said School of Business, Oxford University, UK

Sameer walked down the corridor with a swagger and a smile on his face. He had aced the last case study presentation. The professor told him that he had not seen such a compelling and coherent solution of the case before. He tried calling Tania, who cut his call. She sent him a text message. 'In a meeting right now, I will call you later,' it read. Things between Tania and him had been difficult of late. She was always working with Ankur or hanging out with him. Tanveer, she had told him, was depressed and hardly went out. Vicky met up more often but was quite busy on the weekends. Naina stayed more with her own group of friends since her break up with Vicky, though she kept in touch and met for an occasional coffee. Tanaz was still coming to terms with what had happened to her. Tania often hung out with Ankur on the weekends. She told Sameer briefly where they went and what they did.

Bharat had, in fact, messaged him a few days back asking if Tania and he were no longer seeing each other. He had seen Tania with Ankur a couple of times, once at a party and once at a lounge. 'He is just a friend,' Sameer had messaged him to put an end to the rumours. He was in his room when the phone rang. It was Tania. They hadn't spoken for a week. He told her about his presentation and what the professor had told him.

'I am proud of you,' she said. She then told him her good news about winning the big contract and having to move to Delhi next week for a month to work on it with Ankur. He did not like what he heard.

'You aren't going with him to Delhi! I hate you spending so much time with this guy. I don't like his presence around you so much. Why don't you let him do the project himself?'

'Look, I do not interfere in your decisions and you please do not interfere in mine. I work with him right? Deal with that. I am not heading up to Delhi on a romantic sojourn with him!'

'Who knows, maybe that's what this is. I have little say in what you do. You're always with this Ankur guy who even picks up your phone half the time when I call and says you are busy in a meeting,' Sam said provocatively and continued in an agitated tone, 'You are doing this to get back at me for deciding to take a job here. It's been ages since we spoke. Where is the person you used to be, Tania? It's about our ego and who gives in how much in this relationship.'

Tania began to sob. 'You don't understand me. Ankur is just a friend, while you mean the world to me. We are always arguing and fighting. I cannot even speak to you any more. I don't know where this is going because I am getting stressed out worrying about our future.'

'Please stop crying, Tania.' He realized that he'd made a mistake doubting her fidelity.

'I don't know what to say to you any more, Sam. I have sacrificed a good deal in this relationship with you being away. To top it all, you get so insecure and possessive about Ankur. I don't know what to do or say any more. Let's take a break from this and think about what we want for our future.'

'Look, please relax, Tania. I am sorry, okay? Go to Delhi if you have to and good luck with the project. I will be okay. Forget we had this conversation,' Sam said calmly, reflecting for a moment on what she had just said.

'No, Sam. Let's give each other a break and not chat for a while. I'm happy your presentation went well,' she said with quiet resolve. She needed some space to think about where they were headed.

'Okay, well, goodnight then. I love you. Sleep well,' Sam said, hanging up reluctantly.

He did not sleep much that night. He sent flowers the next morning, which were to reach Tania at work, wishing her luck and asking her to please call him. Ankur threw them out before Tania got to the office. She knew nothing about them.

Sameer decided to make a three-day trip to Mumbai to surprise her but he was unable to do so. He was to start work in a few days and the joining date could not be deferred as all recruits would come in on the same day and go through the same training programme which would not be repeated. What he did not know was that Tania was thinking of doing the same. She really wanted to spend time and work things out with him. Ankur, however, stopped her, saying that the project in Delhi was a priority and the client would be unhappy if they failed to meet the deadline. He requested her to put off her trip till after the project.

~

13
Distance

'You've got to know your limitations. I don't know what your limitations are. I found out what mine were when I was twelve. I found out that there weren't too many limitations, if I did it my way.'

—JOHNNY CASH

8 JULY 2005
Liverpool, UK

A battle of egos had begun between Tania and Sameer. Barring an occasional good morning or good night text message, Tania and Sameer had not spoken to each other for weeks. Sameer walked from his office at Great Tower Street to Monument, the underground tube station, to head back to Liverpool where he had taken a room for four hundred and fifty pounds a month. It was a great start for him at work. He had been picked to join a team to work on the brand strategy for a leading law firm in the UK. He had impressed the senior management during training and while completing his first project. He wanted to call Tania and talk to her about his day at work at Smith and Robinson but decided against it. He instead called his dad and chatted with him for a while, telling him about his first big presentation and the client's reaction. Vicky called him and asked if he wanted to go to a play at the Strand that night.

'Sounds like a good plan. I will see you at Coffee Republic opposite the theatre in a couple of hours,' he said cheerfully. Sameer felt good having Vicky in town as he often felt lonely in the city. Samar had moved to Australia to work with a mining conglomerate and Kim had taken a job in Birmingham. He met Kim occasionally on weekends. He had begun spending time with Simone Price who was Kim's roommate and had also gotten a job with Smith and Robinson along with him. She was an attractive blonde from Melbourne and was fun to hang out with. He went for a swim with her now and then, and they also played tennis together on weekends. He got off at Strand and reached Coffee Republic in a short while. Vicky was late as usual and walked in to embrace him cheerfully. He loved London, having taken to the place like a duck takes to water. He was having a nice time playing the field with every possible attractive lonely, single woman he met at college—with no strings attached, as usual. He asked Sameer, 'Did you know, Tania picked up a bright red Swift for herself? She sent a picture yesterday.' He showed it to Sameer on his phone.

'I have no clue,' said Sameer in a low contemplative tone. *I wonder what else is going on with her. Maybe Ankur knows better,* he wondered.

Tania's Office, Prabhadevi, Mumbai

Tania was packing up for the day at work after putting in long hours.

'So what did Sameer have to say about your new car?' Ankur asked her.

'He has no clue. We haven't spoken for a while now. I don't know where our relationship is headed. Maybe I should have made the trip. We are on a break as I told you earlier,' she replied and continued, 'I do not know what to do, Ankur. I feel like calling him, asking how his day was, about his new job and the like. But he could call me too, na?' she asked, looking worried.

He looked at her with concern, holding back a wry smile. 'You are right, Tania, he should call you. He has to make you feel loved and a part of his life. It doesn't seem to me he does any more. Look, I'm a few years older than you. I've seen a lot of this happen to friends in long distance relationships. You should move on, live your life. How long do you want to wait for Sameer?'

'No, Ankur, Sameer isn't like that. We have problems because of the long distance. It isn't just his fault, we'll work things out. Thanks for the chat, I'll see you tomorrow,' she said hopefully. Saying this, she walked out as Ankur began packing up. She got into her car and called Sameer who was returning from a play with Vicky. She chatted with him for a few minutes and Sameer promised to call her on the weekend.

'I'm glad you called, I've missed you a lot. Congrats on the new car. We'll take it for a spin when I come down,' he told her in high spirits.

'Really, when are you coming? I miss you heaps too,' she said softly.

'I'm going to Munich for ten days next week. I will try and come as soon as I can take a few days off. It's been busy with projects lined up. Anyway, you take care. We'll talk in couple of days. Goodnight, love,' he hung up, hearing a sweet goodnight from her.

Sameer's room, London, UK

He paced up and down his room thinking about her. It was the first normal conversation they'd had in a month. He wondered what the future had in store for them. His phone rang. It was Simone.

'Hiya, are you busy?' she asked sweetly.

'No, not really. Shoot. What's up?'

'Well, I am working on this assignment for an apparel chain and I find myself getting stuck. I seem to go around in circles and can't get to a solution. I was wondering if we could sit together and brainstorm a few ideas. It would really help. I have to make a presentation to the client tomorrow.' She sounded stressed out and seemed to be under pressure to prove her worth. Simone and he were very close as friends and colleagues and leaned on each other for support. Samar had told him in the past that she had been quite smitten by his personality. She found him intelligent, suave and charming.

'Sure. Why don't you take the tube and come by with a change of clothes? There's a Starbucks downstairs, we could sit there. You can sleep over and leave with me in the morning. Is that okay?'

'Fabulous! Thanks, Sam, you're a saviour! I'm leaving in ten minutes, should be there by 11,' she said, feeling relieved. 'Sure, see you soon!' He began cleaning up the room and cleared up the couch. He planned to sleep on it tonight as he would let Simone use the bed. After they were done with the presentation, Simone and he came back to his room from the café downstairs. She changed into a pair of shorts and an old T-shirt and walked up to Sameer who was removing the cushions from his couch.

'Well, you don't have to sleep on the couch, do you? There is enough room for one more in your bed.' Sameer turned around and saw her smile invitingly at him. He noticed her shapely bosom and her slender beautiful legs. Although he was tempted for a moment, he looked beyond her shoulder and focused his gaze on a black and white picture of Tania and him in happier times.

'It's all right, you sleep comfortably. I have a habit of rolling around and you might end up on the floor eventually,' he said with a grin, trying not to make her uncomfortable and feel awkward himself. She smiled and looked at him ardently with her hazel eyes.

'Okay, goodnight, sport. Thanks again for all the help. You made me feel better about the effort I have put in.' She got into bed and covered herself with his quilt. *He's strange! No guy has done that before. He's something. Maybe some day it will happen. I hope it does,* she wished. She was used to the opposite—being desired and rejecting guys who were smitten by her, rather than being rejected. But Sameer had been tactful and charming, keeping their friendship intact.

∼

14
Loss and Pain

'Those we hold most dear never truly leave us... they live on in the kindnesses they showed, the comfort they shared and the love they brought into our lives.'

—ISABEL NORTON

21 OCTOBER 2005
Smith and Robinson, Monument, London

Sameer was making a presentation to the client when his phone started vibrating constantly in his jacket pocket. After the presentation, which went well, he headed to the restroom where he checked to see who was trying to reach him frantically. He saw seven missed calls from Tania and two missed calls from Vicky. All kinds of thoughts ran through his mind. He had not spoken to Tania for a week. *Why did she give me seven missed calls? Is somebody ill or has someone got hurt?* he wondered. He called her back immediately to hear her weeping softly on the phone. Thinking something probably happened to her parents, he asked gently, 'What has happened, Tania?'

'Sam, it's very bad. Where are you? I have been trying to reach you for a while.'

'I was in a meeting. Tell me what happened,' Sameer replied

with worry and urgency in his voice. Deep down he felt something was horribly wrong.

'Come home, Sam. Your dad passed away an hour ago. He had a massive heart attack after he got home from office. I am so sorry. I am at your place with your mum right now,' she said softly, getting a grip on her emotions.

Sameer looked at himself in the mirror with shock and anguish in his eyes. He sat down where he was, with his back against the wall, and began sobbing uncontrollably. Memories came back to him—his father teaching him how to cycle, working on his school projects, driving him to school, reading to him as a child, the dining table conversations, the day he first left for London. He realized how different his father had looked on his last trip. His health was failing but he never saw this coming. He held back his tears for a moment and mustered his inner resolve.

'Tell my mum I am taking the next flight out. I want to see him one last time please. I will be there for the last rites.' Tania cried more at the other end, feeling the pain in his voice.

'Please Sam, get hold of yourself. You need to be strong now and support your mother and brother who are shattered. Text me which flight you are taking. Tanveer and I will be at the airport. Vicky is on his way to your place, please call him,' she said.

Sameer pulled himself together and with anguish in his eyes walked to his boss, Peter Smith. He told him about his father's demise and requested a week off from work. Some co-workers, on coming to know of his loss, walked up to his desk while he was packing up and gave him their condolences. Simone, on hearing the news, walked up and wrapped her arms around him. She spent some time consoling him and walked down to the tube station with him. Vicky called when he was getting into the train. 'Sam, I am sorry man,' he said and paused for a moment adding, 'I have booked two tickets on Air India's flight which leaves in three hours. I am on my way to your place. Come over, pick up your passport and let's head to Heathrow.'

The journey back home was painful and hurried. On the train ride to Heathrow, he broke down a couple times while Vicky patted his back. He checked in at the airport, passed through immigration and got on the plane like a zombie. Through the journey, he looked out of the window, staring far out into the distance and stayed up all night while memories from the past kept flowing back. He blamed himself for not going back home more often, for arguing with his father at times, for not spending enough time with his parents as he grew older. He thought of all the good things his father had done for the family and the advice he had given him. He tried to calm his nerves with some strength—his father was not dead, a part of him continued to live in Rajveer and himself who were like Anil Ahuja in different ways.

On arriving in Mumbai, Vicky and he walked out of the airport into the hot sweltering heat where hordes of people thronged at the arrival terminal and life appeared to go on as usual. Tania walked up to him on seeing them approach and took his head into her arms while he broke down and cried like a child. He had not cried like this before in his life and felt a little ashamed of himself. Tanveer, meanwhile, stood behind her, looking at the ground with agony. The drive back to his place was painful for Sameer. All he could remember was the drive to the airport the first time he had left Mumbai for London. His father had regaled the family with his witty anecdotes and jokes about people they knew and he worked with. He sat with Tania in the back seat of her car with her palm on his knee. Tanveer drove quietly with Vicky sitting in front with him. At the traffic signal, they were accosted by street children peddling pirated copies of the latest bestsellers and new film releases. A girl with a bundle of roses pestered Sameer to buy a rose for his 'madam'. Sameer looked away thinking, *don't they understand how my life has changed over the past few hours?* Life goes on—this is something he was yet to accept and realize over the coming weeks. Sameer walked into his home in a daze to witness the saddest and most difficult moment of his life. The helplessness and devastation he saw in his mother's eyes was heartbreaking. It was an image that would be etched in his memory forever. He saw his brother standing nearby, being consoled by his uncle. He walked in and kneeled down next to his father's lifeless body and kissed him on the forehead. His dad had left this world with a smile on his face. Staring at the lifeless body draped in a white cloth, Sameer still could not believe that his father was no more. He had always been around to give his advice, to support him, encourage him and to joke with him. He moved towards his mother who collapsed in his arms.

'Your dad has left us and gone far away,' she said. She was heartbroken and in a state of shock. She began to sob in his arms. This was the first time she had cried in over fifteen hours. Rajveer came and put his head on his other shoulder and broke down. *I am going to look after both you, I will always be there for you,* Sameer told himself.

The next six days were chaotic for the family. They moved from one ritual to the other, surrounded by extended family, relatives and friends, in keeping with the traditions and culture that Indians are bound by. Tania, Tanveer and Vicky stayed by his side, putting aside whatever work they had. Tania's parents dropped in every day and spent time with the family. There was a stream of visitors, with friends, colleagues, neighbours and family coming in through the day to check on them and support them. Tanaz and Naina dropped by with Vicky and Tanveer and spent some time with Sameer. Tanaz came back the next day and helped Tania out in the kitchen to cook for all of them as well as Sameer's extended family from Delhi who were staying with them for a few days.

A week later...

28 OCTOBER 2005
Sameer's home, Juhu, Mumbai

The day before he left, Sameer managed to get some alone time with his mother. She sat on her bed and gazed blankly at the space before her with her thoughts far away. His mum looked depressed and like a pale shadow of the person she normally was. Sameer sat down on the carpet near her feet, putting his head in her lap. *I had last done this as a child,* he remembered. He asked her tenderly, 'Mum, do you want me to stay a few more days?'

'No bachcha, you go back. You have just started work. What will they think? Your father would not have liked you staying away from work for so long. He is not going to come back if you stay,' she said with sadness in her voice. Anil's sudden passing away had been difficult and painful for her given how strong their relationship had been and how much they had loved each other. She blamed herself for not taking care of him. Sameer looked into her helpless eyes.

'You've done a great job, Mum, you have been a great wife to him and both of you have been great parents to us.'

She put her hand on his head. 'Your dad would have liked to hear that,' she said with a sad smile.

'What about dad's office, Mum? Who is going to take things over and run the place? I wouldn't want to see the place go down. Dad wouldn't like that.'

'You don't worry. I will go in and look at the finances from time to time. Business isn't good but it is chugging along. I have asked Mehta Uncle to take your Dad's place. He has been Anil's trusted right hand for twenty-five years. I think he will manage well. He knows the clients and the staff like him too. I don't want you throwing away everything and coming back. You live your dreams, Sameer, that's the way your dad wanted it,' she replied with conviction and finality in her voice. Deep down, she did want him to come back but she did not say so. She wanted him to make his own choices and did not want to influence his life's choices.

'Okay, Mum, I will go back and stay there as long as I can. But it will be tough with Rajveer and you here and me over there,' he said with a worried look, feeling insecure after having just lost his father.

'Don't worry about me so much. Spend some time with your brother. He needs you, Sam. He's still young and needs guidance and support. I'll lie down for a while. You better sit and talk to Tania. I don't know what is going on with the two of you lately. Tanveer was telling me about the problems you are having. Your dad was waiting for both of you to get married. Tania was like a daughter to him. She is a part of the family,' she explained softly, looking in his eyes.

Tanveer had not told her anything. Tania had come over to see her a week ago and had told her about the problems they had been having and that it was likely that Sam and she would decide on the future of their relationship soon. She had, in turn, calmed Tania down and had requested her to be patient. She did not want to reveal this to Sameer to avoid a possible confrontation.

'Don't worry, Mum. I'll take care of Rajveer. Tanveer is here for him in case he needs anything. I'll speak to Tania as well. You please rest, Mum,' he said, trying to make her feel better. He walked to the door, turning off the lights, and slowly closed the door behind him. He went over to his brother's room and sat with him for a while. Rajveer was taking his father's demise with rare strength. *He is growing up fast,* Sameer thought.

Rajveer talked about his girlfriend Jennifer whom he had been seeing for six months. He also brought up the challenging season this year at the Ranji's and his struggling form to stay on the team. They spoke about Sameer's life in London, chatted about their dad's last few days and about fond memories from the past. Sam asked Rajveer to be around their mother and take good care of her. He also requested him to stay in touch more often.

Sameer walked to the dimly lit living room in a sombre mood. He thought about how a few moments had altered their lives completely. It struck him that life would never be the same again. He sat in the living room looking at old albums—his dad as a child, his growing up years, pictures from his college days, his parent's wedding album and family pictures since then. A lot of cherished memories were captured in those photographs. He picked out a few old snaps of his father and of the family in good times to take with him to London.

Samar called him from Australia and they chatted for a while. Tania walked in quietly and sat next to Sam. He looked at her while talking to Samar. Despite the loss he had faced and the pain he was going through he couldn't ignore how stunning she looked. After he hung up, he spread his legs across and lay down with his head in her lap. She asked him about work in London, how his mum was doing and checked if he had eaten dinner. She asked if he wanted to go for a drive and get a cup of coffee.

'Sure, that will be good. We haven't spoken for a while,' he said. They had put their problems aside for the past few days and Tania had been his pillar of strength through the nightmare. They drove down to the coffee shop at the Gateway in what used to be Mr Ahuja's Honda City. After ordering their coffee, they chatted light-heartedly for a while about their friends' lives and things around them.

'So what have you decided now? Are you coming back or staying on in London?' Tania asked him, putting her hand on his folded hands and looking at him with intense eyes.

'I am going back for now, Tania. I honestly don't know what the future holds but I will take each day as it comes,' he said in a pensive tone, knowing how plans could amount to nothing when life changed with losing loved ones.

'Okay, look Sam, I know how hard it is for you right now, but things between us are not working out any more. They haven't been for a while. We have been squabbling since the trip to Goa. We want different things in life. I want to stay here and you want to settle down in London. I am twenty-four now. My mum and dad worry. They want us to get married,' she said softly, hesitating and unsure whether it was the right time to say this, and asked, 'Tell me what to do, Sam? I don't know where we are going! I am sorry to bring this up now. I know what you're going through, but this needs a solution. This cannot be discussed over the phone.' She looked at him with a sense of resolve, determined to sort things out one way or another.

'I cannot get married now, Tania. I am figuring out my own path in life. I have just started working and I live in one room in London. Besides, things are so uncertain now given what has happened. I need time. I cannot commit to marriage and to returning from London now. I will need a year to be in a place where I can talk about marriage and the future.'

He did not want to argue with her and tried to throw in one last lifeline, 'I know things have been tough for you and we've had trouble, but all I can say is I will try to be a better Sameer and change.'

Tania looked distressed and under pressure. She drew on all her strength from within and, with tears rolling down her cheek, said, 'I don't know Sam. I don't think things will get better with you in London and me here. I think its best we end this relationship. I do not want to pressurize you or stress you out more than you already are. You must know that you are still a part of me. I still love you and will be a friend. I will always be there for your family too.'

Sam looked in her eyes with conviction and paused between words, 'Well, okay, if that's what you want, let's do that. I don't want to hurt you or cause you pain, Tania. No more than I already have. It hurts me if I am hurting you. I have always loved you and don't know how I'll live without you. I guess I will deal with it just like I am dealing with losing Dad. I want you to be happy!'

She moved closer and put her arms around him, 'I hope you'll be okay. I am not going anywhere, Sam. When you need me, I am always there. You have been a part of me. I am not going to push you out of my life.' She did not want to push him out of her life. She wished things were better. She wanted to take back what she had just said and give him one more chance. She could not see him this way—it broke her heart. *If we don't discuss this now, there is going to be more pressure for both of us*, she thought. *Why can't she give me some time? I am tired*, he realized. Sam paid the bill and said he would drop her back. She had not driven to his place that day and he did not want her to cab it back alone. They drove back quietly and swiftly to her place. Sameer stopped the car and walked with her to her porch. She pulled him by his collar and drew him close, giving him a passionate kiss. Sam took a step back after the kiss and walked back to his car with tears in his eyes. He half wished to turn around and ask her for one more chance, but he was too emotionally exhausted.

Tania rushed up to her room and cried for a while. She stayed up all night thinking about Sameer and all they had been through in five years of togetherness. Her biggest fear—distance—had finally driven them apart.

Sameer drove back with thoughts of Tania in his mind. He thought about his dad and his passing away suddenly. He wondered if life would have taken a different turn if he had decided not to go back to the UK after his MBA. Maybe his dad would still be alive. Maybe Tania and he would still be together. Maybe his mother wouldn't have looked like she had aged ten years overnight. Maybe everything would have been okay. He worried about his family.

The next evening, Sameer left for London with Vicky. They were seen off by Mrs Ahuja, Rajveer and Vicky's parents. Mrs Ahuja gave a tearful goodbye to her son and asked him to call every day. Tania managed to drop in during the afternoon and spend some time with him. She was civil and comfortable as she had been all week and looked at him with concern, 'I will keep visiting your mum once a week. Don't tell her anything about us for now and take good care of yourself. I am going to miss you. I'm here for you, remember that,' she said sweetly, playing with his short hair.

'Thanks, you take care,' is all that Sam could manage and he gave her a hug before she left. *How could she do this to me? It's been just a week since Dad passed away.*

On the flight back to London while Vicky was asleep, Sameer felt extremely low with thoughts of his mother and Rajveer back home, memories of his dad and not having him around any more, and what had happened between Tania and him. He watched Mumbai disappear slowly with a view of the sea and then the clouds, as the aircraft rose to a higher altitude towards its destination. He found it difficult to sleep, feeling pangs of loss, sadness and guilt.

Tania meanwhile was unable to sleep either. She stayed up feeling terrible about her break up with Sameer. She still loved him a great deal and it broke her heart to see him going through pain—some of which she had inflicted. *It is not working, I have to move on*, she told herself. Ankur called her, 'Hey, do you want to go for drive. Maybe it will make you feel better. Let's go and get a cup of coffee. I'll be there in an hour,' he said.

'No, Ankur, not now. I'm really not up to it. Please cover for me over the next couple of days. I'll see you next week. I just need some time alone, I hope you understand,' she said in a sad voice.

'Sure, you take care. Don't worry about work. I'll see you next week. Call me if you need anything,' he said with concern.

'Thanks,' she said and hung up. *Goodbye Mr Sameer,* he said to himself and smiled.

Tania went over to Naina's place to spend the weekend. Tanaz joined them there as well and the girls took her out shopping and to a lounge to cheer her up. They talked to her about how they had dealt with their break ups and asked her to be strong and be open to meeting other people. Tania continued to be in low spirits over the weekend, thinking of Sameer and all the good times they had shared.

She walked into her cabin on Monday morning to find a basket of orchids from Ankur. Since her break up with Sameer, her parents had moved at a rushed pace to scout for prospective suitors and get their daughter married. They feared the worst for her and felt it was best that she settle down with someone quickly. She had requested them to leave her alone for a couple of months as she was not ready to start meeting the guys they had come up with. She began to consider the prospect of Ankur and her. There was familiarity and friendship between them. He also had feelings for her and she began to consider his advances and opening up to him, as opposed to considering a future with a stranger she would end up meeting through her parents or uncles and aunts.

∽

15
Drifting Along

'In three words I can sum up everything I've learned about life: it goes on.'

—ROBERT FROST

14 APRIL 2006
Trafalgar Square, London

Summer set in, with long pleasant days and shorter nights in London. Sameer was absorbed in his work and focused all his attention towards learning and bettering himself at what he did. He was to catch up with Vicky, who was leaving London the next morning. It had been almost a year since Vicky had moved to London, having come there a few months before Sameer's dad passed away. He left at 7 p.m. from work, which was quite unnatural for him. He usually put in long hours and would be at work till 10.30. It was still bright and sunny outside and Sameer headed to the station to take the tube to Covent Garden where Vicky stayed. After a nice meal and a few drinks at a Spanish Tapas Bar they walked to Trafalgar Square where they sat and chatted for a while.

'What do you plan to do when you go back?' Sam asked.

'I need to discuss things with my dad when I get back. I'm

planning on starting a small venture capital fund owned and funded by the family with the aim of investing in emerging sectors.'

'That's great. Let me know if Ahuja Financial Advisory Services can help you with valuations and assessing potential investments. That's the sort of work we are doing back home.'

'Sure, sounds interesting. I'll do that. Do you remember, back in college we spoke about wanting to set up our own one-of-a-kind hotel and some restaurants? I want to do something exciting like that. I have the funds to back us. Let me know if it interests you,' Vicky said, looking upbeat.

'Sure dude, I will. But you know how things are here. I'm doing well and settling in at work. But let's see. I'll let you know,' Sameer said and added, 'Are you in touch with Naina? What is she up to?'

'We chat on and off these days. It's the usual MTV shows with her. She does three shows now. She's dating this guy Nitin, who is also a VJ at MTV,' Vicky said. He had moved on.

'Okay. Good for her. Tanveer is still in a mess, man. He hates his job and won't change it despite the other offers. He can't be with Tanaz but still lives under the same roof as her. He is making it very tough for her, dude. She's a great girl. I hear she's an RJ on some radio station.' He did not agree with Tanveer's handling of the relationship.

'Yep, same old Tanveer. Sends half of his salary home. Doesn't spend on himself, has not got himself a car. His folks are trying to set him up with some girls now, can you believe that? Tania was telling me. She asked him to go back to Tanaz and beg for mercy. Our boy is still nuts about her,' Vicky said with a grin reserved for Tanveer.

'How's Tania doing? Last spoke to her months ago,' Sam asked eagerly. Tania had called him twice or thrice a week for a few months after his dad had passed away. His mum had also mentioned to him that Tania had stopped by many times. Their conversations were different now—more formal and distant. The passion and warmth had gone out of the relationship while the familiarity remained. Over time, her calls grew less frequent, and after a while she stopped calling. He hesitated and looked at Sameer carefully. He knew how Sam still felt about her.

'She's doing okay. It's going good at work for her. She started dating that Ankur recently.' *She has to move on,* he felt. *Sam could have done a few things differently or done different things and kept the relationship going.*

'Hope you're okay, dude? She and you have to move on, man, it's been almost six months,' he added, putting his hand on Sam's shoulder.

'Yes, I am good. Good for her. Guess that's what she wants. Maybe I was in the way all this while.'

Vikram stopped him, 'Don't think so, dude. I've known Tania for twenty years now. We've grown up together. Moving past you and ending up with that guy has been difficult for her. She's gone through a lot, man,' and continued, 'Anyway, forget what's happened. What has to happen in life will, you and I know that. It's time you gave Simone a chance, at least while you're in London,' and gave Sam a wink. 'Go for the kill mate.'

Sameer rose from the bench he was sitting on, 'You dog. She's a nice girl man, not one of your flavours. Yes we do spend a lot of time together. Let's see. Come on, let's leave. I have to take the train back and you've got to head to the airport early tomorrow morning,' he said.

Vicky walked him to the tube station and they promised to meet in December when he planned to return for a while during the Christmas break. Sam told him to remember to hand over the gifts he was sending through him to his family.

'Will do. You take care dude,' Vicky said, walking away with a wave. He was going to miss life in London and had thoroughly enjoyed the months spent at LSB. But being here had changed his perspective on many things and his outlook. He hated the materialism and class-driven society he had witnessed all his life. The change came in him while he had a fling with Tanuja, a British girl of Indian origin. She had no respect for India or the people back home and often ridiculed and put down the country of her parents' birth and its people. He reflected on the women he had dated and the sort of society his parents were surrounded by. He realized that was not the person he wanted to be and it was not the life he wanted for himself. He wanted to be different from those people, and also to make a difference. He believed he could use his intellect, money and resources to help and partner with those who had the ideas, talent and products but could not take them to the market for want of things that he had—opportunity in the form of funding and credibility. He knew that money alone did not make a person happy, thinking about his parents' lives and the way in which they led their lives separately under one roof.

He remembered one morning, waking up in Tanuja's room after a night of partying. Her Indian maid had come in to clean the room. Tanuja, who was woken up by the sound of the door opening, got up with a frown and shouted, 'How dare you come in without knocking? You stupid villager bitch, when will you learn? I will send you back to your dump!' The young girl apologized and left the room. Tanuja turned to him, 'Sorry. These damn migrants, yeah! They cannot stop acting like peasants. They don't understand a damn thing. It is so pissing off.' Vicky got out of bed, got dressed and left without a word. The way Tanuja had behaved had stirred a mix of emotions in him. He realized that the maid, despite possibly being a better person than Tanuja, had limited opportunities. She would live a life held hostage to poverty and hunger, while people like Tanuja who were more fortunate were becoming obnoxious and arrogant by the day.

He walked into the station and noticed an elderly man peddling *The Evening Crusader,* a tabloid popular with the commuters. He noticed the headline which screamed—'Superman arrested for drunken brawl in a pub!' He watched a number of young people rushing to pick up their copy. This was what most people's lives were about he realized. Read tabloids, work long hours, buy the latest gadgets even if you don't use them, drink more, party more, shop more, sleep with more people… it was a never ending list of maximizing everything which brought little self-fulfilment or happiness. *This isn't the life I want to live,* he said to himself. He wanted to empower people, understanding that unlike him, most did not have the privilege of a good education and the financial support to pursue their dreams. He definitely wanted to work towards his dream of launching his own brand of tourist hotels and resorts too. He was returning to India with ideas and plans and was more focused than he had been when he left it.

Tanaz's home, Peddar Road, Mumbai

Tanaz heard her phone ring. It was past midnight. Tanveer was on the other line, 'Tanaz, can you hear me?' he said in a rushed voice.

'Yes, Tanveer, I can. What's up?' she said, wondering where he was and why he was calling her so late. She was watching a late night re-run of *Sopranos,* her favourite television show.

'I was pushed off a bus on my way back from a meeting! I've broken my arm and bruised my leg quite badly. I will be staying at the hospital tonight. Please tell your mum that I will be back in the evening,' he explained slowly with a groan. He felt God was punishing him for his sins. He had been forcefully sent by his family to see a girl in Kandivili and this had happened. It could have been worse but he had managed to escape with minimal damage.

'Oh my God! That's terrible. Which hospital are you in? What is the doctor saying? Do you need anything?' Tanaz asked, getting worried. She wanted to go over and be with him.

'I am at SJ Hospital. Don't worry, I will be okay. The doctors want me to spend the night. I will be back tomorrow afternoon. Goodnight,' he said in a brave voice before hanging up. It felt good talking to her. It had been so long. He had forgotten about the pain for a minute. The next morning, he woke up lazily to see Tanaz sitting next to him in a red top and faded old jeans. She had brought him waffles for breakfast and looked extremely worried about the state he was in. His arm was fractured, he had bruises on both his knees and his eye was swollen too.

'You crazy guy, look at the state you are in! You're foolish to stand on the footboard of a bus. How could you be so careless?' she chastened him with concern. She called in sick at work and spent all day by his side. Tanaz took special care of Tanveer till the bandages came off his legs and he went back to work the following week. She fussed over him, cooked for him, washed his hair in the sink and got him medicines when he needed them. Mrs Rustomjee did not mind all this—Tanveer had become one of the family and she was upset about his accident, which could have been fatal. His parents or sisters had no clue about his accident.

Tania and Vicky, on hearing what had happened from Tanaz, dropped in to see him one weekend and spent a lot of time by his side and managed to cheer him up. The four of them sat and watched a movie together. Tanveer felt much better. He had felt extremely lonely and depressed before his accident. He was, however, shattered thinking about all that Tanaz was doing for him. He thought, *here is a girl who gave more than expected in a relationship and I had called it off with her because of my own lack of strength to stand up to my parents.* As he recovered, she drew away from him. She checked on him less often and just dropped into his room every evening to see if he needed anything. He missed not having her around and the attention he had been getting from her. Breaking his arm had actually helped him spend some time with her. He realized that the period during which he had been unwell was the best time he had had in months.

16
Traction

'A pedestrian is a man in danger of his life. A walker is a man in possession of his soul.'

—DAVID MCCORD

4 MAY 2006
Radio Chilli's Office, Mediazone Towers, Lower Parel, Mumbai

Tanaz was at the radio station winding up her show. She thought about Tanveer and the narrow escape he had with his accident. She thought of calling and checking how his day had been but held herself back. *Stop putting yourself through this agony. He can take care of himself,* she convinced herself. She thought, *why did he have to do this to me and to himself? Why can't he fight for us?* The Station Chief, Kabir, walked in and said, 'Great show as always, Taz! We have had a lot of listeners this morning. The advertisement rates on your show continue to rise.' Kabir was slightly chubby and was in his mid-thirties. He had been in a live-in relationship with a show producer which had recently gone kaput. He also had been very encouraging and supportive of Tanaz and to her it seemed like he was very fond of her. He had sent her flowers on her last birthday and had thrown a small party in the office a few weeks back to celebrate the success of her show.

'I am glad that more people are tuning in,' she said, smiling at him with a sparkle in her eyes.

'Yes it is. Now there is a marathon sponsored by SMI Bank for a charitable cause. Do you want to go this Sunday? I have invites to the breakfast after the run with a number of dignitaries and celebrities. I could use a run too,' he said putting his hand on his paunch.

Tanaz laughed at him, 'Well, I could too! I now weigh seven pounds more than I did last year. Let's go. Should be fun. Pick me up on Sunday. What time do we go anyway?'

'Nice, look forward to it. It's at 7 p.m., so I'll pick you up an hour earlier. See you later then,' he said. A short while later she received a text message, 'Maybe we could do breakfast at your favourite Moshe's after the marathon. I look forward to Sunday.' She smiled to herself, enjoying the attention he was giving her.

'Sounds nice, let's go,' she replied.

He sent her flowers and a low fat muffin every day till Sunday. It was something she began to look forward to every morning. She felt good about herself, moving away from the memories of a difficult break up with Tanveer. She did, however, decide to be more cautious and take things slowly with Kabir. She found it difficult to trust him based on what had happened with Tanveer. She was also confused about her feelings for him. At times she felt affectionate towards him and at times she felt angry and outraged at his lack of courage. She did not want to put herself out there and hurt someone or get hurt herself.

28 May 2006
Khanna Group, 18th Floor, Phoenix Towers, Lower Parel

Vikram walked into his dad's plush cabin, which offered a view of the skyline of Mumbai alongside the squalor and the deteriorating slums below. His dad, who was busy on the phone, signalled him to come in and sit down. Vicky looked around the cabin noticing modern art paintings, a new expensive Persian rug from Versace and a new picture on the wall which showed his dad receiving an award from the Finance Minister at a CII event. He saw his dad hang up and said, 'So how was the trip to Brussels, Dad?'

'Not too bad, hopefully we have managed to convince these guys to accept our offer for their shares. If it goes through, it will be our second acquisition in three years,' he said proudly.

'That's great! You've been busy a lot these days. I've been meaning to talk to you since I got back. We haven't really had the chance...'

'Hang on,' his dad said, picking up his receiver.

'Susie, can you bring me print outs of the emails I sent Mr Saxena last week? Print our entire series of communications since January in chronological order and bring it fast! Also, I've told you before, speak to the IT guys. Why is my inbox full? I had asked these guys to auto transfer read mails to my personal folder,' he barked on the phone, sounding stressed and tired.

'I have a meeting in twenty minutes. I need to talk to our bankers about a shipping credit facility. Okay tell me, when do you plan to start coming to office? With this acquisition in Belgium, I really need you to get into the thick of things. Your experience with this course in London will really help us,' his dad explained.

'Actually, Dad... I'm happy things are going great with the business. But I really want to do something on my own. I've been thinking of starting a venture capital firm focusing on emerging sectors as well as funding social entrepreneurship businesses,' Vicky said, sounding reflective and growing in confidence.

'What's all this? This is not why I spent twenty lakh rupees and sent you for the course you wanted to do. Get serious, Vicky! I am working twelve hours a day and I have been told to slow down after my heart surgery. I need you to get involved and learn the business. In a few years, you have to take over this company that we've built over three generations. Leave all this social work to your mother and sister.'

'Dad, this is what I want to do! Running an auto components business does not excite me. I'm not saying it isn't good. Many people would like to do it, to run a business of this scale and build it. But I want to do something on my own terms. I also have ideas and interest in the hospitality sector. I want to evaluate starting a chain of exclusive resorts,' Vicky said in an attempt to persuade his dad, who looked at him with disbelief.

'Oye, sudhar ja! When will you settle down and take life seriously? At your age I was on the road meeting suppliers and customers twenty days in a month. Apne business pe focus kar! You got a second class in college. Even before going to London you were busy roaming around with your girlfriend and following her on fashion shoots. It's my fault to have been so lenient with you. How many times did you come to office last year?' he asked sternly and added, 'Now you want to take hard-earned money and invest in start-ups and open some hotels! People are going to make a fool of you and waste our money. You don't have the experience to do this. You are foolish to think that I will invest in this for people to use you.'

'You don't have to invest, Dad. From what I know, I own ten per cent in this company. The value of this, based on the current market value, is four hundred crore. Please give me a loan of hundred crore rupees, repayable in three years at existing bank-lending rates for long term commercial debts. You have my stake in the company as guarantee. I also want you to let me set up my company in the office space you own two buildings from here. Here are the business plans for my planned venture. I look forward to your feedback and your blessings,' he said with confidence, handing his dad a bound copy of his business plans. 'You want to risk doing this hundred-crore venture instead of leading a four-thousand-crore company. Youngsters would dream to be in the position that you are in. Think about it, the world is not so easy. In a few years you will lose all this spirit of idealism,' he said with a frown, reflecting on his experience.

'I don't want to do or believe in what the whole world does, Dad. This is an opportunity I see and, given the position I am, in I believe I can succeed and make a difference to our people while I do it.'

'Did you prepare this document yourself? Or did you get your friends Tanveer or Sameer to do this? It seems like there has been substantive research,' he said, raising his brow while flipping through the pages.

'Have faith in me, Dad. I'm not the same as I was before I went to London. I prepared this document on my own,' he said, getting a bit impatient.

'Okay, let me run through it tonight on my flight to Delhi. I will need to think about what you said and discuss it with my management team.'

'Thanks, Dad. See you at home,' he said before walking out of the cabin. *That was difficult*, he thought. Three days later, his dad called him over to the Colaba Club where he usually spent most of his evenings with business associates and friends.

THREE DAYS LATER... 31 MAY 2006
A Cut Above, Colaba Cosmopolitan Club, Mumbai

Vicky walked into the exclusive lounge to see expatriate business leaders and fat cat bankers sitting around at the tables with fake smiles and an air of arrogance, drinking scotch, enjoying the sea breeze and negotiating important business deals. He realized that this was where sound fundamentals were traded for reckless profits. This in turn generated big bonuses used to splurge on sushi brunches and expensive wine, pretentious new age art, fantasy romps to Thailand, sports cars, maintaining their mistresses, their hair jobs and their wives' cosmetic surgeries. Thanks to liberalization ushered in by a mild-mannered and a well-intentioned Finance Minister fifteen years ago, a lot of people's lives had become easier while increasing their waistline. Free market capitalism was the buzz word, with deals being struck and companies moving at a scorching pace to grow and diversify their businesses through acquisitions fuelled by private equity investment, foreign direct investment and IPO issues, which small and foreign institutional investors were lapping up with frenzy.

However, many people's lives remained more or less the same despite furious claims of the now defeated former political rulers who claimed that 'India is Shining' thanks to them. Socialism was taboo now and was considered a modern evil while free markets and less regulation was the oft-quoted mantra for lifting millions out of abject poverty. *Not completely true*, he thought. On his way to the lounge he saw the 'slaves' of these real beneficiaries of 'Shining India' standing in the parking lot, discussing with excitement the affairs and opulent lifestyles of their masters and mistresses. The recent purchases made by the great masters and the holidays that they had planned were being discussed, while the group also vented out the frustrations of their everyday struggles with rising food prices and higher cost of living.

'Come, come... What will you have, whisky or gin?' his dad asked, seeing him walk up in a smart business suit and sit opposite him.

'Actually, a diet coke, dad. I've decided to have a drink only once a week. Besides, I have to drive back. I drove down here myself,' he said with a calm smile. *Who got to this boy in London?*

his dad wondered.

'Okay, the reason I called you here is to tell you about my decision. I think your plan is interesting. I am willing to invest the hundred crore you need. I don't need you to secure your shares or take it on as a debt and pay interest. It will be a fully owned subsidiary of Khanna Industries headed by you, of course. I have two conditions—one, Mr Senapati, our head of treasury, will be your financial advisor. He will report to me directly for now. There has to be a joint approval by him and you on investment decisions. Secondly, I will also have Ms Smita, from corporate performance and analysis, work with these companies you take on to put in the right processes to measure success and report performance. Both of them will be very helpful till you have your own team in place. They will devote thirty per cent of their time to your company.'

Vicky looked at him with reverence and affection. His dad and he had always had an awkward and distant relationship. He saw him now in a different light as a thinker and a strategist who deserved respect.

'One more thing. The office space you want is yours. But remember, this business has to run on sound commercial principles. It has to make business sense and generate a reasonable return as stated in your plans, while doing whatever else you want to achieve in giving back to society or helping our small businesses to grow.'

'Sure Dad, I'll make sure that happens,' Vicky said with determination in his eyes.

'For the first time I've seen you want to be responsible about something. I like your passion and I hope you succeed. You better work very hard at making it a success now. Cheers, puttar!' his dad said with emotion.

'Cheers, Dad. I am also happy to help out on the acquisitions you're evaluating. Let me know whenever you need me.'

His dad sat back and enjoyed his drink, taking in the view of the Arabian Sea and feeling optimistic about his son's future. *At least he wants to be different from those obsessed with maximizing profitability and squeezing the most out of their employees at a cost to their health and happiness.*

∽

17
Different Directions

'Most of the things we decide are not what we know to be the best. We say yes, merely because we are driven into a corner and must say something.'

—FRANK CRANE

30 SEPTEMBER 2006
Tanveer's Room, Peddar Road, Mumbai

Tanveer woke up after snoozing three times for five more minutes on his alarm. It was getting difficult for him to drag himself to work each day. He looked at the time on his watch with a yawn. It was 8 a.m. He decided to get out of bed and get ready, otherwise he would be really late for work. He had been getting in to the bank after 10 a.m. these days and staying in till after 9 p.m. There was nothing to go back to, where he lived. He had closed the door on the best thing that had happened to his life. He turned on the radio to 101.2 FM. Tanaz was on air. He listened to both her shows—*The Breakfast Show with Tanaz* and *Top of the Charts* while he lazily got ready. It was the best part of his day—to wake up and hear Tanaz's voice on the radio. He had received many offers from leading banks with offices in Bangalore and Delhi over the past few months. He had, however, turned all of them down. He had also managed to get a few offers from banks in Bahrain, Abu Dhabi and Singapore offering him better prospects and a higher salary. He turned these offers down too. A part of him wanted to stay close to Tanaz even if it meant they could not be together. He feared that this situation was likely to change soon. His mother had been persistent of late and wanted him to get married and settle down. He was made to go and see two girls over the past three months in Mumbai. One of them was pleasant-looking and amiable but seemed to have an overbearing father who wanted Tanveer to take over his import–export business and come and live with them after the marriage. The other was overly conservative and someone he could not relate to. He found her outlook on life very regressive and it was contrary to who he was as a person. *I wouldn't want to raise kids in that environment and with those ideals,* he realized. The bottom line was that he was looking for the first negative point to get out of the arrangement his mother was trying to set up for him.

He turned off the radio and left his room with his bag. On his way out, he turned on the FM on his phone and put on his headset. He rode down the elevator and walked out into the street with the blazing hot September sun in his eyes. He headed towards the end of the lane where the old and battered Fiat Padmini taxis were parked. He wondered what Tanaz was wearing right now and wondered if she had let her hair loose or had it tied up as usual. He remembered what it was like kissing her. He tried to get thoughts of her out of his head. He started thinking about Mitali, the girl in the credit rating department. Everyone in the office thought Mitali and he were in a relationship. The fact was that she was engaged to be married to an investment banker in Singapore—a deal which her parents had sealed for her, much against her wishes. She was getting back at them by sleeping with Tanveer who was a confused soul himself. He thought about the movie they went to the last week and about making out with her in the cinema. *She is quite slutty. She isn't a nice person like Tanaz*, he thought.

'Yaar, what is your chakkar with Mitali? She used to go out with two other fellows I know some years back. You had a nice girlfriend before, chutiya. First time I'm seeing someone sell a BMW and buy an Ambassador!' Vinod had told him last week with a wicked grin, which embarrassed Tanveer.

'You focus on your work, yaar! I don't have time for frivolous comments,' Tanveer had told him. Tanveer reported directly to Mr Gupta now and was to be promoted at the next appraisal to the same level as Vinod. *Was it improper and wrong to make out with Mitali? What impression would Tanaz get if she saw me? She is a girl engaged to someone else,* he wondered. He told himself— *shut up Tanveer, your apprehension about others' impressions of you have ruined your life.* He paid the cab driver and walked past the newspaper seller and the commuters waiting for the next bus on the crowded payment. *I am going to avoid Mitali from today,* he decided. *I am not being true to myself. She isn't my type of girl. Even her waistline is bigger than mine,* he thought. He felt that, while his friends had moved on past their relationships, he was stuck in the same place, pining for Tanaz. The memories of their break up after he returned from Sholapur continued to haunt him.

Lower Parel, Mumbai

Vicky drove to work with his new-found steely determination.

'You have changed so much,' his mother had told him after he got back from London. He managed to catch up with Naina a few days after he got back from London. They spent a few hours laughing about the old times and people in show business.

'I wish I had dated this version of Vikram Khanna.' She looked at him in his smart suit and a crew cut approvingly with a flirty smile.

He told her with a grin, 'Too bad, sweetheart, this ship has sailed.'

They were very comfortable with each other now and promised to stay in touch and catch up now and then. Vicky also mentioned how he had a carton of *Star & Style* magazines, which featured her on the cover and his attempt to buy every copy off the streets and bookstores to the extent he could. Naina was in splits and she said with a smile, 'No wonder that month's issue did so well. They sold a few hundred more than they normally did in Mumbai and I thought it was because I am so hot. But now I know why. It was the Vikram Khanna effect. Go buy some copies of *Maxim* next month. I'm on the cover,' she said cheekily.

'Sure, I'll buy a whole carton of them for old time's sake,' he said sportingly. She gave him a warm hug and a kiss on his cheek before leaving. He thought about her interview which he'd read that morning in the entertainment section of the newspaper.

'Take 5 with Model and VJ—Naina Jaiswal

BT—*Naina, tell us about your foray into Bollywood. Which movies have you signed?*

Naina—*At this point I'm reading some interesting scripts and I am talking to various producers. Hopefully, there will be something in the news soon!*

BT—*You were shooting for the movie* Tanha *with superstar Nitesh Kumar three months ago. We heard you were replaced as the producer was upset with you for coming late and throwing tantrums on the sets. Can you please clarify this rumour?*

Naina—*Well I wasn't replaced! I walked out of the film as I felt uncomfortable working with the 'superstar'. I haven't heard of any such claims from MTV where I've worked for two years or from choreographers and designers whom I have walked the ramp for. They will vouch for my professionalism.*

BT—*No actress has walked out of a film with Nitesh Kumar. He's known to be a family man. He claims you were unprofessional and non-cooperative to creative suggestions.*

Naina—*Well I'm sure he is a 'family man'. I didn't feel comfortable working with him and I returned the advance before I walked out. I'm happy with what I did, I have no regrets whatsoever. I want to work hard and succeed but not at the cost of compromising my values. I'm in no rush to sign new films. To me the script and the professionalism of the cast and crew are of paramount importance. There are good people here, too, who are not part of cliques and camps. There are a lot of good films being made by young directors.*

BT—*Those are strong words coming from a rank outsider to Bollywood. Why are you not doing any more new shows on MTV? A new VJ replaced you on* Smash Hits *which was your show with your boyfriend VJ Nitin.*

Naina—*Be that as it may, I believe new talent has to be given opportunity and it was time for a change. The audience wants to see something new. Besides I'm happy with the* Morning Request Show *and* Bunking Kya? *These are way up my street. I enjoy meeting people, interacting with them and playing their favourite songs so I'm in a pretty happy place. I am also doing ramp shows, a few endorsements and a couple of plays too. VJ Nitin is a nice guy and a good friend. I enjoyed working with him on* Smash Hits.

BT—*You made a big splash a few years ago with endorsements, ramp shows and a sexy cover shoot on* Star & Style. *We don't see you in that avatar today and your* Maxim *shoot recently was very timid compared to your more revealing cover shoots in the past. Why the change?*

Naina—*Everyone today is doing the kind of shoots which I and a couple of others dared to do two years ago and I don't want to be in the business of shedding clothes and doing so called 'item numbers'. Anyway, the point is I was twenty-one then and I'm not twenty-one today. Then it was a decision to be noticed. Having done that, today I want to be appreciated for my talent in acting, hosting shows and making an impact on the ramp. Everyone today has a size zero figure. I prefer being talked about for the way I carry myself on the ramp, the popularity of my shows, my screen presence and my acting skills.*

BT—Do you feel this approach of yours will work?

Naina—The fact that I am still being featured despite a 'timid' cover shoot means that I have done something right and people want to see me. I am thankful for that and hope to continue to do good work.'

He drove on with 'Always' by Bon Jovi playing in the car, thinking about how politically correct one had to be in tinsel town. Naina had called him a few days back telling him that Nitesh Kumar was using his clout to prevent producers from signing her on. Nitin had also told her not to talk about their relationship as he was shooting his debut film. Naina had also told him about a few lines from her interview, which the newspaper refused to carry citing editorial decisions—'*The 'family man' was urging me to do intimate scenes and dance sequences, which were not in the script I signed on. He also advised me that if I take it easy and have fun with him, I could be with him in three upcoming films where he plays the lead. Some might want to do all this to get to where they want, I certainly do not. If I have to succeed here I'll do it on my own terms. If things don't work out I'll move on with my life. It isn't the end of the world.*' The superstar's publicist had told the editor to remove this or they wouldn't get any interviews, special briefings or see the actor make appearances at their *Starburst* awards. In exchange for editing the interview to his satisfaction, the star was to perform at the awards night and do three feature stories close to his film's release date for the newspaper's sister magazine.

Vicky realized that these were the ways of show business. He remembered the problems Naina and he had when they were dating. He knew that he wanted to settle down with someone nice and with a less complicated life. He wanted to be with somebody who was easy-going and relaxed like him. *Someone who is beautiful too,* he thought, smiling to himself as he did not want to get distracted by the flavours. He wondered where he would find such a girl. Most girls he met through work or socially were easy pickings. If they were beautiful they either lacked refinement or intelligence or both. The ones that were nice were either taken or had too many complications. He wondered about Sameer who was now dating Simone. *She is hot,* he remembered from the time they'd partied together in London. He thought she was quite a stunner but somehow she didn't fit into the picture he imagined for his best friend.

He couldn't think of Sameer without Tania. He remembered how ecstatic she was when Sam had first proposed to her. He remembered having told her, 'Babe, take it slowly. I am happy for you though.' Tania had grown distant from the rest of them since she had begun dating Ankur. He had met her just once since he had got back. He waited a minute and adjusted his tie. He locked up and headed to the elevator with a smile. It was great for someone at his age to head a hundred-crore corpus fund. By industry standards it was a small amount, but he thought, *I need to use these funds to make a difference while making money.* It was not the way most businessmen thought. It most certainly was all about returns on investment and cash flows while valuing a potential deal or investment decision. He wanted to find meaning in life and wanted to make a difference. He wanted to work with people with passion and a drive to succeed at what they enjoyed doing. He remembered his conversation with his dad five months ago when he had spoken about his plans of setting up a venture capital firm. Despite the initial struggle, they had concluded three investments for a cumulative fifty-eight crore with start-ups in retail, digital media and rural distribution and logistics for consumer goods. He was looking at a number of other opportunities, which included a chain of bakeries, a publisher of low cost textbooks for rural schools and a few others. He was optimistic about the future and was excited about the progress made thus far.

1 OCTOBER 2006
Smith and Robinson, Monument, London

Sameer walked into the restroom and splashed his face with cold water. He had just finished an important presentation to a leading car rental agency in the UK. The clients had given him a very good feedback on his work and were keen to adopt his recommendations. He had identified key action points that they needed to initiate to market their service as unique in the mind of potential customers. Peter was extremely pleased with him and asked him to take the rest of the day off and be back the next day to begin a new assignment for a grocery chain wanting to win back lost customers.

'That bloke has real potential,' he heard Peter tell a senior colleague at the firm. *I can go home and catch up on sleep,* he thought. It had been two weeks of working over sixteen hours a day to finish the data analysis and compile the report detailing his recommendations. He sent Simone a text message asking her to be ready by 9 p.m. He planned to pick her up and take her out for a nice dinner. She was the light of his life in London. They had supported each other through the pressures of work and the frustration of being away from friends and family back home. There were no formalities between them. It was an easy, no-frills relationship as there were no high expectations from either side.

Being with her is good, he thought while loosening his tie and looking at himself in the mirror. He wanted to take each day as it came with her, without thinking where the relationship was headed and whether she was the right one. This relationship was different—she needed him and he needed her after going through the stress of a long-distance relationship with Tania and the loss of his dad. The intimacy he shared with Simone had helped soothe the pain and heartbreak in his life.

He thought about the article Vicky had forwarded him last week. It was an interview with Tania on her flourishing business by a leading web portal. She had been shortlisted for 'The Young Achiever Award' by *Indian Design. A smart, self-assured business woman my Tania has become,* he thought, remembering the fragile girl he had once loved. *Or do I still love her?* he asked himself, searching for an answer which wasn't easy. He walked out of the door and headed down the hallway towards his cubicle to pack and leave for the day. He stared at the photoframe on his desk before he left. It was a picture of Tania and him in happier times. He had let it stay on his desk even after they broke up, next to another one with him and his family. *I don't know what happened to us,* he thought as he walked towards the elevator with his laptop bag in one hand and his blazer in the other. His mind was clouded by memories of Tania and soon drifted to thoughts of his mother and Rajveer.

PART 4

ANOTHER LIFE

'Nobody can go back and start a new beginning, but anyone can start today and make a new ending.'
—MARIA ROBINSON

18
Crossroads

'Faced with what is right, to leave it undone shows a lack of courage.'

—CONFUCIUS

24 DECEMBER 2006
Sameer's home, Juhu, Mumbai

Sameer had landed in Mumbai a short while ago and was driving home with Vicky who picked him up from the airport. It was Christmas Eve. Two years earlier, at this time, the gang had arrived in Goa for a holiday. Sameer looked out of the window, noticing billboards on either side of the highway as they crawled through peak hour traffic. He noticed with interest advertisements for the launch of a new car by Fiat, new reality shows on television, upcoming residential colonies, a range of new fruit juices in the market, communication of new international routes by Jetset Air and set his gaze on an advertisement by a popular resort offering a New Year holiday package in Goa.

'Life has changed so much since the last couple of years. Who knew then that so much would change in two years?' Sam said contemplatively, thinking about the Goa holiday two years ago.

'Yes dude, a lot has changed—some for the better and some

for the worse. Tania is getting engaged to Ankur on the fourth of January. Are you going to be around? They plan to get hitched some time in March. She's been out of circulation for a while. She's been really busy with preparations.' Sameer was taken aback and hearing this brought a frown to his face.

'No, I leave on the third evening, dude. I need to get started on a project as soon as I get back. I am working on a marketing strategy for a general hospital that has improved its facilities and services. Please don't tell Tania I'm here, dude. I don't want to make it awkward for her or myself. Hope she finds happiness with that guy,' he said in a reflective tone hiding the pain, and he looked pensively outside the window to see hordes of people moving about swiftly, heading home after a long day at work. *Most of these people live on the fringes. Each day was a challenge for them to get through,* he thought. A hawker pushed the latest issue of *Indian Outlook* enticing him to buy a copy. The cover screamed of a scam uncovered in the Indian Navy and polled for upcoming elections in Goa.

'It will be good if you stay back for a day. It will mean a lot to Tania. At the end of the day, we all go way back,' Vicky said in a persuasive voice. Sameer paid the hawker and refused to buy any more magazines.

'No, dude, please don't say that! I don't believe I am strong enough to go watch her getting engaged to some other guy.' They drove in silence for a few minutes.

'So who is our flavour of the week?' Sameer asked Vicky light-heartedly. Vicky, turning into the lane where Sam lived, said, 'No one, dude. There is no time, man. Seriously, I have been too busy with work. Last week we just funded a social networking portal for rural India. It works in thirty different languages. I am now working on this Tech start-up that makes software useable on PDAs to book flights, hotel rooms, cinema tickets and the like.'

'Nice. Good for you, dude. I knew you were going to make it happen. Trust me there is a lot of potential out here,' Sam said, looking out of the window and staring at hoardings of upcoming movies and reality shows on television. They parked at Sameer's usual spot and took the elevator up to the eighth floor where the Ahujas lived. Sameer walked in to give his mother a big hug and a kiss on her forehead. She had aged significantly, her hair had turned grey and she had dark circles under her eyes.

'I am taking you for a health check up tomorrow morning,' he said to her with authority. She had a nice glow to her, seeing her son back home. She joked with Vicky about how busy he had become and how it was time for him to get married.

'Get Sam and Tanveer married first, Aunty. Actually, get Rajveer married too, and then maybe it will be time for me. What have you got Gopal to make for dinner?' he replied cheekily.

Smiling at him with affection she said, 'Chup, bachcha! I have cooked today as both my sons have come home after a long time. There is chicken kali mirch, kadai paneer, dal and kulchas. I know you boys like all this. Chotu should be home in half an hour.'

'Where is he, Mum? What has he been doing since he got dropped from the team? Is he practising every day?' Sam asked with concern.

'I don't know baba! With your younger brother, I don't know what he's up to. He comes home religiously for dinner every day. He goes out sometimes after that. You should sit and chat with him aaram se,' she told Sameer in her motherly affection and added, 'Go relax for a while. You must be tired, beta. I will call you for dinner once Chotu is home. You must be jetlagged. Vikram is here. I'll sit and chat with him.'

'I'm fine, Mum. I slept a lot on the flight. I'll sit with Vicky and you for a while,' he replied.

Sameer was worried about his brother. Rajveer had become

very withdrawn after the passing away of their father and seemed lost and confused after being dropped from the cricket team. He was practising very little and had fallen into a life of drug abuse, drinking and whiling away his time with the wrong sort of crowd. Sameer wanted to have an honest chat with him. He felt guilty being away and not giving him the guidance and support he needed to sort himself out.

The three of them sat there talking about the city, their relatives and Shweta's work with the slum dwellers when Rajveer walked in and gave Sam a hug. He had gained weight considerably. He clearly looked unfit to be playing on the cricket team. *Boy, this guy looks even older than me now*, Sameer thought.

The family and Vicky had a quiet dinner, with Vicky doing most of the talking—about his work and life after returning from London. Rajveer spoke little and mostly concentrated on his food. 'So, how many days have you come home for?' he asked Sameer with little interest. He seemed lost in his own world.

Tania's home, Cuffe Parade, Mumbai

Meanwhile, Tania and Ankur returned from a play called *New Seasons*. He walked her up to her porch and kissed her goodnight.

'Can't wait for you to come back home with me,' Ankur said.

'Well, you have to wait for three more months. They'll pass. Goodnight. I had fun, thanks!' Tania said with a smile and Ankur turned to walk away, giving her a sheepish grin.

She was struck by the image of Sameer dropping her off on the day they broke up. She walked to her room disturbed by thoughts of Sameer. She reassured herself thinking about how much Ankur looked out for her. She remembered how he did everything possible to cheer her up after her difficult break up with Sameer. He had accompanied her to salsa lessons and even cooking classes. She smiled to herself thinking about their cooking sessions together. *He is a way better cook than I am.* A month ago he had invited her home for dinner. She had walked into his apartment where he had set up a table for a candlelight dinner in his balcony. He'd cooked everything himself—from the appetizers to the dessert—and had convinced her to join him for a dance in the living room a short while after dinner. At the end of the song, he had gone down on his knee and asked her to marry him. Tania had been hesitant. It was too much for her, too soon. Ankur had convinced her saying that he fully understood what she had been through with Sameer and he would do whatever it took to make her happy. With some reluctance she had agreed, at which he had taken her in his arms and kissed her.

Things between Ankur and her were good, but she felt he went out of his way just to please her. She realized that the way he was with her was not exactly his nature and feared there could be conflicts in the future. She had felt a little suffocated by his refusal to socialize with Vicky, Naina and Tanveer. At times he even asked her why she spent time with them. She wondered whether to discuss this with him or to let matters take their course.

~

19
Something Else

'Life is pretty simple: You do something new. Most of it fails. Some works. You do more of what works. If it works big, others quickly copy it. Then you do something else. The trick is the doing something else.'

—LEONARDO DA VINCI

26 DECEMBER 2006
AFS Office, Dadar, Mumbai

Sameer took his mum for a health check-up, the results of which were not encouraging. She had high blood pressure and high cholesterol. From his conversations with his aunt he had learnt that his mother was finding it tough to cope on her own. Rajveer was doing whatever he was busy with and she found it challenging to manage her house, her charity work, the family's investments as well as overseeing Ahuja Financial Advisory Services, which was not in a very good shape. A number of talented people had left after Mr Ahuja passed away and took some of the clients with them to their new MNC employers who had recently set up their operations in the city. After dropping his mother at her office he drove down to his dad's old office. It was located in an old building in Dadar, reminiscent of Mumbai's past glory in garment manufacturing. Most of the new lessees were garment distributors. *This isn't the right location to run a Financial Advisory Services set up. It does not send out the right message to potential clients,* he thought. He walked in to see that things were falling apart on the inside too. Six desks were empty and had just an old monitor on them with a CPU next to it. The last time he had come here, the office was bustling with people. He walked to his dad's old cabin which was now used by Mr Mehta. On his way to Mr Mehta's office he shook hands and exchanged pleasantries with some of the older employees he knew. He had a short discussion with Mr Mehta about how things were going. They discussed the challenges, the finances, the reasons for people leaving, and the competition they were facing. From their conversation, Sam understood that Mr Mehta was an amiable personality but was not able to run and manage a business on his own, especially in an ever changing and fiercely competitive business environment. Mr Mehta was more a relationship person and was more comfortable with working on the business development side of things. Mr Mehta had been at the helm of affairs trying to manage things to the extent of his limited abilities. Sameer moved to the next cabin where Bharat was busy typing away on his laptop. His school friend was now the second in command and managed the technical aspects of finance and research for the company. He told Sameer that the situation was grave and they would need to realign the business to cope with the changing times.

'A lot of the MNC and Indian banks today are offering the same solutions as we are in addition to their core lending and credit facilities for businesses,' he told Sameer.

Sameer had understood the precarious situation they were in from his conversations with Tanveer. He realized from his conversation with Bharat that drastic measures were required for the future. In his mind, Ahuja Financial Advisory Services in its new avatar could provide solutions and advice to small and medium-sized businesses that lacked the bandwidth to take these decisions.

'This is where banks make most of their money,' Tanveer had told him. It was easier to charge smaller businesses higher rates of interest, processing fees and other hidden charges, which boosted profits for banks. They could advise them and act on behalf of these small and medium-sized businesses to best protect their interests. They had to get out of trying to advise large companies, some of which were a pale shadow of their earlier selves. The better poised ones had in-house experts and preferred dealing with large commercial and investment banks, much in line with what the MNCs did. Managing the portfolio of investments for high net worth individuals was also a losing proposition as the big banks had significant inroads into that space.

'Many of the high net worth individuals have a relationship with them in some form or the other,' Tanveer had told him, adding, 'It is the unique selling proposition they deploy apart from recruiting top talent which AFAS cannot attract and retain in its current state.'

The website and logo also gave an extremely poor image of the company. It appeared to him like a relic from the licensing era. He felt he should have taken more interest and helped his father to bridge his old network of relationships and credibility with the modern times. Anil Ahuja was a nuts and bolts man focused on delivering financial advice and managing their investments. The soft fluffy aspects like brand perception were not a priority for him. He was the brand of AFAS known for his wit, intellect and repute. Now he was gone. Sameer knew that someone needed to be brought in from the outside. *Mr Mehta and Bharat have been too long a part of the old system to effectively bring in change; they could be partners in the process though,* he thought. He interacted with a few more employees Bharat had spoken about and mentioned gravely that there was a risk of losing them. Sameer took them out for lunch and charmed them. He sought their views on what changes they expected to see in the organization, in the way it managed its business and dealt with its customers and made a note of their suggestions.

'Hang in there. A major overhaul in the way we do things is underway. I promise you higher pay, better positions and a revamped organization in the next eight to nine months,' he said confidently. The four young managers at the table with him cheered up on hearing the proposition of growth and more money if they stayed.

Café Churchill, Colaba Causeway, Mumbai

He left after a few hours in office to meet Tanveer near the Churchgate Station from where he picked him up and took him for dinner at night at Café Churchill. They relaxed and talked about Tanaz and how Tanveer was still in love with her and could do nothing about it.

'I'm so confused, man. I had a fling with a girl at work who is engaged to someone else,' Tanveer said and added looking away, 'I slept with her and got mixed up in her revenge against her small town folks. Now there is this intern in office from the US, Anjili Kumar. Her father heads our Singapore operations.'

'What's her story? Are you guys seeing each other?' Sameer asked.

'No yaar, not much of a future. I'm just doing time pass. Well she's hot, but she's so different, almost from a different generation. She has a number of piercings and tattoos all over her body. These kids are complicated, they just want to experience new things,' he said and added, 'She goes back to LA in two weeks, after completing her two-month internship. I'm having fun, being a part of her Indian experience but she is nothing like Tanaz. The connection isn't there.'

'It is strange, man, listening to you talk about flings with random girls. These women are so not your type,' Sameer said with a chuckle while chewing on his steak. Tanveer nodded sadly and told him about a beefy Sales Manager for a telecom company called Xerxes, whom Mrs Rustomjee was trying to set Tanaz up with.

'She doesn't appear too interested,' he told Sam with a relieved smile. His expression drooped, remembering Tanaz leave home last night looking drop dead gorgeous in a blue cocktail dress. He had seen her get into a swanky new car from his window.

'She gets dropped home often by this guy called Kabir who is her boss at the radio station. I hear them talking on the phone a lot. I think she is dating him,' he said with regret and disappointment.

'Well, what do you plan to do?'

'What can I do, dude? My Ammi is trying to set me up with women from the stone ages who want to take care of me and cook for me. It is bizarre, yaar! I thought women have changed and want to be more independent. I didn't even know such women existed in these times,' Tanveer replied to him with a frown.

'There are all kinds of women in the world. Try to sort things out with Tanaz, man. You guys are meant for each other. It is not like you to get involved with these women you've been hanging out and sleeping with. You're a serious guy, leave all this,' Sameer cautiously told him with a stern look.

Tanveer sat there and looked downcast and confused. Sameer changed track and told Tanveer with concern about his mother's health, the things his brother was getting up to and the challenges AFAS was facing. 'Business is falling apart. Earnings are down by eighteen per cent from the same time last year. This when our economy is chugging along at nine per cent per annum,' he told Tanveer worriedly. Looking seriously in his eyes he asked him, 'Look, I know you're looking to move from the bank. Are you up to taking the reins at AFAS? It is going to be very different from what it is now. I am considering the option of rebranding it as Sunrise Finance and Advisory (SFA). We need a guy like you—in fact, it is the same job you are doing for the bank, except you are on the other side. You will be supporting and saving money for small and midsized businesses at a fee, as opposed to making money for the bank. We need a trusted insider who knows the inner workings of the banking industry to deliver the right services. The money can be worked out.'

Tanveer looked baffled, not knowing what to tell his best friend who really needed his help. 'Look, I'm not sure. Let me think about it. It's a big step. Meanwhile, keep talking to others. If there is a way to help Bharat or Mr Mehta outside of work and in no conflict with my job, I am always willing to. I manage a team of five now, but to run a twenty-people-strong set-up is something else. I will let you know in a few weeks.'

'Sure, thanks! Do think about it seriously. We really can make it work and build something sustainable,' Sameer said with a wave of his hand and called the waiter to order his favourite cheesecake. He did not want to try convincing him more and embarrass him. They got back to talking about Rajveer and the fact that he needed to clean up his act.

'Yes, let me have a word with him tonight,' Sameer said contemplatively, knowing that this was like walking on a tight rope. Rajveer had more or less done what he felt like, though he had a lot of respect for Sameer.

Vicky joined them in a short while. He was formally dressed and was coming straight from work. The guys headed out to

Shooters for a drink and to catch up on what had been going on around them for the past few months.

Sameer's home, Juhu, Mumbai

Rajveer returned at 1 a.m. to see Sameer sitting and waiting for him. Sameer beckoned him to sit opposite him.

'There are things we have to discuss,' he told Rajveer firmly. Rajveer sat down and his gaze locked with Sam's. His brother looked pensive.

'What's going on with you? I haven't been hearing about you doing anything productive after being dropped from the team. I have spoken to Vineet Mama and they don't mind having you over in Dalhousie for a couple of months. I need you to get off whatever else you're up to and get away from this life. Get back your fitness levels and practice. If there is a team bus you want to get on to, you cannot do it in the shape you are in.'

Rajveer was about to start arguing with him, questioning his decision of continuing to stay in London, but Sam stopped him in his tracks and said with concern, 'Look, I am sorry I haven't been around for you or Mum, but I am thinking about coming back in a year or so. Mum's health is not good. If she goes on at this rate, who knows what is going to happen to her. Business isn't good at dad's office. I need to come back in a few months and get this back in shape too. You've got to grow up. If you feel it's cricket where your interests are, work hard at it and get back in the team. If it isn't, figure out what you want to do but stop wasting your life. It isn't worth it. Tell me, what is it that you want to do?'

Rajveer said with tears welling up in his eyes, 'I need to work on my batting, Bhaiyya. I scored less than twenty runs at an average in every match I played last season. I have lost my touch.'

Sameer put his arm around him. 'Look, I am here for you now.

Go to this rehab centre, which Vicky's aunt runs, for a month. Once you feel better, head to Dalhousie and practise there for a couple of months. Practice hard and regain your fitness levels. Mum will go with you to Dalhousie and after that she can go and spend a few months in Delhi with her family and relax,' he said and added with optimism in his voice, 'You could also go to Australia. I've found out through Samar that John Reid runs a very good Cricket Academy there. Most Australian batsmen have been trained there or have gone there to fix their game.'

'How are we going to afford that? Business is in the dumps you say. I found out it costs close to twenty lakhs for a four- month camp!'

'Don't worry. I have a great deal of my earnings saved up. I haven't spent much really. I could use it now. I should have that much in the next three months. But get out of whatever it is you're doing, stop drinking and start working out. Let's go for a run tomorrow morning and remind me to set up an appointment for you at the rehab centre,' Sameer said, looking at him seriously.

'Thanks. Thanks for everything, Sam! I'll do my best,' Rajveer beamed and got up to head to his room.

Sameer sat there and thought of his dad for a while. *I am making the right decision. I do not want to lead a life of compromises and regrets, not any more than I already have,* he told himself. He sat in his room for a while, looking at pictures of his college days—him with the gang and him with Tania. Vicky had sent him the Goa pictures some time back, which he looked at on his laptop. He browsed through his email and logged on to Facebook for a while. He clicked on Tania's profile. She had a picture with Ankur standing up close with his arms around her neck as her profile picture. Sameer signed out, turned off his laptop and went to sleep.

3 January 2007
Chhatrapati Shivaji International Airport

Mum and Rajveer saw Sameer off at the airport. He noticed a glimmer of hope in his mother's eyes. She was pleased with the maturity her son had shown and the way he was planning to help Rajveer. Sameer boarded the Air India flight and thought of home, his family and friends. He wondered what Tania might look like on her engagement day. He had made it to Mumbai and back to London without speaking to her. Tanveer and Vicky were upset about him not having done so, but Sam found it extremely difficult to call her. *I have only myself to blame,* he told himself. He was to land at Heathrow and head to Simone's place in Paddington to bring in the New Year with her. Life went on. Old relationships ended and new ones were going great guns. But for how long would this last, he did not know. He wondered if Simone was willing to move to India.

3 January 2007
Tania's home, Colaba

Vicky came over for a cup of tea with Tania. It was the evening before her engagement and there was a lot of hustle and bustle at home. People kept coming in to set up a stage, arrange decorative bright lights and flowers, and discuss the catering arrangements. Her family had decided to host a small engagement ceremony at home in keeping with her request to keep things small. He knocked on her door and on hearing, 'Come in,' he walked in to see her sitting with a stressed out look on her face.

'Hey beautiful, what's up? We haven't met for a while. Work has been crazy. You don't have to look so stressed out. Cheer up, I'm here now,' he said. She hugged him and looked at him with confusion.

'I'm so confused, Vicky. I think about Sameer a lot! Things between Ankur and me are good, but I don't know. Why didn't he even call me? If he had come and said, "Don't do this, don't get engaged, marry me instead," I would have.'

'But that didn't happen, right? Look, you are just stressed, take it easy. Relax, things will be okay. It's just that you guys were so close. I can understand how you feel, and given the kind of relationship you had with him and the fact that you were so committed. Sameer has moved on, he's dating Simone and still lives in London. This is how life is really,' he said cupping her cheeks in his hands. He thought, *she is confused, but she has to move on, even if it is with Ankur.*

'But did he say anything about me? What is happening between this Simone and him?'

Sitting down next to her and looking in her eyes, he said, 'Look, Sam has moved on and believes, like I do, that you have moved on as well. Simone and he live together and he's quite committed at the moment. We didn't get into these things so much. He was here for his family and sorting out his dad's business. It isn't good for you to be having doubts about Ankur at this stage.'

'I guess you're right. I hope I'm taking the right decision for the right reasons,' she said softly.

'Well, if you have doubts, let me dial Sameer's number now. He must be at the airport. Maybe if we leave now we can get him in person,' he teased her, with mischief in his eyes.

Whacking his arm, she said with a faint smile, 'Sshhh! You're still a brat. There is no need. This is between us. I'll be okay. I am just a little stressed out. Let's take our tea out to the balcony.'

'I know,' he said and hugged her thinking, *was that the right advice*? He wondered if he should call Sameer and tell him what had just transpired. He decided to let it pass after he met Tania's dad on his way out. Her dad told him how grateful he was that

Tania had met Ankur. The Mishras had undergone a lot of stress when things fell apart between Tania and Sameer. Vicky felt that they needed no more complications or stress and got into his car, wishing that things would work out for her and Ankur.

~

20
Home, a Different Place...

'There is nothing like returning to a place that remains unchanged to find the ways in which you yourself have altered.'
—NELSON MANDELA, *A Long Walk to Freedom*

4 SEPTEMBER 2007
Sameer's home, Juhu and Noodle Town, Khar, Mumbai

Sameer was back in Mumbai for two weeks while Simone was on a trip to Melbourne to visit her family. He planned to go and spend a week in Melbourne before both of them travelled back to London. Sameer felt frustrated back home. He found the traffic situation and pollution difficult to deal with. *Being away from the country for four years makes a world of a difference,* he thought. He realized that it was a good decision to continue living in London. He was busy making arrangements for Rajveer who was leaving for Australia in a few weeks with him for his training camp. Rajveer was to leave with him for Australia and was to stay with Simone's family for a week before going to Sydney where the camp was to be held. The only good thing about coming back, Sameer felt, was the effect it had on his mother. Mrs Ahuja was extremely cheerful having her son around. The trip to Delhi had also helped calm her nerves a bit. Sam had been talking to

Mr Mehta about the business even while in London and thought it was best to leave her out of the stress of coping with the tough times. She was also pleased with the change she saw in Rajveer, who was more focused than ever before. He had lost weight and was working out rigorously to regain his past stamina.

'I am playing with more confidence now than six months ago,' he told Sameer. He had scored a century during a friendly club match, which had many other state-level players on the other side. He was optimistic about returning with a bang the next season. Rajveer was also working on his off-spin bowling. He was a part-time bowler for the Under 21 Team and felt it would help him break in as an all-rounder, he told Sam at the dining table. Sameer told him about Simone and his work back in London.

'So do Simone and you plan to get married?' Rajveer asked with interest.

'Arey no, dude, we haven't really got to that stage. We're taking it as it comes. It's great with her. We'll see what the future has in store for us.'

Sam finished dinner with the family in a hurry and drove out to meet Tanveer regarding the offer letter he had set him via email a few weeks ago. Sameer had sent him an offer which would give him a ten per cent stake in the business, twenty per cent higher salary than what he was at and a new Honda City at his disposal which would serve as Tanveer's office car. Sameer believed this to be a good offer and knew that Tanveer was considering it seriously. Tanveer had also consulted Vicky about it and had taken his views on whether he should accept the offer. Vicky was to step in as a stakeholder in the reorganized business. He was bringing in rupees two crore for a thirty per cent stake. *It is a generous offer,* thought Sam. AFAS (now Sunrise Financial Advisory [SFA]) had generated revenues of three and a half crore rupees and made a profit of fifty lakh rupees that year. It was a twenty per cent reduction from the previous fiscal year but a profit nonetheless. He had plans to move the set-up from the existing office space, which they occupied at a heavy rent, to a small office near Nariman Point in the financial district, as well as three small offices—one each in Bandra Kurla Complex, Pune and Ahmedabad—to be opened over a two-year time period. Of the four people he had taken for lunch, three had remained with the firm. Vicky and he planned to promote each of them and send them to head the operations of these new offices. Bharat was to be appointed as Director—Operations and Research for SFA, while Mr Mehta would step into the role of Vice-Chairman and Director—Business Development and shuttle between Delhi and Mumbai. Sameer was to assume the mantle of Chairman of the company in its new avatar and it was agreed that Vicky would be its Managing Director, overseeing the business and providing strategic advice and business development support. Sameer had spent the last few days writing up the strategy and business plan for the revamped set-up, and was also developing a new brand identity and positioning for SFA with help from Vicky. Vicky was to be the face of the company and represent it at forums and industry events. The employees, sixteen in total, were excited about these changes. Sameer and Bharat were making sure that they were involved and that the transition went off smoothly. In the interim, Mr Mehta was to continue till a new CEO was appointed. Mr Mehta was also being given a five per cent stake in the business. The rest of the Senior Management team, which included Bharat, was to be allotted a total of five per cent stake in the business too.

Tanveer got off the train and walked out of the station towards Café Churchill. He walked with a slouch and a tired look on his face with the stress of managing his own team and delivering on unrealistic targets in a market with bearish sentiments. He felt glad that he had sold his shares in New Yard Shipping at two times the price he had picked them up for two months ago. He now took home a gross salary of one and half lakh rupees a month but realized that, while it had lowered his financial burden and stress, it had failed to bring him any happiness. He had been buying nicer clothes. He had furnished his room at Mrs Rustomjee's with the latest designs from Living Centre. He was also taking salsa classes and working out in the plush Fitness Planet gym. However, happiness and peace of mind eluded him. He still hated his job and pined for Tanaz. He walked into Café Churchill and sat down, undoing his collar button, and ordered an orange juice.

Sameer parked his car in a spot which, fortunately, became vacant in front of Noodle Town. He walked up to Tanveer who was already at their table and gave him a firm handshake. They got to the point quickly. Tanveer said in a sombre tone, 'Listen, I had a serious discussion with my parents and they don't want me to take the job. It is too much of a risk, yaar!' He averted his gaze from Sam who tried not to look disappointed. He continued with a smile, 'But I feel it is the right thing to do. Who says we cannot make a success of it? Give me a month to move to SFA. I also will bring a couple of guys with me who have operational expertise in lending and credit control—they, too, could bring in new business.' An elated Sameer got up and embraced him.

'Thanks, thanks a lot man. You won't regret it. It's going to be your ship to run now. You're the boss, you take the decisions. Vicky and I are going to step back and support you in any way we can,' he said.

'We'll do it together, dude,' a smiling Tanveer concluded. Sameer updated him about the current progress at SFA, the plans to grow and expand the business which Vicky and he were discussing, and the team they had in place. After a few moments of silence, while eating their dinner, Sameer decided to broach the topic.

'Tanaz sounds sweet on the radio. I was listening to her show on my way here. Why don't you take your own decision on her as well? If there is any girl that is right for you, it is her. She's been with that Kabir chap for months now. Do something before it is too late. I keep saying this to you because I want you to be happy. You look like a pale shadow of your former self.'

'I wish that decision was so easy to take, dude. I still love her and still think about her all the time. But my parents are so opposed to it.' Tanveer felt torn between his parents' dreams and his own.

'Well, you have decided to take the plunge and join SFA despite what your parents think. You did it because you know that, despite the brand name and a relatively secure future, you hate your life at the bank. Similarly, you love Tanaz and you want to spend your life with her. Your parents, blinded by society's norms, cannot see that. It's time you do something about it, man!'

Tanveer looked at him pensively. He had had similar thoughts over the past few months. But he could not get himself to intrude in Tanaz's life. She seemed occupied with her job and busy with Kabir.

7 September 2007
Vicky's family home, Colaba

Vicky was busy packing his things in his room. Tanveer and Sameer were to join him in a while and they were to go out for a drink. He had bought a small apartment in Pali Hill and was to move out of his family home and move into his own little pad in a few days. Vicky had grown used to living by himself in London and felt it was time to move out and start living independently. He felt that he was too comfortable and pampered in the family home. Tania was to come over and help him decorate the place. She had called him a while back and said she would be coming over to discuss some designs.

'Great, come over. It will be like the old times. Sameer and Tanveer are coming over to chill for a while. Then we might go for a drink. You should join us. It's been forever since we met. We've seen very little of you after your wedding,' Vicky said.

Tania had kept in touch very little since she had begun dating Ankur, and even less after her marriage. She spent most of her free time with Ankur. Vicky had only disdain for Ankur who had made a play for Tania's affections at a point of time when Sameer and she were trying to work things out and Sameer was hoping to save their relationship. Through Naina, he was now aware that it had been Ankur who, under the guise of friendship and concern, coaxed Tania to break up with Sam a week after Mr Ahuja passed away. If he had been aware of that earlier, he would have given Tania better advice when they spoke before her engagement. Sameer and Tanveer walked in when Vicky was packing his books into a box. He asked Tanveer to take home the carton of *Star & Style* copies featuring Naina on the cover. 'She's my bhabhi, dude, I can't do that,' at which the boys laughed. They joked about Tanveer quitting the bank finally, and settled down to play *FIFA 2007* on Vicky's PS III till Tania joined them. Vicky was leading 2-1 against Sam in a game of Arsenal vs. Liverpool.

Tanveer thought about his meeting with his boss Mr Gupta that morning, after he had sent in his resignation letter.

Earlier this morning…
Mr Gupta's Office, Oceania Bank, Flora Fountain, Fort, Mumbai

'I don't know why you want to quit. You are doing so well. I promoted you two months ago and you are at the same level as Vinod who is three years senior to you. Anyway, tell me what can I do to keep you? Who has offered you a job? Is it IDFC Bank or Swiss International Bank? These buggers have come in and are trying to take our staff away. I won't let that happen! Tell me what they are offering you. I can match their offer. You are a rising star and we have invested so much in you,' Mr Gupta said, trying to be charming and persuasive while looking at Tanveer.

'It is not about the money, Shekhar. This is about me. I don't want to do this any more. I am grateful for the opportunities you have given me and all that I have learnt in my years here,' Tanveer said confidently and added, 'Besides, I am not joining IDFC Bank or any other bank for that matter. I will be moving to head a boutique financial advisory firm owned by a good friend.' Mr Gupta almost sprung out of his chair.

'I don't know what the problem is with young people today. You people want to become the boss at a young age. Don't be swayed by your emotions and get over-confident. You have a good career in banking. Go and sleep over it. We can talk tomorrow.'

'My decision is made, Shekhar. I don't want to look back ten years later and wonder why I didn't follow my heart. Though we are a small set-up, we believe we can deliver value to our market and succeed. I hope you can release me next month. I will be happy to put in extra hours and ensure a smooth handover.' Mr Gupta looked at him with disappointment. 'Anyway, it's your decision. I am sorry to see talent like you leave. Think about it. We will be happy to match whatever benefits this firm can offer you. I can tell you off the record that you are the favourite to take my job in a few years. On relieving you early—I wish I could let you go in a month, but you know the HR policy of three months' notice period. I doubt they will consider exceptions,' he said with a toothy grin.

'Tarun and Vijeta, who left recently, served a one-month period. I feel the same should apply to me as well,' Tanveer spoke, fully aware of the good boy–bad boy routine in corporate culture.

'That's right, but if I had someone of your calibre and

experience to take your place I would let you go tomorrow. It isn't like I want to hold on to people who do not wish to work here any more! You have a responsible position and targets to deliver. Once we manage to get someone and you have discharged your responsibilities, you can go,' Mr Gupta said with some hostility. Hearing the way in which he was being dealt with, Tanveer was reassured of his decision to quit.

Back at Vicky's room, Colaba

'Hey guys, good to see all the boys chilling together,' Tania said while walking in cheerfully. The boys stopped the game and focused their attention on her. She was wearing a short maroon kurta and a pair of old jeans, and to Sam she still looked like a breath of fresh air. He painfully averted his gaze from her. They said a muted 'hi' to each other and Sameer moved away to take a look at a copy of *The Economist* lying on Vicky's table. Tania, after she exchanged pleasantries with Tanveer and Vicky, walked to him and asked if they could sit down and chat for a few minutes, to which Sameer nodded. They moved outside to Vicky's balcony which had a couple of chairs. Meanwhile, Vicky pulled out an old tape from their Goa trip which he had shot on his Handycam. He put it on to show Tanveer his reaction on being bitten by a crab—hopping around on one foot, holding the other in one hand. Tanveer cringed, remembering the shooting pain in his foot and how Tanaz had spent a couple of hours holding his leg in her lap and doing everything to make him feel better. Sameer discussed work and the purpose of his trip to India with Tania. He remained very aloof and distant and avoided looking at her directly, instead looking straight ahead at the view of the street from the balcony. Tania began to feel impatient.

'You can barely look at me, Sameer. Don't know how you and

I have become like this! We've become strangers to each other. You came down four months ago for a week and did not bother to call. You've been here for a couple of weeks and you cannot call and say hi or congratulate me on the wedding. Why have you pushed me out of your life, Sameer Ahuja? I thought we were still friends, if not anything more….'

She had hoped that Sameer would try and woo her back after they broke up. What she did not know was that he had tried, but Ankur had thrown out the flowers and gifts he had sent to her office. Neither of them knew about the trips they had planned to surprise each other then.

Fixing his gaze on the floor, Sameer said in a deep voice, 'Sorry, Tania, I didn't mean to upset you. I just felt it was best to stay away and not mess with your head. You're with someone else now and I don't want to get in the way. Congratulations anyway, I hope you are happy and you stay happy.'

Tania calmed down knowing how intense Sameer was and how hard their separation had been for him. She hugged him. 'It's good to meet and chat after so long. Your mum must be really happy that you've come home. It's great what you've been doing to revive AFAS and get Rajveer back on track. Your mum and I still chat, you know. She told me about you seeing Simone.'

She wondered how serious he was about his relationship with her. Sam walked to the other side of the balcony and said in a brooding tone, 'Yes, I am seeing Simone and I have come back in time to set a few important things right—but I am too late for some other things. You were right, Tania. I should have finished my MBA and come back.'

Tania moved to where he was standing and said to him in her gentle soothing voice, 'Hey, stop second guessing your decisions. We cannot go back and change what happened. It's our destiny and was meant to be that way. On hindsight, I think you working there and staying longer has given you a good experience. It's given you a wider perspective on life and the short spiky hair makes you look smarter too.' She touched the ends of his spiked hair and both of them laughed.

Vicky looked at Tanveer who appeared lost in some other world after watching the old tape from a different and memorable past.

'Dude, you better work things out with Tanaz! Go convince your parents, convince her old lady if you have to. The world has changed. You don't want to be Sameer right now. I know what he is going through. I was with him in London too when things fell apart—it wasn't pretty,' Vicky said to Tanveer in a hushed voice, while Sam and Tania were catching up.

Tanveer heard him out keenly, hanging on the every word that was said. Tanaz had grown more popular by the day and had won various industry awards for her work. She was extremely popular among the youth and an SMS opinion poll by Megafone had found that she was the hottest RJ in the city. Vicky had teased Tanveer about it, saying that he had engineered the votes in her favour. But Tanaz had remained her old self despite the hype and hoopla surrounding her. Success and fame had not gone to her head and she remained as sorted as she used to be.

Sameer and Tania came back into the room, interrupting their conversation. She moved towards Vicky and asked him if he was ready to look at the work she had put together. Vicky checked out pictures of designs which Tania explained to him for a while. All of them were too tired to go out for a drink and decided to call it a night. Tania left to go home and after a while, Sameer dropped Tanveer home and headed back himself. Simone called him and he talked to her about Tanveer's decision to come on board as the CEO of his dad's company. He was speaking to her after three days. They chatted about what each of them had been up to during their holiday. Sameer also told her about meeting Tania at Vicky's place while Simone listened to him without emotion. She was not too happy with Sameer going back to India more often and constantly talking about the opportunities there.

'I miss you heaps! Now that you've finished your work, try and get here a day or two earlier than you had planned.' She was insecure about his relationship with Tania and them spending time together.

'No, my mum will get upset, Sims. I will be there soon, yeah? It's just a few days more,' he replied.

'Well, you have your priorities, it's your call. Goodnight, Sam,' she said and hung up. *Why does he have to spend so much time in India? Two trips in eight months*, she thought.

21
A New Start

'Life is like a game of cards. The hand you are dealt is determinism; the way you play it is free will.'

—JAWAHARLAL NEHRU

22 DECEMBER 2007
SFA Office, Dadar, Mumbai

Tanveer was busy settling in at the old SFA Office. It was his second day at SFA and his release from the bank was as expected—long and frustrating. He had to complete the three-month notice period. Mr Mehta and half the team had already moved to a smaller office in Fort and were settling in there, while a couple of staff had moved to Delhi and taken over the operations from a small business centre. Tanveer was, along with Bharat and the rest of his team, working out of the old office while they were still looking for office space in Bandra Kurla Complex and in Pune. The transition phase for a small outfit like SFA was difficult—getting signboards prepared, getting the new office furnished in a better design, getting people used to the new systems and internal processes and getting all of this working was a challenging task. Tanveer and his team were pushing ahead with these changes while ensuring business went on with minimal disruption. Tanveer was in the process of sorting out some contracts and paperwork. He realized that he had to rush to the *Business Times* office with Vicky. Vicky, through his contacts, had arranged an interview with a feature writer to publish an interview showcasing SFA's new plans and the new leadership. He quickly signed the documents and handed them to Sandra, who had been Mr Ahuja's secretary for twenty years, before he headed for the meeting. *Little did I know that I would head an organization I once interned in as an eighteen year-old*, he thought. Vicky was to join him directly, driving in from his office in Fort to Lower Parel where the magazine's office was located. Vicky had, over the last few weekends, done a lot of analysis on SFA's business and customers and had fine-tuned the strategy and business plans which Sameer had prepared with the team at SFA. He was getting his hands around the problem. Close to thirty per cent of the business generated no profits for SFA and they had no competitive advantage in those particular segments of services. The key, he believed, was to build scale and focus more on what the business had a good position in and make that more profitable.

Business Times *Office and Sicily, Phoenix Mills, Lower Parel, Mumbai*

Vicky parked his new Honda Civic in the visitors' parking area and rushed up to meet Supriya Sen Gupta. He was immaculately dressed in a smart black suit and looked very impressive. He was ushered into the room where Supriya was waiting for him with a notepad and a cup of strong black coffee. Vicky shook hands with her and requested her to give Tanveer ten to fifteen minutes to join them, as he was stuck in traffic on RJ Flyover. Supriya was a young business reporter with shoulder-length curly hair, kajal in her eyes and a cute smile. She was slightly plump but managed to carry herself well and appeared confident. She was instantly attracted to Vicky.

'You must be really intelligent to have become the Managing Director of a company at twenty-seven. How long have you been with SFA?' she asked cheerfully.

Vicky adjusted the buttons on his blazer. 'Well, I don't know about that. It is a position I was nominated to, given my investment in the company. I head a venture capital firm called Sunrise Investments, which is part of the Khanna Group. We started this after getting back from London where I studied at the London School of Business over a year ago. I used to work in Khanna Industries in the role of a Finance Director before that,' he said confidently and smiled at her.

Supriya saw him as a serious-minded guy who meant business. 'Well, you are just a couple of years older than me really. I think I have seen your CEO, Mr Tanveer, some years back. If I am not wrong, he used to go out with a friend of mine, Tanaz Rustomjee. We were together in Xavier's. Same batch, same class. I wonder how she is doing these days. She was such a sweet and simple girl, very easy to get along with.' She smiled at him before taking a sip of her coffee.

An office boy walked in to check if Vicky wanted something to drink. Vicky waved him away politely, asking him to get a bottle of water. He turned his attention to Supriya and said, 'Yes, of course I know Tanaz! She is a good friend. I was actually listening to her show on the radio on my way here. It's a small world.'

'You bet it is. I haven't met her for a while actually. It's a busy life here at the magazine, meeting deadlines that depend on meeting and interviewing businessmen who are busy making money themselves—and some are quite eccentric too,' Supriya said, giving him a flirtatious smile.

'Ouch. Hope you don't put me into that eccentric category. So what do you do for fun?' *She is not seductive and sexy like Naina, but she does have pleasant features and seems interesting. She is attractive in her own way and appears sweet,* he thought.

'Not much. Most weekends I work as we often have interviews lined up, depending on when people are free to talk. I love to sleep, watch TV, and maybe go for a movie. I am quite a lazy and boring girl,' she said and looked at him with a modest smile.

Tanveer walked into the room in a grey suit, looking smart and apologizing profusely. Vicky introduced Supriya to him as a friend of Tanaz who went with her to college. Tanveer gave her an uncomfortable nod and smiled at her thinking, *I wonder what she thinks of me.*

'Why don't we take this interview outside? Let's go over to Sicily for lunch. I am going to call Tanaz too. She works a couple of buildings away and it will be fun catching up. It's been a while since I met her. What do you say, Supriya? Is that ok, Tanveer?' Vicky asked.

'Sure, I'm starved,' Supriya said.

Tanveer did not get a chance to respond. He did not need to. He felt odd at the prospect of Tanaz joining them for lunch. They had barely spoken after he had recovered from the injuries sustained in his accident, though they had eaten many a quiet lunch and dinner at the same table under the watchful eye of Mrs Rustomjee.

Vicky hung up after speaking with Tanaz. She wouldn't be joining them for lunch but would drop in to say hi and maybe join them for dessert. They walked over to Sicily nearby, where Supriya completed her interview while they waited for the food. She decided to include a picture of both Vicky and Tanveer and was moving the one-page interview up to page ten from the initially planned page fifty-four. The article was to be titled, 'Winds of Change—Sunrise Financial Advisory—an old warhorse gets a new boss and a new direction.'

Tanaz soon joined them while they were eating and gave Supriya a hug. 'It's been a long time. Good to see you,' she said. She gave Vicky a peck on the cheek and said a cordial 'hi' to Tanveer and sat opposite him. *She smells like fresh flowers,* thought Tanveer, looking at her. He slipped into another world while watching her smile and chat with Supriya and Vicky. She had a new, short hairdo that, Tanveer thought, suited her immensely. He mumbled, looking at her, 'Belated happy birthday. Hope you had fun.' Tanaz was stung and responded with a cynical smile, 'Dude, my birthday was a month back. I guess you were too busy to remember it till now! Sameer and Vicky did, by the way. Anyway, thanks for your belated wishes.' She went back to poring over the dessert menu. She sat there wishing that Tanveer would make an effort to talk to her. She wanted him to make her feel special like he had done so long ago. Supriya grinned, finding the look on Tanveer's face quite funny.

Vicky, to avoid the awkwardness, lightened things up by saying, 'Tanveer is one of your eccentric corporate honchos. He gets so absorbed with work that he gets absent-minded about other things. Once he called me in London to wish me on our friend Sameer's birthday.' All of them laughed at this and Tanveer sportingly joined in.

'So how do you guys know each other?' Tanaz asked Supriya and looked at Vicky with interest. 'I did not know you were friends with Supriya.' Vicky and she had remained good friends even after she and Tanveer had broken up. He had played the role of a protective older brother and she had continued to look up to him. She had remained good friends with Sameer, Tania and Naina too.

'I am interviewing them for a feature story on Sunrise Financial Advisory's new leadership and strategy. It is to be published in the next issue of *Business Times*,' Supriya told her.

'I didn't know her till this morning,' Vicky said jovially and looked at Supriya, enjoying the attention she was giving him.

'So who is their new CEO? Have you taken over the mantle, Vicky?' Tanaz asked eagerly.

'No, not me. I am the new Managing Director. I have picked up a stake in the business. But I won't be spearheading the change agenda,' Vicky said, putting an arm around Tanveer, who was busy eating his blueberry cheesecake. 'Tanveer is the new CEO,' he added, beaming with a smile.

Tanveer gave her an uncomfortable nod. He was nervous on his second day in the new job. He had moved from a safe, stable environment to one that was in flux—and he was at the helm of that change.

'Oh, wow! This is huge. Congrats!' she said looking at him with her hand against her mouth. 'When were you planning to tell me? I had no clue you quit your job! I have no clue what is going on with you any more. We live in the same apartment, Tanveer!' she said, reproaching him. She was happy that he had left his mundane job, but felt terrible that she was no longer a part of his life. Even though she was in a relationship with Kabir, she still felt connected to Tanveer, a connection and longing she found hard to explain to herself. Supriya gave an inquisitive smile to Vicky, wanting to know what exactly their living arrangement was.

'Well, I joined just yesterday. Everything has happened so quickly. I was planning on telling you tonight, Tanaz,' Tanveer said in a feeble voice.

'Nice try,' Tanaz said icily and turned her attention to Supriya to chat with her about their common friends. *I'm in trouble again*, he thought. Unexpectedly, Tania walked in the door looking for a place to sit. She looked beautiful in a salwar-kurta. Ankur soon followed her in. She was surprised to see Vicky and Tanveer there, dressed formally and having lunch with an attractive girl and Tanaz. *Tanaz! How come she is sitting opposite Tanveer and eating a brownie*? She wondered, *are they back together*? Ankur appeared civil and uninterested and was introduced to Supriya by Vicky as 'a friend and a business associate.' *Since when*? wondered Tania, giving Vicky a searching look and said wryly, 'You look smart today, a little over-smart.' She turned her gaze to Tanveer, giving him an affectionate tap on his shoulder. 'Good luck on the new job Mr CEO. You better take us out for dinner to celebrate,' she said merrily. She bantered with Tanaz over the bags and shoes that they were sporting and talked about going shopping over the weekend. She watched Supriya flirt with Vicky. 'I'll catch up with you later. Give me a buzz when you guys want to go over the designs for the new office,' she said before leaving. She gave Vicky a wry smile.

'The new flavour seems nice,' she messaged. Ankur kept his distance from the group as he did not like hanging out with them. He stood there hearing everything Vicky and Tanveer said closely. No words were exchanged between Ankur and the rest except a 'hi'. Vicky took care of the cheque and decided to walk Supriya back to her office where his car was parked.

'If you aren't meeting some eccentric corporate boss tonight, do you want to come for this play called *Twisted* at St Andrew's? The play is at 8 p.m. A good friend is in it and I have a couple of passes,' he asked Supriya casually. Jitin, a friend he knew through Sameer, was the lead in the play and it had garnered a good response. He had been persuading Vicky to come and watch the play for the past two weeks.

'Sure, I would love to,' she beamed. 'Pick me up at 7 p.m. I'll text you my address. I stay in Bandra myself. Maybe we could grab dinner at someplace after the show,' she said in a matter-of-fact way.

'Sounds like a plan,' Vicky shot back with a grin. 'You have my number from my card. Give me a call later and we'll work out the agenda for tonight.'

Tanveer's car and Wasabi, Taj Royale, Mumbai

Tanveer, who was walking a few steps behind Tanaz, offered to drive her home and then go back to work.

'Don't take the trouble. I'll cab it,' she told him.

'It's no trouble, Peaches,' he said to her with a warm smile. 'Can I take you and Mrs Rustomjee out for dinner tonight to celebrate my new job?' he asked.

'Well, if my mother is okay with it, I don't mind,' she said carefully, with a confused smile, pushing a strand of hair behind her ears. She was surprised with what he had just said—it was unlike him. He had kept to himself a lot since she began seeing Kabir and they had interacted very little since. Tanaz and Tanveer drove back in silence. Tanveer complemented her on being polled as the hottest RJ.

She was in splits at his comment and said, 'Nice try again. That happened a month ago too!' *It feels so normal with him. We are so comfortable and at ease with each other,* she thought. He stopped the car on the way to her place and, on an impulse, walked into a flower shop that Tanaz visited every week and came out with a bunch of orchids.

'Sorry,' he said with strength in his voice and continued, 'About everything. I have been a terrible person and it's entirely my fault.' Tanaz took the flowers and looked out of the window with tears in her eyes and said, 'If you weren't cute and I didn't once love you, I would have killed you for how mean and rude you have been. I guess it's too late for us, Tanveer. I am with Kabir right now, you have to remember that. Besides, I don't believe your mother's position on us has changed, so what is the point?'

'I know, but let's at least be friends again like we once were. I miss you, Tanaz, I feel like a part of me has died without you,' he said, his voice choking with emotion. He turned to look at her while he was driving, while she displayed a mix of emotions—looking confused and slightly smiling at the same time. He felt crushed on hearing that the prospect of them together in the future was unlikely. He also felt that his way back into her heart would not be easy, given what he had put her through. He realized that if it did not happen, it was never meant to be. Tanveer, on reaching home, asked Mrs Rustomjee to go out for dinner with Tanaz and him. He told her he would not take no for an answer. The three of them went out for dinner to Wasabi, a famous Japanese restaurant at the Taj Royale. Mrs Rustomjee smiled to herself about the camaraderie that Tanveer and Tanaz shared. *It's been such a long time,* she thought and wondered how they would look as a couple. *They would look very nice,* she told herself and got back to her food, while Tanaz and Tanveer fussed over her and each other. Nobody had taken her out to a nice place for dinner in over twenty years. She opened up and entertained them, telling both of them stories of her youth in Mumbai and what the city had looked like in those days. She also spoke with a glimmer in her eye about her crush on Clint Eastwood many decades ago.

Supriya's home, Sky Garden Apartments, Bandra

Vicky and Supriya enjoyed the play and headed to China House for dinner. Supriya looked trendy in a black tube top and a pair of white, low-waist jeans, while Vicky wore a smart dinner jacket. He ordered wine and relaxed enough to flirt with her about her eyes, hair and the things she liked. He was relaxing on a date for the first time since moving back to Mumbai. It had been quite a challenge getting a new business started and adjusting to life in his new apartment. Supriya sipped her wine and smiled dreamily, flirting with him. After dinner, they went on a long drive. She leaned in and kissed him when they reached her building. While getting out of his car she asked, 'On a different note, do you think I can get an exclusive interview with managers in your dad's company on their acquisition in Brazil? Also, maybe if you could introduce me to a couple of businesses you've invested in. I could do a story on them. I hope you don't mind.'

Why do I have to move so quickly? Vicky thought. 'Yeah, no worries, Supriya. You don't have to be so formal. I will speak to you tomorrow after I chat with him. I'll get a couple of these CEOs to call you too. I had fun, good night.'

'Thanks, I appreciate it! Goodnight,' she said. 'Let's do this again some time soon.' She walked away, turning around and grinning at him. She noticed the way he looked at her. *Nice catch*, she said to herself.

'Sure. Goodnight, sweet dreams,' he said with a smile and started to drive away. *Well that's one nice girl of the twenty or so I've met since I got back. Smart, pretty, simple. Not bad, Vicky*, he told himself.

∽

22
Someplace Else

'In dreams begins responsibility.'

—WILLIAM BUTLER YEATS

20 MARCH 2008
Brent, London

Sam and Simone were enjoying a romantic meal at their favourite restaurant, San Pedro's at Brent. It was drizzling outside and was too dour an evening to be out on a night about town, but Sameer and Simone were enjoying a romantic meal celebrating Sameer's promotion at the firm. Sameer was to leave for Belgium in four days for a three-month-long assignment, and was making the most of the time available to unwind with Simone who, along with him, had completed a year and a half at Smith and Robinson. The guys at work had thrown him a party the previous evening to celebrate his promotion at Devonshire House, where Sam had a drink too many and had told them emotionally how much he loved all of them, especially his boss, Peter. Simone thought how adorable he was and how much of a support he had been at work and otherwise. They had been getting serious in their relationship and were planning to move together from the shared apartment they stayed in now to a small apartment for themselves.

Though the relationship for her began as a fling, she had grown very attached to Sameer. Simone adored his intellect, kindness and how sorted he was at his age unlike most guys, while Sameer was smitten by the way in which she made heads turn, her warmth and her free-spirited nature. *She does not need anyone to make her happy, she has always stood on her own feet and found a way out,* he thought. They planned on heading to Amsterdam for the weekend to let themselves loose and have a blast in the eerily beautiful city. The city had its dark side, but Amsterdam was a beautiful place in many ways and Sameer loved the vibe of the city with its history and culture, which was unparalleled and unique, besides its many picturesque canals. Sam leaned in and kissed Simone on her lips and rested his palm on her bare thigh. She looked seductive in a sexy grey and silver dress which showed off her beautiful legs and her enviable curves. With her hazel eyes and her shiny brown locks, she could make most men crumble.

'The hottest thing about you is how oblivious you are to your sex appeal,' Sam told her flirtatiously, leaning in to give her another kiss.

'All right honey, let's leave. You've had a lot to drink tonight. I won't be able to carry you if you pass out, you know,' Simone said, smiling at him sweetly. Before they settled their bill and left, two drunk middle-aged guys who had been gazing in Simone's direction for the past hour rose from their bar stools and walked up to them.

'Hey sexy legs, why don't you come by to my place tonight?' the bald one asked her with a toothy grin.

'Yea, what's a delicious broad like you doing with this Paki bloke? Go on, mate, why don't you go someplace that plays bhangra, yeah?' the stout one joined in, giving Sameer a tough look while the bald guy laughed with a snort and added with a wolfish grin, 'Yeah, this isn't Southall yeah. Run along mate.' Sameer, who was drunk himself, rose from his seat, outraged to hear racial slurs directed at him.

'Why don't you losers take your comments someplace else? Leave the lady and me alone.' He rolled up his sleeves and watched them carefully to see if they had a knife or a gun as was commonly the case. The bald guy stared him in the eye and refused to back down.

'Go back to your country, Paki. Why do you come here and take our jobs, yeah? Go on, will you?'

Simone pulled him away before Sameer could react. 'Come on, Sameer! Let's just get out of here. Guys, leave us alone, yeah,' she said, taking his arm and leading him to the exit. The two guys staggered out behind them, following them outside. After mumbling a couple of racist comments directed at Sameer, they went back to the bar for another drink. On getting out, she looked at him with surprise.

'What were you doing? These guys could have attacked you with a knife or a bottle. These things are happening every day. You don't have to get into altercations with a bunch of Hooray Henrys. Take it easy. These little things happen everywhere.' Sameer looked disturbed and walked with haste.

'It's not a little thing to be discriminated against. It is really annoying! Imagine their nerve, walking up to us and making a pass at you. It doesn't happen everywhere, Simone—it sure hasn't happened to me in Mumbai.' He was deeply enraged by what had just happened and tried to calm down. *'Go back to your country Paki....'* rang in his ears.

'Come on now, Sameer, get over it. Let's just go back home. Don't let them get under your skin. They are insecure, jealous and so drunk that they have no clue what they are talking about. You are a better person than them.' She kissed his cheek and took his hand in hers which helped him calm down. Sameer went back to her place. He had given up his rented room a couple of months ago and was living in with her. This way, they had more time to spend with each other and it was a lot more fun. Sameer now knew what it was like to live with a girl. The money saved on rent was used to pamper her. He usually took her out to a nice place on weekends and bought her designer bags and footwear.

They undressed and made love in her large bed. Simone moaned in pleasure and pleaded with him to go on. The noises they made undeniably bothered the burly guy from Jaipur—a student who had rented the room next door to hers. He often gave Sam a look of wanting to kill him when they crossed paths in the hallway. *It is so near and yet so far for him,* Sam thought with a smile every time he saw him in the hallway. It was easy for him to get it on with Simone—at her place, at his, in parks, on a flight to Iceland for a holiday, in the shower and at the cinema. She had no inhibitions and, given the status of their relationship, he liked this. While he stayed at Liverpool, they took the train back to his place a few times during lunch and enjoyed many a quick love-making session.

He cuddled with her and said, 'Remind me to take this sweatshirt from you in the morning and pack it with the rest of my stuff. I really like it and it will have your sweet smell as well.' He remembered that it was the sweatshirt Tania had given him many years ago and nodded off to sleep, looking forward to the weekend with Simone in Amsterdam. He was to fly out to Belgium the day after they returned. He planned to come over every fortnight and spend the weekend with her.

Tania and Ankur's apartment, Khar

Ankur was cooking pasta in the kitchen, having managed to return home early from work. The firm Tania and he had started had been sold by them to a larger competitor, Supreme Spaces in Delhi, who found it to be an interesting and lucrative business, which helped them consolidate their presence nationwide. Supreme Spaces focused on the commercial end of the market and did work primarily for offices, hotels and restaurant chains. Ankur had stayed on as a part of the deal to head operations in Mumbai while Tania decided to leave after the sale of their stake. She did not like working in a corporate set-up and was more at home designing homes and boutique restaurants, which allowed her greater scope for creativity. She also wanted to slow down after her marriage with Ankur and was now a freelance decorator running a small set-up of her own. She also taught twice a week at the RJ School of Design. She enjoyed her independence and felt it was better not to work with Ankur as they had begun having a number of clashes over the approach to work and the future direction of their business, before they had sold it off. They planned to sneak away to the Maldives for a week in a couple of days, to celebrate a year of marriage. The intention was to work things out as they had had a number of arguments and had clashed over little things. Many times, they went without talking for days and more or less led independent lives.

Tania walked in and, seeing Ankur at the kitchen, walked towards him to give him a hug. 'So you're early today? Not bad. But why are you cooking? Don't you remember we have to meet Naina and Vicky for dinner? We had planned on this last week,' she asked.

'You had planned on this—it doesn't include me. I'll eat at home. Besides, I'm tired of eating out all time. Besides, they are your friends. I don't see the point of coming and sitting there. I've told you, I don't really like hanging out with these people,' Ankur told her in a reproachful tone.

'I don't see why not, Ankur. We've never gone out as a couple with my friends for a lunch or dinner. Can't you make this much effort for my sake? I get taken at least once a week for dinners and parties you're invited to and have to schmooze with people I cannot relate to. Do I complain?' Tania wanted to try and reason with him. She felt like she was the one giving in all the time.

'Look, I'm bloody tired after a day's work! It isn't like I'm pleading that you accompany me. I can always take someone from office. These are business dinners and parties at the end of the day. You can go have fun. Now let us drop this subject,' he said in a tone of finality.

'Well, what I want to do is never important, is it? You have become very different from the guy I decided to marry. Maybe you have a good reason for not coming tonight, but the way you speak to me these days is rude and insensitive,' Tania said, sounding upset.

Ankur, with a menacing look on his face, screamed, 'What nonsense, yaar? Goddamn, give me some peace, you nagging bitch! Can you not see I'm home from work early one day? Can I not relax? Please cut this emotional bullshit. I cannot deal with this constant whining about how rude I sound. It's fucking irritating. You are irritating me. Do you get it?'

Tears started rolling down her eyes. 'How can you say something like that? If that's how irritating I am, why did you marry me? How hard is it for you to treat me with respect and talk to me nicely?' she asked, hurt by his outburst.

Ankur turned off the cooking range and put the dish he was about to bake in the refrigerator. He picked up his car keys and headed for the door. 'I can't have any bloody peace in this house. Don't wait up for me,' he said and shut the door behind him. Tania sat down and cried for a while.

China Joe's, Bandra, Mumbai
> *'Love people, not things; use things, not people.'*
> —SPENCER W. KIMBALL

Naina and she met after a couple of hours for dinner at China Joe's. Naina, who was now a very successful VJ at MTV, continued to be good friends with Tania. Vicky was also joining them for dinner. It was a nice way for him to catch up with the girls he'd been closest to, since he had not been able to meet either of them for the past three months, being busy and absorbed with work.

'Something seems to be bothering you tonight, Tania. I hope everything is okay with you and Ankur? Is he screaming about something again?' Naina asked, aware of similar instances in the past. Tania looked helpless and worried.

'It's getting difficult with Ankur. We keep having these fights and argue all the time. He gets very aggressive and even abusive these days. He curses a lot and screams and shouts all the time. I wonder what happened to the Ankur I knew till a year ago.'

'Well, he's just being an asshole because his wife is a sweet girl who takes everything lying down. Give it back to him in equal measure. Throw a few pots and pans, or maybe break his phone—that should set him right. He is just being pushy and you're letting him walk all over you.'

Tania continued, looking harassed, 'I'm not made that way, yeah? I don't scream, shout or abuse anyone. We really need to sit down and talk. He wants his way all the time. I feel like I'm living in a prison with him sometimes! We only do what he wants, when he wants. It's like I have very little say in everything. I was pushed in a corner to sell the company we had both built together to serve his ambitions, not mine.'

'Look, it appears to me that you guys have serious issues. Find a way to talk and work things out. If you feel that things continue to be the same, then you really have to think.' Naina touched her arm and looked at her with concern. *The guy is a moron to behave with her like this,* she thought.

Seeing Vicky walking into the restaurant, Tania said, 'Yes, we need to. For now, I'm just going to get some space and go spend a few days with my parents. It will help me relax and will ease the pressure.' She put a smile back on her face and hugged Vicky who kissed her on her forehead and settled down to order something. The girls fussed over Vicky who had just broken up with Supriya after dating her for three months. He found his feelings towards her to be forced and the two of them were squabbling over Vicky's approach to work and life. Supriya was fun-loving and wanted her spot in the sun. She wanted to climb the social ladder and be seen with important people at important places, while Vicky, having all of this, stayed away from it. He saw his relationship with her heading towards a roadblock in the long term and decided to end things before it was too late. He told them about the last time they met, when Supriya had come over to his place after work.

One week ago…

She had been spending the night at his place on and off, which he did not mind. He walked into the apartment after she had come in a while earlier. She said, 'Hey handsome, how was your day? Should I make you a cup of coffee?'

'No, sit down. We have to talk,' he said in a tired voice and sat down next to her, watching her smile at him.

'Look, my dad called a while back. My parents do not know about us being in a relationship. His business associates are pestering him and media guys are requesting him for interviews and sound bites. All because you went and printed an article about how his company was in talks to acquire companies in China and the US. Our evaluation of these companies was confidential. Whatever I discuss with you or while you're around is not fodder for furthering your position at the magazine.'

She tried to say something but Vicky stopped her. 'Let me

finish talking, I'm not done! I've been okay when people are called to give exclusive access to product launches, business awards and the like using my name. But this I'm not happy with. How could you? You know how sensitive these things are! You picked up sensitive bits from the financial statements of potential acquisitions I was studying at home last week. You should have checked with me. Couldn't you have asked me? What you did isn't right at so many levels.'

'Come on dear, big deal, man. That's how things work here. When you know people, you can get things done. I'm not sure why you're upset. I'm only doing my job. Sooner or later, these things come out. I wrote a very positive article on how an Indian company is going great guns and expanding beyond our shores,' she said, trying to downplay the situation.

He cut her off, 'Look, I know how things work in this world. I don't want to be used! We have just begun seeing each other and we need to figure a lot out. What you did makes me uncomfortable. I don't know if there is a future for us together.'

'Well, I think I'll leave now, Vicky. It surprises me that I cannot use your help if it furthers my career. Or if being with you benefits my work,' she said, standing up to leave.

'News channels and business newspapers are criticizing the move. They say we have no experience in managing large acquisitions. Managing the press is diverting our attention from closing these deals. Our share price has nosedived thanks to these negative reports. I figure you were only thinking on how having this information would help you. It's better you leave. Take care,' he said with a grimace, watching her walk out of the door.

Back at China Joe's, Bandra, Mumbai

'I called her the next day and said it was best that we part ways. I feel

Supriya breached my trust. She used me. These were discussions to be kept out of the public domain. It was really irresponsible and selfish on her part. The best part is, she wasn't even apologetic about it,' he said.

'It seems like she was really using the opportunity of being your girlfriend. I mean, some of these things could be unintentional. But you're not wrong about doubting these intentions. Anyone would, in your place. Don't worry. You did the right thing,' Naina said, touching his arm. Vicky told them he was okay and was busy with work and some new exciting business opportunities he was funding. He just wanted to stay away from women for a while. He asked Tania where Ankur was and enquired if everything was okay, to which Tania replied evasively, 'He is having dinner with a client, something he could not get out of.'

Tanaz's Home, Peddar Road

Kabir drove Tanaz home after dinner at Kabab King. Kabir said, feigning a look of irritation, 'Why can't you stay over at my place for one night? All we get to do is make out in the car and anywhere else where we can squeeze in a kiss.'

'Getting me into bed is all you have in your mind! You want me to spend the night at your place, you want me to move in—it's nuts, Kabir! Why can't you wait to a point when I'm more comfortable?' Tanaz chastened him. Tanaz had yet again spurned his attempts at trying to persuade her to come over to his place for the night. It was something she hadn't done till now, despite the fact that they had been dating for eight months. She still felt guilty about lying to her mother and going to Goa years ago.

'Yes. What you are comfortable is with your ex-boyfriend living under the same roof as you! He must be waiting for you to come back, right?'

'Why are you dating me if you do not have trust? Anyway, Tanveer was never touchy-feely the way you are. Leave him out of this. The poor guy stays out of my way. You have to understand who I am as a person. I'm not your ex-girlfriend who will move in with you on a whim and get used by you and move on a few months later,' she said, giving it back.

While turning into her lane, he looked at her angrily and said, 'Leave her out of this. We didn't work out. That Tanveer is a chutiya! That's what he is and you still don't see that despite what he has put you through. What about me? I have to beg and plead for intimacy.'

'Well, don't beg and plead then, and get over it, will you? You don't have to bring Tanveer into every fight we have. Goodnight. I don't think I'm up for the movie tomorrow, sorry,' she said and got out of the car, walking away quickly. Kabir took a sharp U-turn and sped down her street in a huff, wanting to run down anybody who came in his way.

PART 5

LOVE AND LONGING

'How I wish you could see the potential, the potential of you and me. It's like a book elegantly bound, but in a language that you can't read just yet.'
—Lyrics from 'I Will Possess Your Heart',
Death Cab for Cutie

23
Lucky Storm

*'Love does not begin and end the way we seem to think it does.
Love is a battle, love is a war; love is growing up.'*
—JAMES BALDWIN

18 JULY 2008
Domestic Terminal, Delhi Airport

Vicky's flight on Air India had been cancelled as the departing flight was unable to take off from Mumbai. He scampered around for tickets on other airlines and managed to get a seat on Indus Air at three times the normal price, given the demand due to Air India's cancellation. He was relieved to be on the flight back, having managed to successfully complete meetings that were set up, relating to an important deal. The captain requested all passengers to strap on their seatbelts as it was likely to be a bumpy ride for the next two hours before they landed. He reclined on his business class seat, sipping orange juice from the tall blue plastic glass the air hostess had given him. Vicky spilled a little orange juice on his shirt due to the turbulence on the flight. An air hostess, noticing the spill, walked towards him with a cheerful smile and wiped his shirt with a tissue. He looked at her and thought, *what a knockout*. She had a tiny nose and a broad beautiful smile.

Her light brown hair was tied in a bun behind her head and her full black uniform showed off her svelte figure. Vicky muttered, 'Thanks,' without saying anything more. *I can't think straight any more,* he realized, smitten by her presence. He watched her with a dumbfounded look as she went about her duty in the business class with single-minded dedication. She came back a few minutes later with the same friendly smile. 'Do you need an extra pillow? You seem uneasy. Is there anything I can get you? Sorry about the turbulence,' she said with warmth and concern in her voice.

'No, I am fine. Could you please pass me my laptop bag? It's up in the overhead baggage space.'

'Sure,' she said. He watched her remove his bag from the overhead cabin. *I want to talk to her, want get to know her better, want to make her sit on my lap and feed her grapes.* She interrupted his thoughts saying, 'Here you go, sir,' and walked away a bit before turning around. 'That's a nice tie. Do you fly with us a lot?' she asked, also noticing that he was looking at her.

'Thanks. No, I more often take Air India—our company has a tie up with them. But I guess I will in the future,' he said and smiled at her flirtatiously.

She walked away smiling back at him. *Stop killing me with that look in your eyes,* his eyes told hers. He turned on his laptop and began reviewing some reports he had received from Tanveer. His Venture Capital Firm—Sunrise Investments—and all the set-ups the firm had invested in were now clients of SFA as a result of Tanveer and his relationships and business development efforts. For Vicky, SFA made sure the funding was used prudently and the finances were in place, supported by the expertise which SFA had. Tanveer was now helping these businesses raise debt at the lowest possible costs. Vicky stopped his imagination from running wild. *What are you doing, Vicky? Hitting on air hostesses now? She's stunning though,* he thought. He could not think or focus on his work. He had not seen anyone as exquisitely beautiful as her. She was a rare combination of sex appeal combined with an innocent face, expressive eyes and a mesmerizing smile. She interrupted his thoughts again with her sweet voice, 'What will it be for you, sir, veg or non-veg?'

'Veg,' said Vicky guiltily, thinking she could possibly read his thoughts. 'No, non-veg,' he said and then, in a confused tone, changing his decision once more, said, 'No, sorry. Actually, give me a vegetarian meal please, thanks.' She laughed with a gleam in her eyes. *The sound of her laughter has a nice ring to it,* he felt.

'Do you want both?' she asked him innocently.

'No, vegetarian will do,' he said with a sheepish smile. *I better shut up. She thinks I am a doofus,* as she went about laying a tray with his meal before him. Due to the turbulence, she almost tumbled over and leaned onto Vicky's shoulder for support. *She smells intoxicating,* he sensed and put his hand across the aisle and held her waist to prevent a fall.

'Sorry,' she said in a sombre tone, feeling awkward now. Vicky wanted to say, 'Any time,' but just nodded along saying, 'Don't worry. Hope you're okay. Take it easy.'

She came back later to pick up his tray and asked him if he wanted tea or coffee or both with a mischievous smile. *She does think I am a doofus,* Vicky thought.

'Coffee would be great, thank you,' he said in charming voice. He continued working while sipping his cup of coffee when she stopped by again.

'You look really tired. We are an hour from landing in Mumbai. It may delay by a further thirty minutes given the turbulent weather. Why don't you take a short nap?' She looked shy and felt awkward while she said this, realizing that advising a passenger on what to do with his time was beyond her call of duty.

'Okay,' he said, obeying her cheerfully and turned off his laptop.

'That's considerate of you. Yes, I am really tired. It's a good idea to catch a few winks. I've had a long day,' he added. She nodded, feeling better about it and put his laptop bag back into the luggage cabin overhead. She went back to her seat at the front of the aircraft, a few seats away from where Vicky was. *Stop! Don't cross the line. He may be dashing, but he is a passenger*, she told herself. Vicky was indeed tired and nodded off to sleep. She woke him up after the aircraft had landed in Mumbai.

'Thanks,' he said taking his blazer from her and pulled out his laptop bag from the overhead cabin.

'Hope to see you again on board. Thanks for flying with us,' she said, reserving a genuine smile for him as opposed to the one she gave to the others.

'Sure, I hope to see you again. Bye, Sarah,' Vicky said, noticing the name on her badge—Sarah Anwar, it read—as he disembarked from the aircraft. He turned around to look at her while he was climbing down and she was looking back at him with her cheeks a little flushed. He waved goodbye. He walked towards the Indus Air bus under an umbrella. There was torrential rain in Mumbai. The ground staff had thick raincoats on and advised passengers that most parts of the city were flooded.

Tanaz's home, Peddar Road

Mrs Rustomjee was sitting at the dining table looking extremely anxious when Tanveer walked in after getting drenched from just walking across the street from the parking spot to their building. It had taken him an hour to complete what was a fifteen-minute drive home. He looked at her wondering why she appeared restless.

'What is the matter, Mrs Rustomjee? Why are you worried? Do you need anything?' He was like one of the family now, as the old lady had warmed up to him considerably since the dinner at

Wasabi. Of late, she had been getting his laundry done for free and not charging him for electricity as she usually did.

'Tanaz is not back from the pharmacy. She left an hour back, before the rain started. It's just down the street and my baby has such a bad cold too. What am I to do?' she said, pacing up and down the room and looking out of the window.

'I'll go down and bring her,' Tanveer said readily, taking the umbrella and walking out without waiting to hear a response. He had called her from work and checked on how she was doing. They had been talking a lot these days, especially since she had broken up with Kabir a month ago. However, he wasn't sure if she had forgiven him, given what he had put her through. They had been drawing close to each other but Tanaz was holding back, not sure if she could put herself out there and trust him again.

It was pouring heavily outside and the winds were blowing at twenty-five km/hour. He heard the monstrous clouds thunder threateningly above him while he rolled up his trousers to knee-length and walked towards the pharmacy. He saw empty packets of biscuits, chips and plastic bottles flow by in the water next to him. His knee was below the water and he knew he had done a smart thing by putting on his old boots instead of his leather shoes. He walked ahead towards the pharmacy which was about three hundred and fifty metres away from their building. He waded through the flooded street, watching his steps carefully to avoid walking into an open drain. A few metres from the pharmacy, he saw Tanaz across the street, standing under the shelter of a closed hardware store with a few other poor folks who were also stranded. She was in her track pants and a sweatshirt. She hadn't gone in to work as she had been down with flu and a sore throat since the previous night. He saw her shivering in the cold, her nose was red and she gave him a relieved smile and waved out on seeing him walk towards her. *He looks so cute. It is sweet of him to come,* she felt. He removed his windcheater and made her put it on despite her protests and brought her under the umbrella. They walked back slowly, with his one hand holding the umbrella above her head and the other arm tightly around her. She walked along with him, watching her step and shivering with Tanveer's arm around her. It was 6.20 and was getting dark outside while the downpour was getting worse. Tanveer drew her closer and reassured her that they would be home soon. She buried her head on his chest and felt warm and protected. They got into the building and into the elevator. Tanaz got in first and smiled at him. He was completely drenched, having focused only on protecting her from the rain.

He got into the elevator, looking at her smiling face and cupped his wet palms around her cheeks, leaned forward and gave her a long, fervent kiss. The door was still open but neither of them cared about this—the residents of the building were either at home or stuck outside. She wrapped her hands around his neck and kissed him back. Looking at him adoringly, she said, 'Your hands are so cold, and you're going to catch my cold too by spending so much time inside my mouth.'

'I sure don't mind,' Tanveer said, wrapping his arms around her and running his fingers through her hair.

'This feels nice,' she gushed, forgiving him in a moment for all that she had been put through. They went up to see a worried Mrs Rustomjee standing with towels by the door. She made Tanaz and Tanveer sit down and wiped their hair. She had hot soup ready for both of them. Tanveer slipped into Tanaz's room an hour after Mrs Rustomjee retired to her room. Tania was sniffing with a runny nose and he got into bed and cuddled her, keeping her warm. He put his hand under her sweater and rubbed her back.

'Rub my back a little more, this feels good,' she whispered in a low moan. It had been close to thirty months since they had made love and their bodies longed for each other. With one hand, he pulled down her pyjamas under the sheets and ran his hand down to the soft touch of her thighs. He cuddled with her and held on to her while their legs intertwined. They made love with passion and longing. She ran her fingers through his hair and moaned in pleasure before they lay back with their arms wrapped around each other. They lay in her tiny bed, staring at the ceiling with smiles on their faces. Both of them had come a long way since Goa. She took his hand to her lips and kissed it.

'I've missed you big time, Mr Loser,' she said drowsily.

'I'm not going to leave you at any cost this time, Peaches,' Tanveer said with deep emotion before Tanaz fell asleep with a smile on her face. He covered her with a quilt and went back to his room after a while.

Arrival Terminal, Domestic Airport, Santa Cruz, Mumbai

Vicky drove his car out of the airport thinking about Sarah Anwar. His mother called to check if he had landed safely and asked him to get home as soon as possible. He walked out of the terminal, feeling glad that he had driven his car to the airport in the morning. It was pouring heavily outside now and there seemed to be fewer taxis than were required outside the airport. He got into his car and drove out. A little distance ahead, he saw a figure in black on the side of the road, desperately waving out to a moving mini-bus to stop. He lowered the window glass on the other side. It was Sarah, drenched from head to toe. He quickly drove over to where she was and opened the door, telling her to get in.

'Are you sure?' she asked, gasping for breath.

'Absolutely. Get in quickly, you're getting drenched.' She was drenched from head to toe, having run from the terminal to the street in the downpour outside. Drawing deep breaths, she told him in a sad voice, 'I went over to the coffee shop for five minutes and they took off without me. I tried to stop them but with no luck. These crazy people even took my bags with them! Thank God for you,' she added warmly with her doe eyes. *Thank God,* he told himself. *What luck! Of all the crew they had on board she had to be left behind,* he thought.

'Sure, no worries. Where do you need to be dropped?' he asked, giving her a box of tissues. She took a couple of them to wipe her wet face and removed her hair clip. He turned on some music. 'Sailing to Philadelphia' by Mark Knopfler played in the background.

'I stay as a PG in Prabhadevi. Could you please drop me there if that isn't a problem?' she asked him in a gentle but anxious voice.

'That's a problem. From Mahim onwards, the area is flooded. Most people are stuck this side or that side. I just got off the phone with my mum. My family home is in Cuffe Parade, but I have my own apartment in Pali Hill. That's where I am headed,' he explained. *Nice lie Vicky,* he told himself.

'Oh,' she said worriedly. She tried her co-workers' numbers too, but the lines were jammed.

'Don't worry. Come relax at my place and I'll drop you when the rain slows down,' he added in a matter-of-fact way while she looked at him with hesitance. He gave her a look of reassurance which said, *trust me*.

'Thanks,' she replied, feeling assured.

'So where are you from, basically? When did you move to Mumbai?' He took turns looking at her and the road ahead which was a blur, given the stormy weather.

'I'm from Mussoorie and I started working for Indus Air a year ago,' she said.

'Mussoorie? Wow! It's a far cry from here. Way more beautiful and peaceful,' he beamed at her.

'Yes, I miss it so much. I went to boarding school there as my dad was in the army and moved a lot. My parents have settled there now after my dad retired from the army three years ago. By the way, I don't know your name,' she asked in her cheerful voice, giving him an inquisitive look. Vicky was trying hard to focus on the road as clarity was abysmal. 'Vikram Khanna. I head a small Venture Capital Fund here in Mumbai,' he said, charming her with his confidence. 'So why did you decide to become an air hostess?'

Sarah put her finger on her chin and pretended to think a lot. 'I don't know. It just happened. I wasn't too keen on studying any more. I didn't want to go end up in a call centre or a bank or just get married. I wanted to travel and see new places, experience life and meet different people—so here I am. My folks let me make my decisions, so thank God for that,' she said with charm and confidence, and it was quite clear where her life was headed. *She is not one of those girls who do things because someone else thinks it's a good idea*, he thought. Vicky drove into his building and parked his car in the basement.

He took her bag and his and led her to the elevator and she meekly followed him. In the elevator, he smiled and continued to flirt, 'Sarah—has a nice ring to it. It's a beautiful name, it suits you really.'

She blushed. 'I guess my mum and dad picked an appropriate name then,' she said. They entered his apartment. They could still hear the storm raging outside. He showed her to his room and said, 'Please feel comfortable. Go and take a shower if you want.'

'I don't have a change of clothes,' she said. 'I really want to get out of this uniform,' she added while making a baby face. He went into his room and pulled out a nice sweatshirt and a pair of old track-pants. He walked over to where she was standing and said to her in a friendly voice, 'These may not be your size but you should be comfortable.'

Her eyes lightened up, 'Thanks,' she said. 'Give me a while. I'll freshen up, take a shower and get back.' He opened the drawer and gave her fresh towels and shower gel, and turned on the geyser while she stood behind him looking shy and embarrassed. She came back ten minutes later looking adorable in loose track pants and a sweatshirt twice her size. She had let her hair loose which made her look even more stunning than before.

'Veg grilled sandwich or chicken grilled sandwich?' he asked her with a mock grin. '

Anything will do. You have a really nice apartment. Whatever you do you've made a success of it in a short while,' she said, looking around the room, noticing the plush furniture and the art that adorned the wall. She went into the living room and reclined on the couch. Vicky popped in with a naughty grin, 'Would you prefer tea or coffee?'

'A cup of tea, please. Cardamom or peppermint tea if possible, with a spoon of sugar,' she shot back. She looked at the pictures framed on the walls. It had pictures of Vicky with his mum and dad and the rest of his family—his sister, cousins, grandparents and others. There were quite a few with Tania, Sam and Tanveer, one with Sam and Simone in London, a few snaps of the gang in Goa and a couple of snaps with Naina framed on the wall.

'How do you know her? Isn't she a VJ on MTV?' She looked at him with curiosity.

'We dated for a couple of years and broke up during a holiday in Goa, two and a half years ago,' he replied, being open about things as he always was.

'Sounds like an interesting story. Come sit down and tell me about it,' she said amiably, directing him with her gaze. Vicky and she moved to a couch near the window with their cups of tea and a plate of grilled sandwiches.

'Nice sandwiches. The tea is great too. I've been starving all day!' she said, taking a bite.

'Thanks,' Vicky responded. He told her about his relationship with Naina and how things fell apart. She took her palm and placed it on his folded fist. He talked about Tania, Sameer, Tanaz and Tanveer and how their relationships had taken a different turn after their Goa trip some years ago.

'They seem like a really nice bunch of people. You're lucky to have a nice set of friends,' she said warmly and added with a faraway look, 'Everyone isn't that lucky.'

'Yes, but it's so different now. I'm close to everyone and keep in touch, but the equations within the rest of our group have altered. Being in different cities, seeing different people and our chosen career paths have changed our lives. We don't have time for each other like we used to once. I meet Tanveer and Naina sometimes, with Tanveer more so now because we work together. I've seen very little of Tania after she got married or Tanaz after she broke up with Tanveer. Sam is in London. We used to meet while I was there and now when he comes home to see his family. We used to go out and party at the drop of a hat, now we only make plans to meet up and end up cancelling them.' He felt lonely at times.

'You haven't gone out with anyone since you got back?'

He turned his gaze to the raging storm outside and sat back. He told her about Supriya and how his dad had gotten upset with him for sharing confidential information with the media. She laughed a little and he shook his head and smiled.

'Sorry. I'm laughing at her! How can she do something like this and expect to get away with it? The world is full of strange people,' she said contemplatively, taking a sip of her tea. He found it difficult to take his gaze away from her. *She's the whole package. She isn't just beautiful, she has a nice personality and she comes across as sensible too.*

'Now maybe you can tell me about you. I figure it could be

almost as interesting as my life…used to be,' he said, hearing which she laughed with a glow in her eyes. *Boy! She's irresistible,* he felt, telling himself, *slow down, dude.*

'Well, almost! I used to be in this rock band called 'Pepper & Jam' in Dehradun a few years back. I went to college there, where I went out with this guy—Ricky Lobo. I played the keyboard and Ricky was the lead guitarist and was the lead on the vocals too. A very talented guy, but very messed up in his head,' she said, pushing back strands of hair behind her ears while Vicky listened to her with interest. 'We had a lot of fun as a group—three guys and I. The four of us were joined at the hip, jamming every weekend. We went and played at campus gigs in Bangalore and Pune. During the summer break before our last year of college I took him home to Mussoorie, and a friend who went to boarding school—Gita—came over as well to spend a week. I walked into my room after running an errand one day to see him in my bed with my friend!'

Vicky looked shocked. 'What are you saying? A guy must be nuts to go cheat on you!'

'Okay, stop flattering me and listen to what happened! Seeing me, Ricky got up and tried to pretend nothing was going on. I threw both of them out of my house. My parents were confused, wondering why they left suddenly. So that was the end of rock bands in my life. I sleepwalked through my last year of college avoiding even running into him. He was very sorry for what he did and tried to make it up to me. But you cannot take all that has happened back, you know. I was like, this is it! He handled it badly, dropped out of college mid-way through the final year. He was always stoned.'

'That's a shame. Where is he now? What happened with your friend Gita?'

'Well, he is in rehab somewhere for drug addiction. I did send him a get well note. I hear, through the other guys, that he's getting better. For a while, I felt responsible for what he went through but I realized that he had brought it upon himself. It was tough for me to forgive something like that. That's one thing I can't do,' she said, looking at him with those doe eyes. With the majestic air about her, she looked like a princess from an age-old legend.

'I bumped into Gita at the Delhi airport a couple of months back. We just said hi. She was with her husband and her baby. It's miserable to lose friends like that.'

'True. When you trust someone, it is hard to move past that. But if you can't move on, it's best to say goodbye.'

'Yes, that's what I had to do like a year back again. I was with Easyfly then. I'm sure you've never flown with them. The service and customer experience at Indian Railways is better! The work was rubbish too—delayed flights and frustrated passengers. Anyway, I was seeing this guy Rohit, a fellow crew member. We were friends for a bit and hung out a lot. I was new to the job and he gave me a lot of support. He stepped in when some jerk tried to misbehave with me. We went out for eight months, but one day some crew member told me he had a wife and kid in Baroda. I was mortified! I mean, lying to this extent? I quit a week after I heard this and stopped talking to him. He claimed he would leave his wife and kid for me, which was very disturbing. I wouldn't have even had coffee with him if I knew he was hitched. He never spoke about it. I find it very hard to trust guys after all this,' she said, looking exasperated. 'I was lucky Indus Air was ramping up and I walked in from one flight to another in a different uniform. It's infuriating though, to be lied to and be cheated on. I don't do it to other people and don't expect other people to do this to me. Sometimes girls bring it upon themselves. I've seen a few crew members go out with businessmen, cricketers, or movie stars just for kicks. To cling on to guys who will buy them expensive gifts. I could write a book! You won't believe the compromises which some people will make to afford a designer bag or Prada shoes while there are some who put their heads down and work to support their families and give them a better life.'

'Yeah, there is so much of consumerism today, isn't it? But all guys are not the same... maybe you met the wrong ones,' Vicky said, testing the waters, to which she gave him a knowing smile.

'Achcha, this coming from you Mr Khanna, after all you've told me! Your flavour of the week adventures and living it up in London included?'

'That's different,' he said. 'While I was committed in a relationship I didn't cheat on anyone,' he added with a sheepish smile and continued, 'But it must still be disturbing for you to remember what these guys did. I can imagine how difficult it is, especially with that guy who had a wife and a kid.'

'Well, it was for a bit. Now I'm okay, really. I learnt my lessons and it's all right! My life is okay, I'm more fortunate than a lot of people. So many have no access to education or basic health care and lack job opportunities, while there are other people who fly from Mumbai to Bangalore to play golf with a friend. I feel blessed to have a nice life and yet not be as self-centred as some who spend more on one meal than what an average slum dweller earns in a month,' she said emphatically and added, 'People feel that by looking away and focusing on themselves, they can wish poverty away.' *She is compassionate too*, he thought.

'True, the gap between those who have it all and those with very little or nothing has only widened. It's perverse sometimes. I keep hearing about this one and that one buying penthouses for crores of rupees. What do these people do? Many of our people have lost their senses. It's all about show and making a statement these days. It's up to us to make a difference, which is what I want to do.'

She set her gaze on him and smiled. He looked out of the window. The storm was tearing down mercilessly. It seemed like an operation clean-up for Mumbai. Being with Sarah felt like a dream. He told her how he felt one morning in London with Tanuja and how she had spoken to her maid. He explained how that experience shaped his objectives in life. They chatted for some more time about life, friends, love, his relationships and hers, music—co-incidentally, they both liked soft rock and jazz.

'It's thanks to my "propah" upbringing in a boarding school where pursuing varied tastes is much encouraged,' she chirped.

Vicky told her how he met Naina by pulling a fast one on Tanveer, which had her in splits. 'I didn't think you were this funny when I first saw you,' she said, looking at him dreamily.

She fell asleep after a while and Vicky carried her to his room and tucked her under the sheets. He walked back and lay on the couch himself, wondering if he was awake or if it was a dream. She was not just another beautiful girl—she was a nice person who was grounded and had her heart in the right place. He felt connected to her in a strange way.

Tania and Ankur's Apartment, Khar

Tania was alone at home and Ankur was stuck in his office with the downpour preventing anyone from the office block from getting out. Ankur was in a bad mood. He called Tania and cursed the rains, saying how it had ruined business for him—important meetings in Bangalore had to be postponed as flights had been cancelled. They chatted for a while and Ankur fell asleep on a couch in his cabin, while Tania was sitting at her desk at home and was completing some designs. She wondered what her life would have been like if she had married Sameer instead. She remembered a situation four years ago when she had been stranded at Ambience Mall where she had gone shopping and got stuck in torrential rain. Sameer had driven from Juhu to Worli for two hours to pick her up from the mall and drop her home. She wondered if Ankur would do the same for her. She wondered if it was wrong to compare Ankur to Sameer. But being with him for so long and having connected with and understood each other so well, it set her expectations for her relationship with Ankur.

Things were difficult with Ankur. They communicated very little on most days. When they did talk or spend time together, they would more often than not end up having an argument. She also sat and thought about the day when Sameer dropped her home and could not leave as it was raining heavily. They had sat down in her room and had played chess for hours. Her mother had made hot samosas and tea for both of them. She wished to go back and relive those days again. Today, her relationship with Ankur was fraught with conflict and raging ego battles which she found hard to live with.

∽

24
Bright Shiny Morning

'Twenty years from now you will be more disappointed by the things that you didn't do than by the ones you did do. So throw off the bowlines. Sail away from the safe harbour. Catch the trade winds in your sails. Explore. Dream. Discover.'

—MARK TWAIN

19 JULY 2008
Vicky's Apartment, Pali Hill, Bandra, Mumbai

Vicky woke up the next morning to the sound of soft music. Sarah had put on one of his old U2 albums. He woke up with a smile and headed to the restroom to freshen up and brush his teeth. It was bright and sunny outside and the city seemed to be going about its business as usual. Vicky remembered that it was a Sunday morning and that he did not have to go to office. He sat up and saw Sarah dressed in the same tracks and sweatshirt, walking out of the kitchen.

She turned around and gave him one of her dazzling smiles. 'Did you sleep well, Vicky?'

Lifting himself out of the couch and walking towards her, he said, 'Good morning, my beautiful dream. Oh yeah, I slept like a baby.' He rubbed his eyes and looked at her intently. 'So you aren't a dream after all, huh?'

She nodded with a sexy pout and a warm smile.

'Guess Shanta bai isn't coming today. She is normally here by this time.'

He saw that Sarah was at least four inches shorter than he was. She had seemed taller with her heels yesterday. He kissed her on her forehead, smelled her beautiful hair and put his arms around her. She stopped making the toast and turned around to face him. 'Okay, are you mixing me up for someone else or do you remember we met just yesterday? How do you like your eggs?' she asked seriously.

'Any way you make them, sweet bottoms. What are your plans today?' he asked, keen to spend time with her.

'I will take a shower in a bit, after which I don't know. I'm yet to hear from the airline if I am on the roster today. What do you have in mind?' she asked.

'Well, let's go out for dinner to some nice place. What do you think?' he asked her flirtatiously while she was making an omelette for both of them. She took out the carton of orange juice and poured it into two tall glasses.

'Actually, let's stay in watch some movie. You have a nice collection. We could listen to music. Only problem is, I do not have a change of clothes,' she said with a self-conscious smile and added, 'Please drop me home tonight.'

'Well, I have some other T-shirts and shorts too,' he said after turning her around and looking deep into her eyes.

'Yes, that would be better. I am floating in these track pants of yours,' she said, grinning at him. He drew her up close and his gaze met hers. He wanted to kiss her but held back. *She needs to trust me first—she's not some flavour,* he thought and pulled her cheeks affectionately. She looked puzzled and giggled, anticipating that he would try and kiss her. She was attracted to him and was finding it difficult to hold herself back.

'The toaster will be on fire, let me check on it. You are very mischievous! I wonder how many other girls you bring home like this. I'm not one of your flavours, Vicky Khanna,' she said, pushing him away affectionately.

'Yes, ma'am. I'm aware. I've given up on flavours though,' he said agreeably. *You're a flavour for life,* he thought.

Sarah cut him off, 'Breakfast is ready. Stop the badmashi in your head and please come to the table.'

Vicky followed her, carrying the two glasses of orange juice, with his eyes following her move across to the table. He could not take his eyes off her. They enjoyed a scrumptious breakfast and joked about Vicky's misadventures with the different girls he had gone out with, his general outlook and attitude, and what he wanted from life. He asked her seriously on an impulse, 'Can I take you out for coffee and a drive before I drop you home tonight? It'll be fun.' At one level he felt that they were moving quickly while the longing he felt to spend every waking moment with her overpowered those thoughts.

'Okay,' she shrugged. She added with a cheerful smile, making a gesture with her expressive hands, 'You will have to take me out to buy a dress first. I can't come wearing what I am right now! I'm kidding. We'll go over to my PG, I'll change in a bit and we can go from there.'

Am I moving too quickly? He moved across to where she was sitting, put one arm on the table and looked at her intently. She smiled shyly at him while talking to her dad, reassuring him that the storm had blown by and that she was safe in Maximum City.

'I have a hunch you're good on your feet,' he said while she cleared the plates and he followed her with the glasses.

'I do love dancing. I have taken lessons in salsa and ballroom dancing,' she turned around and said cheerfully.

'Impressive. We should go out and party some time, you know, like just you and I,' he said.

'I know,' she said laughing. 'It sounds like a plan.'

He put his arm on her shoulder and turned her around, 'I am getting into the bathtub, I'll be back soon,' and walked away with a brat-like grin.

She smiled at him sweetly, not saying anything. She was taken aback a little by their flirting and him asking her out so quickly. *Vicky seems like a really nice guy and what is life if one doesn't take risks?* she felt, smiling to herself, unable to ignore the sparks flying between them. She heard her phone ring and was asked to report to the airport in two hours. She took her purse and left Vicky a quick thank you note with her phone number before rushing out.

'Thanks, call me—98502—9786xx. I've got to get on a flight in two hours. Got to rush home and change quickly. Dinner and dancing some other time!' it read.

Radio Chilli's Office, Mediazone Towers, Lower Parel, Mumbai

Tanaz was in the middle of her show and saw Tanveer standing outside the broadcasting room, smiling at her broadly and holding a bunch of orchids. She laughed, noticing how uncomfortable he looked and watched some of the production crew giggle at him. She finished the show and went outside where he was standing patiently.

'These are for you. I picked them up from your favourite florist before coming here,' he said, giving her the bunch of orchids.

'Thanks. This is unexpected—and it's very sweet of you! How come you came by? I thought we were meeting for coffee in the evening.' She looked at him starry-eyed. She loved the way he made her feel.

'Well, I was missing you at work a lot and I couldn't wait till evening, so I took the rest of the day off. Things are slow this week anyway. Let's go grab some lunch, then maybe a movie. We could still do coffee and be back home for dinner.' He looked around to see the staff watching him with interest. Kabir was standing a few metres away with his arms folded and a frown on his face.

'Okay, sounds like fun. Give me ten minutes and I'll see you at the reception.' She turned around and walked to her desk to pack up for the day with a smile. She felt like she was beginning to live again. What was missing in her life had been brought back to her by a twist of fate. She hoped they would manage to make it last this time.

∽

25
Progress

'True love is night jasmine, a diamond in darkness, the heartbeat no cardiologist has ever heard. It is the most common of miracles, fashioned of fleecy clouds—a handful of stars tossed into the night sky.'

—JIM BISHOP

20 JULY 2008
Simone and Sameer's Apartment,
Liverpool Street, London

Sameer kissed Simone goodbye. He had a flight to Mumbai in three hours.

'I still feel you can book some last minute tickets and come. Mum will be happy to meet you. It's a little weird that both of us are heading on our holidays separately.'

She feigned a smile but was unhappy with the fact that he was going to India instead of on a holiday with her. 'It is okay, love. I'll pass. I've already been to the Himalayas and went to Goa too when I was twenty-one. I would prefer it if you came with me and the gang to Jordan, Turkey and Syria. It will be fun—definitely better than a trip to Mumbai at this time of the year,' she said, hoping he would change his mind at the last minute.

'You don't understand. I haven't seen mum for months and she likes me to stay for a while.'

She kissed him on his lips and said, 'Well, go have a nice time then. Call me when you reach, yeah?'

He nodded and walked out of the door with his duffel bag.

A week ago, Sameer had discussed with her his thoughts about going back to India. He could not see a future in the UK any more, driven by how things were back home, the opportunities he was thinking about and the looming recession which was around the corner. Simone did not warm up to the idea as he had expected. She was okay about spending a year or two, but could not see herself settling down in India for the long term. They had decided to take time off and reconsider their options over the next few weeks while on holiday and get back to discuss things. Simone had begun to draw herself into a shell since the discussion, and Sameer had decided to do the same—to give each other space before making a decision.

Vicky's Office, Lower Parel, Mumbai

Vicky walked out of the conference room and went back to his cabin. He couldn't concentrate on the new business idea—for a courier company covering the rural landscape—that was being presented. His mind was preoccupied with thoughts of Sarah. He remembered their breakfast two days back and the late night coffee and conversation on the stormy night. He had tried calling her yesterday but her phone was switched off. He decided to send her a message.

'Hey, hope you're having fun flying around looking at us mortals from the skies above! Thing is, I'm missing my sweat shirt and track pants. It may have to do with the fact that they were worn by you! How about I take you out for dinner and come by to pick these up as well?' His phone rang five minutes later.

'Hey, lifesaver, am I disturbing you? Sorry I've been unreachable. I've been flying around for the past two days without a break. It's been crazy with the rain and flights getting delayed. Sorry about the other day. I had to rush,' she said with warmth and familiarity while entering the arrival terminal.

'That's okay. It seems like you had a busy few days. So are you game for dinner tonight?' he asked.

'Hmm, no, I have other plans. This guy is picking me up in a while and I'm spending the rest of the day with him. We might be going for dinner and maybe a drive too.'

He tried not to sound disappointed. 'Well, all right. I didn't know you'd started seeing someone.' He sounded jealous and the disappointment showed.

'Well yeah, there is this guy who is suave and dapper. He heads a venture capital firm and stays in Pali Hill. I could be seeing him soon if he tries not to waste time and comes to the airport quickly. I'll wait at the Barista near terminal three. Call me when you are outside,' she chirped with a smile.

'Oh yeah, is that right? Smart girl. Man, you had me there! I was thinking "what the heck?" Okay, I'm leaving now and should be there in thirty minutes. I'll call you when I'm outside,' he said cheerfully, sounding relieved. He listened to the sound of her crackling laughter at the other end while he walked out of his cabin in a rush.

'See you soon,' she said before hanging up.

A fellow colleague who was walking with her asked, 'Who was that? Haven't heard you talk to any guy like that. Captain Harpreet only gets snubbed by you. He can take me out any time! If only he asks,' she said with a little disappointment.

'Well, Vicky is adorable and a nice guy—unlike Mr Harpreet who is a skirt-chasing mongrel. Stay away from him, yeah! He's married and has two kids. His wife used to be an air hostess with Air India,' she warned her colleague before taking her bag and walking towards Barista with a smile.

26
Commitment

'Somewhere over the rainbow, skies are blue, and the dreams that you dare to dream really do come true.'
—THE WIZARD OF OZ (1939), LYRICS BY E.Y. HARBURG.

1 AUGUST 2008
Banyan Tree Café, Fort, Mumbai

Tanveer and Tanaz were at Banyan Tree enjoying a light breakfast. It had been a couple of weeks since they had gotten back together. This morning, for the first time in many years, they'd left for breakfast together, making it explicit to Mrs Rustomjee that there was more than friendship between them. It was a beautiful Sunday morning in Mumbai, a day when most people stayed in bed reading one of the newspapers, with bulky weekend supplements setting the mood for the day. It had been drizzling since both of them woke up and it had rained all through the previous night. They had spent the previous evening tucked in on a couch watching an old Hindi movie and a re-run of episodes of *Friends* after which he had taken her out for dinner. Mrs Rustomjee had taken kindly to Tanveer and seemed to accept the fact that over the past two weeks Tanaz had been happier than she had been for a very long time. She consoled herself, realizing that Tanveer was a nice guy and would keep her happy. She decided, *I am not going to bring religion and tradition in to make life difficult for them.* Her daughter had had a problematic childhood to begin with and she did not want to make it harder for her. Tanveer had sent text messages to Sameer, Vicky and Tania telling them that he had worked things out with Tanaz and that they were back together. Vicky called Tanveer, congratulating him on getting back together with her. He asked him where they were and what they were up to, telling them that he would drop in and have breakfast with them. Sameer, who was returning to London in a couple of days, called in and told Tanveer that he would be joining them as well.

'I guess everyone is excited about us getting back together, Peaches,' Tanveer said, showing her the text messages from Tania and his younger sister Zoya, congratulating them.

'I guess they are. We are the lone surviving couple from Goa,' she said with a smile.

Tanveer and she had spoken nineteen-to-the-dozen all morning. They had so much to talk about, having been away from each other for over two years. They shared laughs over the prospective suitors their parents had set up for them over the past few months and Tanveer's awkward flings with women at work, which he apologized for as 'immoral' and 'inappropriate' behaviour and asked Tanaz to forgive him. She was briefly upset with his fling at work with Mitali but she forgave him after a couple of days, deciding to let bygones be bygones and work towards a better future together. She loved him deeply and fate had brought him back into her life.

Sameer walked in, congratulating them and settling in to order breakfast. Tanaz blushed with a radiant glow on her face and Tanveer acknowledged his wishes with a sense of pride and happiness at what he had done.

'What has Vicky been up to? He normally comes over a lot. I have hardly seen him since I've come this time,' Sameer asked him. He signalled to the waiter to come and take his order.

'No clue, dude,' said Tanveer and, putting his arm around Tanaz affectionately, added, 'As you can see, I have been busy over the weekend.'

'He should be here as well in a short while. It will be good to catch up,' Tanaz said.

Tania walked in, wearing a white and green salwar and a green dupatta. She had begun to wear Indian attire more often these days. The guys felt it was possibly Ankur's doing. He had grown extremely possessive of her as she had revealed to Vicky. She had to lie to him when she came out once in a while to meet the group of friends. Ankur did not want her to have anything to do with Sameer and was extremely upset over her decision to help Tanveer design the new SFA office given Sameer's links with the business. Tania gave Tanaz and Tanveer a big smile and was exuberant about them getting back together.

'It's good to see you guys back together,' she said elatedly. She said a cordial 'hi' to Sameer and talked to him about work and asked, 'Do you have any clue why Vicky has asked all of us to be here? He insisted that I be here now, no questions asked.'

'No clue, Tania, it's good to see you though. How is married life treating you?' Sam said consciously, trying not to sound too familiar.

'Good. There's so much to do! I'm doing my own freelance work and I teach as well. It keeps me busy,' she said, measuring her words carefully. Shifting her gaze to Tanaz she added, 'Hey, Tanveer and you have to be there and do a couple's dance at my cousin Bunty's wedding. Please replace Ankur and me as he doesn't dance anyway,' she said. *Ankur was too busy to practise for a sangeet. He couldn't care less really*, she thought.

'Sure we will, it sounds like fun. Call me tonight and we'll work it out,' Tanaz assured her. 'Tanveer will probably do some Rajesh Khanna or Dharmendra dance for you. The same moves he displayed when we partied in Goa, remember?' Sameer said to Tania.

The rest of them laughed at Tanveer who was busy chewing on his cheese toast. 'Stop dude, the women think I am a clown,' Tanveer shot back and looking at Tanaz, said, 'I was drunk that night. I don't normally dance like Rajesh Khanna or Dharmendra, you know that.'

Sameer and Tania laughed more while Tanaz almost choked on her pancake. Sameer nudged Tania. 'Well, normally it is Jeetendra, right Tanveer? Remember the talent show in college, Tania? One by one the crowd kept leaving as Tanveer continued dancing,' he said, grinning at Tanveer. It was fun pulling Tanveer's leg like the old times.

'You guys are mean,' Tania replied, giving him a mischievous smile. She added, looking at Tanaz, 'They convinced him to take part in the talent show, telling him he's a great dancer.'

'So we're chatting about our hot stepper's retro moves,' said Vicky, walking up to their table with a beautiful girl in tow who smiled shyly at them. Vicky wore a 'best FCUK in town' T-shirt and ripped-at-the-knee designer jeans, while Sarah walked in wearing a black and white salwar-kurta sans make up, coming across as demure but nevertheless looking stunningly beautiful. *They look like they're in love*, thought Tania. *Man, who is this beautiful girl*, thought Sam. *Wow*, was all Tanveer could think, while Tanaz stood up and walked towards Vicky to hug him thinking, *they look great together*.

He looked at the group like a school boy showing off his prize. 'Everyone, this is Sarah. She works as an air hostess with Indus Air and is basically from Mussoorie,' he said and added, 'Sarah, these are my best friends—Tania, Sameer and Tanveer, and next to him is his beautiful Tanaz. It's good to have all of us in the room at the same time and same place, without anyone wanting to kill each other.' The rest of them smiled at him and at each other. He turned to the group who watched them with shameless interest. This news was out of the blue for them as Vicky had been solely immersed with work since returning from London. Bringing a girl over to meet all his friends was a big move for him. The only other girl from the past who had had this privilege was Naina.

Looking at the menu, Vicky said, 'We're here just for a bit—we are heading to my parents' place for the family lunch. Haven't seen you in a while, Tania, how have you been? Glad you're here now and we can catch up. Sam leaves in a couple of days too,' and continued with a gleam in his eye, looking at Tanveer, 'Our loser is back. Nice, rocking! We've got to chat about this later.'

He thought that though he'd been seeing Sarah for two weeks, they had been taking it slow and were getting to know each other. He liked the fact that the more he got to know her, the more he was falling in love.

Tanveer acknowledged his wishes with a nod. Sarah congratulated him too and asked him whether he still enjoyed the scooty rides, at which all of them laughed. Tanveer could not stop thinking how Sarah was a combination of Tania's beautiful smile and air of innocence and also Tanaz's svelte figure and hazel eyes. *Vicky is a stud, man, first Naina, then Supriya, now this. It just gets better for him,* he thought.

Sarah chatted with Tania who was sitting next to her, telling her about where she was from, work and how she had met Vicky. Sarah was initially apprehensive about meeting Vicky's friends and was worried about them being judgmental, since she had met him only a couple of weeks ago. She soon realized that they were easy to get along with and she liked all of them instantly.

Tanaz chatted with Sameer who was sitting next to her and

appeared a bit lost. She thought about the chemistry between Tania and Sameer, who was sitting on her other side, thinking, *they look sweet together*. Tanveer interrupted the different conversations going on and said self-consciously, 'Guys, there's something I have to say. It's important.' Everyone turned to look at him.

'Tanaz and I plan to get married in November. We will do a registered marriage. We feel Mrs Rustomjee will be okay and I am going to tell my parents in a couple of weeks.'

Tanaz put her head on his shoulder and smiled. Tanveer had proposed at dinner the previous night.

Last night at the Ginger Bay

'I know I have been a complete a fool to hurt you in the way I did. But the time I have spent trying to push you out of my life has been the most miserable. It made me realize how special you are. Without you my life is a meagre existence. Please marry me,' he said, getting down on his knees.

'Yes, I will. Now please get up and don't make me cry,' she said, looking in his eyes and smiling.

Back at the Banyan Tree Café, Fort, Mumbai

Tania was shocked and gave a shriek of surprise and happiness. Sam and Vicky got up from where they were and moved to give Tanveer a bear hug and embrace Tanaz. Tania got up and hugged both Tanveer and Tanaz at the same time. Tears rolled down her eyes and she was embraced by Vicky followed by Sameer. Tania looked at Sameer for a moment thinking, *what if this could have been us*. Sam knew what she was thinking and looked uncomfortably at his phone, which displayed a picture of Simone and him.

Sarah gave Tanveer an affectionate squeeze. It was like she had known them forever. Vicky had done a terrific job last night, when they stayed up late talking about their friends and what their lives had been like. Tanaz and Tanveer, as Vicky had earlier told her, were victims of their parents' beliefs in their age-old customs and traditions. Sarah was happy to see this victory of love over barriers of caste, creed and religion, which had divided humanity. These were the values she espoused and stood for. Her mother was a Christian school teacher who had fallen in love and married her father, Irshad Anwar, who was a commander in the Indian army—despite family opposition from both sides. She had been brought up to learn about and respect both religions. Gradually, her parents' families had come around to accepting their relationship.

'You really are very beautiful,' Tanveer told her in his typical awkward tone reserved for people he did not know but would like to get acquainted with.

'Thanks,' Sarah said shyly while the rest laughed. The focus of the group was back on her.

'We are planning to have a small reception dinner at the Mayfair for family and friends after the wedding. I'm hoping that Tanveer's family will be there too,' Tanaz said, feeling excited.

'Guess I can help you with my experience in wedding shopping,' Tania said.

'I knew this dude would be the first amongst us guys to get married,' Vicky said to Sameer.

'Well, I better get going, guys. I have to go pick up some books from Chapters and then take my mum to my uncle's for lunch,' Sameer told the group while getting up to leave.

'I'll come too. Need to pick up my monthly dose of *Wallpaper* and then go home for lunch. Ankur gets edgy if I am late,' Tania said, reflecting for a moment on Ankur's moods.

Smiling at Tanaz and taking her hand, Tanveer said, 'Yes, let's all leave. We have to go and have lunch with Mrs Rustomjee and discuss our plans with her. She has no clue. Wish me luck.'

'Good luck with your prospective mum-in-law, dude. Wish we could come and watch the fun. Do you want me to talk to her on your behalf? I could help you,' Vicky said with a grin.

'No way! I'll handle it. You'll end up doing what Jai did to Veeru in *Sholay*,' Tanveer said with a worried laugh, while the others smiled.

'I have no clue what Jai did, dude! You've been talking about that movie for eight years. I should watch it some time. Let's go, Sarah. My folks will be waiting too. I told them I have a beautiful little surprise for them,' Vicky said, putting his arm around Sarah while she put her head on his shoulders.

Vicky looks like he is in love, thought Tania, while Sam was thinking, *I hope he's thought this through*, and Tanveer felt, *Sarah looks special. She has such a natural chemistry with Vicky while with Supriya it did appear to be a bit forced.*

Tanaz's home, Peddar Road, Mumbai

Mrs Rustomjee took the news of her daughter wanting to marry Tanveer very calmly. 'I am happy for both of you, but I have one condition which you need to accept,' she said, choking with emotion. Tanveer and Tanaz looked at each other, wondering what the condition was. 'Both of you please stay on in this house after you get married, and put up with this old lady till she is alive. I do not want to live alone,' she said, looking vulnerable, showing a side to her which Tanveer hadn't seen.

Tanveer hugged Tanaz and her at the same time. 'Of course. We aren't going anywhere, Mrs Rustomjee. We are here and will continue to be with you,' he said. His parents were never going to move to Mumbai and they did not like to visit the city either. He wanted Tanaz to be happy and close to her mother, and he was at home living with Mrs Rustomjee, being used to her moods and her eccentric ways.

Vicky's family home, Colaba, Mumbai

Vicky and Sarah enjoyed a friendly lunch with his family. She bonded with his grandmother, sister and his cousins, though his parents initially felt awkward as it was the first time Vicky had brought a girl home for a family lunch after Naina. They gradually opened up and chatted with her, asking about her life and her parents. Vicky's mother noticed that she was unlike any other girl her son had dated, while his father was pleasantly surprised that his son had fallen for a sweet and grounded girl as opposed to the social butterflies who surrounded him.

'She appears to be nice. Hang on to her now,' Vicky's mother told him, while his dad said to him in hushed whispers, 'She's beautiful,' and winked. His grandmother doted on her. 'Kisse ki nazar na lage,' she said before Sarah and Vicky left. 'She is sophisticated, beautiful and charming. Where did you find her?' his hard-to-impress sister said, giving her nod of approval to Vicky who chatted about Sarah gleefully.

On their drive back to his apartment, she said, 'Can we go to Mount Mary's and light a candle? I promised myself I would do that if it went well with your parents. I was so nervous about it.'

He looked at her ardently. 'Sure love, I've never been inside the church. Let's go.'

'It's nice, it makes me feel calm and at peace. We could go to Haji Ali on a Thursday when I'm not flying. I go there when I can, it's a nice feeling,' she added, looking at him while he nodded along in approval.

'What do you want to do tonight? Do you want to go out for

dinner or a movie and coffee?'

'Hmmm… how about we go to Jazz and Blues tonight? Maybe I'll sing for you. It's karaoke night. But I'm taking you out tonight, huh? Also, I'll make dinner. We can eat and leave. We eat out all the time—it isn't good for our health,' she said.

'Yes boss, let's spend some time at the church and head back. We can hit the gym together in the evening and you can get back and cook. Let me call and reserve a table at Jazz and Blues.'

∽

27
Standing Up

'Do what is right, not what is easy.'

—A QUOTE FROM *Reader's Digest*

1 AUGUST 2008
Chapters, Kemps Corner, Mumbai

Sameer and Tania finished their book shopping, with Sameer picking up a number of fiction and non-fiction books as they were three times more expensive in London. He walked Tania out to find her a cab as she did not want him to drop her home. Outside the bookstore, as it began to drizzle again, they looked at each other with a sense of loss and longing. Almost as a natural reaction, with thick drops of rain coming down on them, they both leaned in and kissed briefly on the lips before Tania pulled back with confusion in her eyes and Sameer turned his gaze away from her.

'We cannot do this, I'm married now, Sameer. I have to give my marriage a chance,' Tania said, looking into his eyes with a pained expression.

'I'm sorry, Tania. I'm still seeing Simone as well. I don't know what came over me. It was nice catching up with you. Have a relaxed weekend and take care,' Sameer said reluctantly. Tania and he hugged and she kissed him on his forehead. 'Take care Sameer. You have a nice trip back to London,' she said and got into the cab which drove away. She turned around to see Sameer still standing there, watching the taxi disappear around the corner.

She reached home in a state of confusion, thinking about the emotions that had come over her outside Chapters. Leaning in and kissing Sameer was like a natural reaction to her. They were drawn to each other like bees to honey or a moth to a flame.

Ankur asked her sternly as she walked in, 'How come you got so late? It is almost 2 p.m. and I am very hungry. I thought we are having lunch together?' She walked up and put her magazine on the table.

'Sorry baba, there was just too much traffic. Anyway, you're not going to believe this. Guess what? Tanveer and Tanaz are getting married this November! Vicky is now seeing a sweet girl called Sarah who he is serious about. A lot is happening at same time. After breakfast at Banyan Tree, Sam and I just rushed over to Chapters to pick up some books,' she said sweetly.

'You went with that Sameer? You hung out with that son of a bitch! Didn't I tell you not to have anything to do with him? What the hell, Tania! This isn't right. You go and do shopping with your ex-boyfriend while I wait here—and you pretend it's all cool,' Ankur said looking infuriated, while pacing up and down the living room.

'I don't think you paid attention to anything else I said apart from hearing Sameer's name. Please don't spoil my mood, Ankur! I'm in a good mood and I'm happy for my friends. Why make an issue when there isn't one? Besides, I'm not taking any orders from you okay? I'm thirty minutes late and I'm sorry. Please let us eat now,' Tania said, while setting up the table for lunch.

Ankur grabbed her hand. 'What the fuck? You cannot walk away. This is unacceptable behaviour. I'm warning you. I am not going to sit around and watch you hanging around with Sameer,' he said, pulling her and twisting her hand as she tried to free herself. Raising her voice in pain, Tania said, 'Leave me! Ouch, you're hurting me, you brute. What is acceptable to you? Pictures of you getting splashed over page three with socialites and some shameless hags? I've had enough of being pushed around by you.'

She felt her face get hot, and the next moment she was on the floor with a burning sensation on her right cheek. He had struck her in a fit of rage, making her collapse on the floor. She looked up at him with shock and bitterness, while running her palm over her cheek, which was turning red.

Ankur continued, 'I'm sick of this bloody life and I'm tired of trying to live up to your expectations! You want to see your ex-boyfriend in me? Well, I'm not that guy, get it? I'm Ankur, not that damn Sameer Ahuja from London who was probably sleeping with women while you were sitting here fussing over your commitment for him.' He took her favourite vase and smashed it to the ground, looking at her threateningly.

'Stop it! If you are bored of me and tired too, why don't you leave, Ankur? How much can I put up with? You went and sold our company—which I'd work so hard to build—against my wishes. There are limits to my patience. Go to hell! Get out of this house. I'm not going to leave this time. It's my apartment if you remember. Please leave. I need time to think about us. I cannot live like this any more,' Tania screamed hysterically, with tears running down her cheeks.

Ankur walked to his room and packed a duffel-bag with his clothes and toiletries and stormed out, banging the door behind him. Tania sat down holding her head with both her hands, thinking, *what have I done with my life?*

On the way to Tania and Ankur's Apartment, Mumbai

Naina was on the road with her boyfriend Nitin, who was dropping her to Tania's place before heading to a film premiere his publicist had asked him to come to. She looked tense as Tania had called her a while back sounding upset about the fight she had had with Ankur. They navigated through peak hour traffic and Nitin turned his gaze to her with concern.

'What happened with Suresh Lalwani? He mentioned to me that you refused the offer to do a special appearance in the movie. He was offering you five lakhs. Why did you turn it down?' Nitin asked her, sounding irritated. After a lot of struggle and circulating in the party circuit, he had been cast as the second lead with a meaty role alongside big stars.

'It's not about the money. It was some item song with his fifty-year-old leading star, on the beach in a bikini. It's weird. It doesn't work for me,' she said, looking at him, not ready to be convinced.

'You walked out of *Mumbai Talkies* as well. It was your big break—a golden opportunity to star opposite Nitesh Kumar. You were the second lead, with forty minutes of screen time.'

'You already know the reason why! Why do we have to discuss this again and again? He would coax me to use his trailer with him. He was creepy and passed lewd comments. I was uncomfortable!' she said, looking flustered.

'Calm down. These people have a big ego. You'll ruin whatever little goodwill and connections we have. He got another actress to replace you the next day. I mean, this guy is a big action hero with a fan base. You've got to be more diplomatic with these people! He's got a wife and kids and the glossies were reporting your side of the story which he denied, claiming you were unprofessional. He's been telling people not to work with you.' He looked at her with concern. 'You know I've got a movie now and another one after this. I am also doing three shows. You've got to move forward.'

'Okay, you're big and famous. You have a good thing going. I'm happy for you! I still have my countdown show, which keeps me busy. I'm also going to Delhi for the fashion week. I have money saved up so I don't need to take these shortcuts you are suggesting to success,' she said, sounding agitated.

'I'm not suggesting anything! You had three shows till six months back. The days of hosting request shows and countdowns are numbered. People want reality shows now. They want to see people like them succeed or make a fool of themselves or others. You refused to do *Locked up* with me. Mandira agreed and it's a big hit. Now she's on for another reality show.'

'Good for her! I don't believe in these scripted "reality" shows anyway.' She took out her packet of mild cigarettes and lit up. 'You've got to turn right here and stop. I'll see you later tonight, thanks,' she said, getting out of the car.

THE NEXT DAY... 2 AUGUST 2008
Mumbai Club, Colaba, Mumbai

Vicky, Sam and Tanveer walked off the court, sweating profusely and panting after a long basketball game. They headed towards the coffee shop at the club. All Vicky talked about was Sarah and his feelings for her. Tanveer went home after a cup of coffee while Vicky and Sameer decided to go and have dinner and discuss things. Vicky told him that he was planning to ask Sarah to move in with him.

'Moving in together, huh dude? Nice. You're moving fast with Sarah, man! But you're happy and it shows. She seems to be really nice,' Sameer said with enthusiasm.

'Yes, it's great with her. I haven't felt this way before. We connect at so many levels and feel like we've known each other forever. How's it going with Simone?' Vicky asked with interest.

'Well, I am happy for you. I am not in the same place as you. Simone and I live together but we're moving with the flow and taking things as they come. We've been together for a while and she's a nice girl—friendly, sexy, great to spend time with,' he said contemplatively and added, 'I am thinking of moving back to India now. I believe I've learnt what I wanted to and anyway, things have slowed down considerably in London. I've had to fire two really good people on my team. Tough economic conditions lie ahead with the credit crisis and what's been happening in the US.'

'Hmm, well I hope it works out. You do seem like you're having a good time. What do you plan to come back and do? Things at SFA appear to be going well as far as I can see,' Vicky said.

'That's good. I have been getting some positive feedback from Tanveer, Mr Mehta and Bharat. Tanveer signed three new contracts last week. Can you update me a little more?' Sameer asked.

Vicky explained to Sam, who listened with interest, 'Well, yes. Mr Mehta and Bharat are likely to sign one this week. Sumeet, our man in Delhi, is likely to sew some thing up as well with Mr Mehta, and there is another one which Rohan, the Pune Head of Operations, and Tanveer are working on. It should be finalized sometime this week. It's good actually—we have the new offices up and running, services are streamlined. We now provide advice and consulting as opposed to managing people's investments. We've gotten rid of a lot of unprofitable business and should improve our profitability by the end of this year by ten to twelve per cent.'

'That's fabulous, dude. I will have a detailed run through of the numbers with Tanveer later. What about expansion plans for next year?' Sameer asked.

'We are evaluating opening in Hyderabad and taking over one boutique set-up offering similar services in Bangalore. We could look at Kolkata too. The business plans are being prepared by Tanveer in co-ordination with the operational heads. Tanveer and Bharat are getting us brand recognition, working closely with the media on different items of news, analysis and features,' he said and added, 'We have twenty people now and we plan to add five more people through the acquisition and redeploy a few of them to Hyderabad.'

'Good, that's the right way to go. We shouldn't expand in a frenzy and add unnecessary fat. I wanted to chat with you about some offers I want to run through with you. Look, SFA is more or less back on track. You've done a great job providing oversight and supporting business development. Tanveer has things covered pretty well,' Sameer said while their dinner was being served.

'That's right,' Vicky said, wondering what was coming up. He did have a few ideas in mind.

Sam said excitedly, 'I have a proposition in mind which we could consider doing together. I am keen on getting the chef from San Pedro's in London down to Mumbai. He's a nice chap, basically from Lucknow—Aditya Prasad. We will need to be involved as investors mainly. The operations will be taken care of by the other partner. I love their food and Simone and I go there a lot. It has a great cosmopolitan vibe, an amazing Italian wine list and I can't seem to get over their Mexican food.'

He added, 'I have a place where we could do this. My dad had invested in a retail property on Waterfield Road in Bandra, which is a great location for this. I have been in touch with Aditya and he is keen to partner on a fifty-fifty basis. We invest and he operates and runs the place.'

Chewing slowly on his pita bread, Vicky said, 'It's a great idea dude. Why don't we fly him down and talk business. I am willing to invest equally with you. I think it is a great concept and it would potentially work. You took me there a couple of times. I remember gorging on their chicken fajitas and chicken with south-western rice. No one makes it like that here and if he can create the vibrant environment like it is in London, it will work great. We could get Tania to design the look and feel of the place.' He added, 'And this Aditya must be interested—at the end of the day, India is now where the opportunity is.'

'Sounds like a plan. I know Aditya quite well now—honest chap, passionate about what he does and wants to come back home,' Sameer said. Vicky leaned forward and said, 'Well, there is this other opportunity—to do an eco-tourism resort near Pune and one in Alibaug. We have a plot near Pune, while in Alibaug we own a heritage building with a view of the coast a few minutes' walk from our beach house. What do you think about heading the business? Bringing the plans to fruition? We can bring in some good people from the hospitality industry to work with you. I wouldn't be too keen on going ahead without you as we have the same tastes and a common vision. Besides, there is a level of trust we share. It's not just about profits at the end of the day for us. It has to be exclusive, provide quality of service, be environment-friendly and contribute to the society around it. I think you have a gift, the way you've held things together at Smith and Robinson—and you've helped re-align SFA's business and convinced people to stay despite the changes and chaos.'

Sameer, looking away from the screen of his PDA, said, 'Sounds exciting. There is so much we can do and create a space for ourselves. There are so many different kinds of customers looking for varied value. There is a lot of untapped potential at tourism destinations in India. Let's research this and begin working on a business plan. I am with you. Let's work on it.'

'Great, good stuff. Let's go and check out the locations when you move back and we could start visiting similar set-ups like we aim to build in India and outside. We'll work out the formalities regarding registration and the like while you're in London. I will get the corporate affairs team rolling on the set up of the company and registration formalities. Headhunting the senior team needs to follow that. I reckon we could get the Alibaug place up and running very quickly,' Vicky said, sounding upbeat and driven to succeed.

'Great dude, let's get these ventures rolling. I'm excited. I look forward to coming back home,' he said, looking optimistic. *I need to talk to Simone and tell her about my decision,* he thought.

'How is Rajveer doing?' Vicky asked.

'He's good. He has picked up his game. His coach in Australia will be the coach and manager of Hyderabad Hurricanes—one of the recently launched CPL teams. It's likely that he will make the team at the auction as a middle order batsman. His coach really is impressed with him. He will try out with the Mumbai Ranji Team as well and should hopefully make it back in the team soon,' Sam said proudly. He was happy to see Rajveer get back on the right path and succeed.

'Great, I'm happy for him. Good he is back to doing what he loves,' Vicky said, as both of them stood up to leave. Vicky asked, almost as an afterthought, 'Is Simone on board with your plans? Does she know about you moving back to India and the restaurant plan? Will she move with you?'

'Well, she does have an idea. We have talked about it. I'm not sure if she'll move. We've got to work that out. She is trying to convince me to move to the Middle East where Smith and Robinson are planning to start an office. Peter has been asking me to consider moving there to head it, and take Simone with me too,' Sameer said, unsure of what the future held for him and Simone.

'Clearly, they don't want to let go of you. But you don't want to do it, right? You better speak to her. This could drive you apart,' Vicky warned Sameer with apprehension in his voice.

'True, I don't want to move there. I'm not too excited about it.

There's enough in India we can pursue. I'll speak to Simone and try convincing her,' Sameer concluded.

'Do that. Let's go, dude, Sarah's flight must have landed. I need to go pick her up,' Vicky said while they walked out together.

~

28
Life is a Mixed Bag

'Experience is not what happens to you. It is what you do with what happens to you.'

—ALDOUS HUXLEY

8 August 2008
On a flight to Bangalore

Sarah had been on duty for the past three days, during which she had a layover in different cities. Vicky missed her a great deal. She was on the phone with him each time she got off the flight and when she got back to the hotel. She ordered food to her room and spent most of her time talking to him on the phone while the rest of the crew went out partying. He shifted his gaze away from his laptop screen and looked at his iPhone wallpaper, which had a picture of Sarah smiling at him seductively.

He shut his laptop and left for the day. *Why waste a beautiful day at my desk when I can barely concentrate*, he thought. After a couple of hours, he boarded an Indus Air flight from Delhi to Bangalore via Mumbai. From what Sarah messaged him that morning, he knew she was on duty on that flight. On an impulse, he decided to take the flight to Bangalore to surprise Sarah—and surprised she was when she saw him. She almost dropped her tray filled with glasses of orange juice and lemonade when she saw him sit there and grin at her. She looked stunning as ever in her sexy black uniform. He was the only passenger in the business class on the flight. She gave him a thousand-watt smile and asked with a naughty gleam in her eyes and a tray with glasses of juice to serve the only passenger, 'Welcome on board, Mr Khanna. Will you have orange juice or lemonade?'

'How about a taste of your lips?' he asked with persuasive charm. He took a glass of lemonade from the tray and took her hand to kiss it. Sarah blushed and looked around to make sure she was in the clear.

'Behave,' she chastened him in a hushed whisper, 'I'll lose my job.' She walked away smiling to herself.

After the take-off was complete, Sarah started to walk past him towards the economy class passengers on the other side of the curtain. Vicky held her hand and said, 'You have to know this—I love you, really do and I'm damn serious about it,' and let her go, loosening the grip on her hand. The way she looked at him and walked away gave him the answer he wanted. While she served him his meal, he asked her, 'Will you move in with me, please?'

'Yes,' she said, slowly biting her upper lip, looking scared but giving him a reassuring smile. She came back to him before they landed and with an affectionate look said, 'Let's meet outside the airport, by the café outside. We'll find a cab and get to the serviced apartment.'

'I have the Grand Manor booked,' Vicky said, at which she looked at him and shook her head in disapproval.

'You didn't have to do that. You're spending so much money on all this,' she said worriedly and added, 'Can you cancel it? It's unnecessary to spend so much for one night! We aren't on a honeymoon, mister! The serviced apartment is nice.'

'Chill. Okay, I will if it makes you happy. I'm on the flight with you back to Mumbai tomorrow morning. I'll come over and help you pack and move in.' He had it all figured out this time. He was head over heels in love and it showed.

Sarah took her seat at the front of the plane and announced that they would be landing shortly in Bangalore and thanked the passengers in Hindi and English for flying with Indus Air. Vicky and she glanced passionately at each other with a smile on their faces, sitting a few metres apart.

Tanveer's family home, Sholapur, Maharashtra

Tanveer was having lunch with his parents and sisters. He had just told them about his decision to get married to Tanaz. Despite Sameena's emotional pleas and cajoling, he did not relent this time. His sisters supported him through the argument, which strengthened his case. His father Ibrahim's stance on the issue had changed considerably. He quietly accepted his son's wishes saying warmly, 'Well, you have been a great son to us and a good brother to your sisters. You've done more than most others I have seen who have married people of their parents' choice. I don't believe it really matters any more and if it makes you happy, go and marry her! I want you to have happiness and peace at the end of the day. I do not care what the society comments about your decision. At the end of the day I am proud of what you have accomplished and the responsibility you have shown.'

These comments made Tanveer smile and he embraced his father. Ibrahim and Sameena mentioned that they would not be making it for the registered marriage but would come in with his sisters for the small reception Tanaz and Tanveer were planning to host after the wedding.

While he was leaving, his mother said, 'She is very beautiful. I hope and pray she will be a good wife to you.'

He walked out and hailed an autorickshaw to take him to the railway station. He felt on top of the world having managed to accomplish what he once believed was impossible.

Simone and Sameer's Apartment, Liverpool Street, London

Simone and Sameer were sitting and having a cup of tea. They had decided to stay at home and enjoy a quiet weekend. This was the first time they were spending time together after Simone had returned from her Turkey–Syria–Jordan trip. She had extended her trip to spend two days in Dubai. There were undercurrents of tension in the air. Simone had been quiet and aloof since she got back and Sameer found it difficult to bring up the topic of his decision to move back to Mumbai. Simone put her copy of *Glamorous* down and looked bravely at Sameer who was engrossed in reading a book about the economic meltdown.

'Sameer, there's something I've been meaning to tell you. Please hear me out before you react. I met Steve who is from Melbourne in Petra. He is Stuart's friend who works in Dubai in a shipping company. We had a few drinks and hit it off, and I slept with him…' she said carefully, taking her gaze away from Sameer and added, 'He's asked me to move to Dubai and live with him. I think I really like him and with you it's been tough since you've been saying you want to go back to Mumbai. I'm sorry it's happening this way. We've had a great run. It has been good with you, but we want different things really. It is difficult. I wish it hadn't happened this way.'

Sameer shut his book and leaned across with an agitated look on his face. He stared at her and shifted his gaze to the painting on the wall behind her.

'How could you do this to me? After all we've been through together and given what we have. I can't believe this.' He got up and walked out of the apartment with his coat, without saying a word. She tried to stop him from leaving but he ignored her pleas and pushed her hand away. He ran down the stairs and walked for a few blocks over to the park where they normally went on weekends in spring and summer months. The air was chilly and the sky was overcast with dark grey skies. Despite it being summer, the temperatures had dropped considerably over the past three days. Feeling tired, he collapsed on the first bench he saw in the park. He watched people jogging while they listened to music on their MP3 players and couples walking their dogs. He noticed some families with their toddlers leaving the park as it began to drizzle. He thought about his life in London and the time Simone and he had spent together. He thought about the last trip back home when Tanaz and Tanveer got back together and Vicky started seeing Sarah. He reflected on the kiss with Tania and how he felt after it. He was confused in that moment and longed to hold her in his arms. He still did. He felt that at that point and in that moment he had cheated on Simone too. *What was I thinking? Simone and I would never have lasted*, he thought. He sat there for a couple of hours lost in his thoughts. The drizzle turned into a steady downpour and it began to get dark. There were just a couple of teenagers in the park apart from him. He quickly walked out of the park and hailed a taxi to get back home. Sameer walked in and took off his coat. He didn't feel as devastated as he had felt when Simone had first told him. He moved over to where she was sitting with a worried look on her face and red eyes. He put his arms around her and hugged her.

'I will be all right. It sometimes is difficult to comprehend the things we do. Don't be hard on yourself. When do you plan to leave?' he asked with warmth and tenderness in his voice. She broke down in his arms and they stayed wrapped around each other on the couch for a while.

Simone left for Dubai after a week and Sameer dropped her

off at the airport.

'Do finish the macaroni I've kept in the fridge for you. I'm going to miss you heaps,' she said with affection and kissed him.

He came back to an empty apartment and thought about the twenty months they'd spent together. He was to leave London in six weeks, having resigned from his job at Smith and Robinson a day after Simone told him about her little affair. He called Vicky and told him that he was coming back and, on the weekends, began working with Aditya on the India plans.

10 DAYS LATER... 18 AUGUST 2008
Tania's Apartment, Khar, Mumbai

Tania was sitting at home with Naina and Tanaz by her side. Ankur had come in for a while and had packed his things and left earlier in the day. Both of them had decided to separate for now and take a call on the marriage in the next few months, based on her lawyer's advice.

'I think you did the right thing. No point holding on to something when you aren't happy,' Naina said.

'Yes, it does give you time to think and work things out. You could meet after some time and talk. Once he and you have had a chance to think this through,' Tanaz said.

Tania sat there looking stressed out. Her parents did not know much about her situation with Ankur besides the fact that they had arguments and fights, which was normal in a marriage. They did not know that things had gotten this far. She planned to have a serious discussion with them in a couple of days.

'We are all with you, okay? Don't worry so much. Whatever is for the best will happen,' Tanaz added, putting her arm around Tania.

'She's right Tania. Let's go shopping now, it will cheer you up.

It sure works for me,' Naina said. The girls smiled at this and got up to leave.

'I hear Sameer is returning in time for your wedding?' Tania asked Tanaz.

'Yes, he is getting back like a week before the wedding. We are really happy that he is going to be there. Though he's been in his own world after Simone cheated on him. Tanveer has been travelling so much with their company expanding and everything. It's been very busy for him,' Tanaz said while they walked out of Tania's apartment.

'That's how Sameer is, deep and intense. How is it going between both of you?' Tania asked. Tanaz looked at them with repressed glee.

'It's been great. Sometimes I can't believe we are back together and things are happening. Tanveer has changed so much too,' she said and added, 'His mother has been telling him to ask me to convert and change my name and religion. Tanveer was quite firm with her. He said, "I'm not changing my religion or beliefs for her. Why should she do so? I don't think this is necessary, it doesn't matter to me. Please stop asking me this." When he told me this I was shocked!' A smile came to Tania's face and she remembered how traditional Tanveer used to be.

'Not bad. Our Tanveer seems to be on fire!' Naina said, at which they laughed as they got into her car to leave.

∼

PART 6

LIVING YOUR DREAMS

'The past is a ghost, the future a dream,
and all we ever have is now.'
—BILL COSBY

29
Bliss

'You don't love a woman because she is beautiful, but she is beautiful because you love her.'

—ANONYMOUS

13 NOVEMBER 2008
Marriage Registrar's Office, near Marine Drive, Mumbai

Sarah, Vicky, Sameer, Tania, Naina, Mrs Ahuja, a couple of Tanaz's friends and Mrs Rustomjee accompanied Tanaz and Tanveer to the noisy and chaotic Marriage Registrar's office on the morning of their wedding. Tanveer was in a simple sherwani, while Tanaz was wearing a white and pink salwar-kurta.

'I've never seen you look so beautiful, Peaches,' Tanveer said before leaving in the morning and kissed her. Tanaz glowed radiantly. Her dream had finally come true. Despite the odds stacked against them, Tanveer and she were finally together. Tanveer was taking her to Sri Lanka for their honeymoon for ten days the following evening. His parents were to come that afternoon in time for the reception at Mayfair with his sisters and a couple of other relatives. Tanaz felt nervous about finally meeting her prospective in-laws. After the registration, they prepared to head to the Trident Hotel where a room had been booked, to relax before the reception at night. Sam and Vicky, who were wearing matching black and brown sherwanis, hugged Tanveer with warmth and pulled his leg about how he looked.

'Guys, leave him, at least on his wedding day,' Tania warned them. She was extremely happy for Tanveer who had finally followed his heart and chosen love over everything else. 'This is the only way he could be happy,' she said to Sarah in a conversation they shared while the guys caught up.

'Chal, we're off. Sarah and I will pick both of you up and we'll head to Mayfair from Trident at 8 p.m. I'll need to go get the car decorated with flowers now,' Vicky said sounding rushed.

'Sure dude, thanks buddy,' said Tanveer.

'I'll pick your folks up with Rajveer from the railway station in a couple of hours and take them over to my place,' Sam said to him.

Tanveer and Tanaz left for the hotel after embracing Mrs Rustomjee who looked regal in her green and white dress and stood teary eyed through the proceedings, overcome by emotion. It was the happiest day of Tanveer's life. The sky was blue, birds chirped merrily and the city of Mumbai was a beautiful place again. Tanveer looked unusually comfortable and cheerful on his wedding night. Having too many people around often made him nervous and resulted in him making awkward comments. Tonight though, he was charm personified and made conversation with every guest. He looked dashing in his grey suit, wearing a blue shirt and blue tie, while Tanaz glowed, standing next to him in her blue wedding gown, designed by Sheetal Mirchandani. Tanveer's parents were immaculately dressed in traditional attire and stood near the entrance to greet guests alongside Mrs Rustomjee who had taken to them immediately. She took them around introducing them to all her Parsi friends and family. Ibrahim requested Tanveer to have a nikah the next afternoon and solemnize the wedding, which Tanveer and Tanaz agreed to do for their happiness and peace of mind before they left for Colombo.

Sameer made an entrance with Naina and was followed by Vicky and Sarah who couldn't spend a moment without each other. Tania, in a blue and black sari, was the last of the group to come in—an hour late, and without Ankur. She appeared to be stressed but managed a cheerful façade. She appeared distant and stuck with Naina most of the time. Sameer sat with them but remained absorbed in his BlackBerry through the evening. Tania spent a few minutes chatting with Mrs Ahuja who hugged her warmly, complimenting her for looking like a 'pari'. She had a short exchange of words with Sameer as well about going down to Alibaug the following day to check out the heritage property they were to convert into an exclusive resort with thirty suites. Tania was to redecorate the place which she agreed to do at a nominal rate.

A number of close childhood friends and people from their respective workplaces were there to wish them as well and Tanveer also had a few people from Oceania Bank whom he was still friends with. The celebrations and the dinner went pretty well with everyone joining in to shake a leg with the newly married couple. Tania and Sameer danced together for a few minutes and in a short while she moved away and Naina stepped up to shake a leg with him. Vicky and Sarah danced quietly in the corner while Tanveer had everyone hysterical with his impersonation of Dharmendra and Rajesh Khanna's dance moves till Tanaz pulled him away from the dance floor and made him dance a slow waltz with her. His mother looked embarrassed and thanked her stars that most of her relatives were not among the audience for her son's dance performance. Tanveer also danced with Mrs Rustomjee who enjoyed the attention.

Tania went with Naina and Sarah to the powder room after

dinner. Looking upset and hurt she said, 'My parents and I had a huge row before coming for the wedding. They want me to reconcile with Ankur. They want me to compromise and adjust a little more. They feel that if he doesn't want me to have anything to do with Sameer, I shouldn't. There is too much pressure for me to handle.'

Sarah put an arm around her. 'Look, understand their position. There must be pressure for them too, having to face society. Take it easy. You are trying to work things out. Be patient and give it time.'

'She's right, don't get upset. Let things be for a while,' Naina added calmly.

Tania left shortly after that and drove back quietly. Ankur was to move back to the apartment as he was unable to find a good apartment, and she had decided to pack her things and move to her parent's home. She wanted to live separately till they sorted their differences out. Tania stood at her doorstep for a moment and remembered again the night she had broken up with Sameer before he left for London. She remembered their passionate kiss and how helpless and forlorn he had looked. The memory of that night constantly haunted her. Fraught with memories of time gone by she wondered, *have I made a big mistake?* She opened the door and walked up to her room.

Sameer drove Naina home and walked her up to the elevator in her building. His mind was far away, thinking about Tania and the way she looked tonight when she had kept looking at him dancing with Naina.

'Tania looked very disturbed tonight. Is everything okay with Ankur and her? I didn't ask as it might seem intrusive,' he said, looking troubled. A tired Naina looked at him while pressing the button for the elevator.

'They are living separately till their problems are sorted out. Things have been quite stormy of late between them,' she said looking into his eyes and added, 'I feel you should let her be for a while as, otherwise, it might just end up complicating things further. I can't figure Ankur out. He's always had issues and has been tough on her. You take it easy. Thanks for the ride.'

She got into the elevator and waved him goodnight. He turned around and walked away thinking, *I wish things had turned out differently.*

Honeymoon Suite, the Trident, Mumbai

Tanveer helped Tanaz take off all her jewellery to help her undress and get into bed. She giggled while he fumbled with the pins.

'Ouch! Slowly now. What is the hurry?' she asked.

Tanveer could not believe that his dreams were coming true. They heard a knock on the door. Tanveer pulled away from Tanaz's arms to see who it was at 3 a.m. It was the room service attendant and he brought in a bottle of champagne, courtesy Sarah and Vikram. Tanveer thanked the attendant and saw him away with a tip and a friendly nod. He came back to uncork the bottle and poured two glasses of champagne. They took their glasses and moved to the bathtub where Tanaz got in after him with her back resting against his chest. Tanveer took a sip of his champagne thinking, *boy, I am in heaven! Life can't get better than this.*

30
In the Skies Above

'For you I know I'd even try to turn the tide.'

—JOHNNY CASH

14 DECEMBER 2008
Indus Air flight to Delhi

Sarah was on duty on an early morning flight to Delhi. She was extremely sleepy and thought about the late night they'd had. Vicky and she had gone home at 3 a.m. and she had managed to get two hours of sleep. To her surprise, Vicky who had come to drop her off at the airport was sitting in a business class seat, making eyes at her. She smiled at him affectionately with her eyes asking him a question, *what are you doing here? I'm coming back home tonight.*

Surprise, Vicky's eyes told her. Again, he was the only passenger in business class. He had booked all the business class seats Indus Air had on this flight. After the take-off was complete, she came to him, giving him a friendly whack on his arm and asked, 'Why are you here?' She gave him her characteristic beautiful smile and looked stunning in her black uniform. He always imagined her in her uniform, looking sexy and seductive. Vicky removed his seatbelt, stepped out on to the aisle and went down on one knee, taking out a glittering diamond ring, 'My sexy Sarah, will you please marry me?' he asked her tenderly.

'Yes, of course yes!' Sarah quivered and began to cry while he placed the ring slowly on her finger. The curtains were drawn open and a number of other passengers were smiling at them, while Sarah's colleagues walked up and congratulated her. He ecstatically hugged some of the other crew who stood there smiling amongst the excitement. The captain's voice came on the overhead microphone, 'Congratulations, Sarah. Wish you happiness from all of us at Indus Air!'

She was given the rest of the flight off and she sat next to Vicky and cuddled with him. *I need to call my parents when we reach Delhi*, she thought. This was the best moment of her life. She was thirty-five thousand feet in the air with Vicky next to her who was now taking a picture on his iPhone with tears rolling down her cheek and a picture of the beautiful diamond ring on her finger, which added that extra glow to her smile and eyes. Tania had helped him pick up the ring a week ago.

'I love you and always will,' she said with intensity.

'I love you too, my sweet bottoms,' he quipped back, kissing Sarah on her cheek and resting her soft little head on his shoulders, which made her smile. He loved the dreamy look on her face and those doe eyes, and knew that he would do anything to keep her happy. He had already booked a flight out to Dehradun from Delhi for both of them and had arranged a car to drive them to Mussoorie where her parents lived. Vicky was excited about his future together with her. He could not wait. His parents, who knew of his plans to propose, were planning an engagement ceremony at the Four Seasons in a few weeks. It was something Vicky was against, but he agreed to it by getting them to agree to let Sarah and him plan and have a small wedding without their interference and their page three crowd.

Heritage Bungalow, Alibaug, Maharashtra

Tania, looking demure and petite in a simple salwar-kurta, walked behind Sameer who was showing her around the old heritage bungalow. This was the site for Vicky's and his proposed first resort. Vicky and he had agreed to form a company called Future Forward Hospitality Ventures which was to conceive, build and operate heritage eco-tourism resorts under the Sunsets and More brand all over India, as well as partner with and run theme fine-dining restaurants, which included their plan of setting up Mexikhana, the desi version of San Pedro's, in partnership with Aditya in Mumbai. Aditya was to come down to Mumbai in a week to finalize the agreement and plan things out with both of them. Sameer asked a number of questions to the civil engineer who was with them to assess the kind of restoration that was required and the additional work that needed to be completed to get the place operational. The business plans and budget to get the resort up and running were being worked out by a team at SFA led by Tanveer. Sameer was to be appointed as the CEO of Future Forward Hospitality Ventures. He had head-hunters working on bringing in experienced people in the hospitality sector to spearhead senior management roles.

'We could do a smaller version of our Mexican restaurant here in Alibaug too. We can keep the kitchen inside and set seating up on the beach overlooking the sea. It should be a great draw,' he thoughtfully explained to Tania.

'Good idea,' she said, listening to him intently with the wind in her hair. She put on her sunglasses. 'Any idea what time Vicky lands in Delhi? I want to call and wish him. I am so excited. Naina is more or less settled too. So that leaves you, Mr Ahuja—the last of us to take a decision on marriage,' she said, smiling at him.

'True, though I don't think I'm there yet,' Sam said in a

reflective tone thinking, *you are more or less single now too.*

Both of them received a text message from Vicky saying Sarah had said 'yes' and that they were flying out to Dehradun and then driving to Mussoorie to meet Sarah's parents. Sam dialled his number and both Tania and he wished Vicky and Sarah, who were in high spirits. Tania and Sameer were excited about the prospect of Vicky getting married.

'You've finally belled our lady-killer,' he said to Sarah who looked at Vicky while walking out of the airport with her hand in his and smiled.

Tania completed her survey of the location after which she discussed plans in detail with Sam who had already seen pictures of similar places. She was to go with him to Goa, Shimla and Dalhousie to take a look at other resorts that operated on similar lines. Their planned trips to these locations were a matter she was yet to discuss with Ankur and she knew they would be a sore point given the trouble they were having. They had met last week to try and discuss their problems with a marriage counsellor but Ankur had walked out in a huff midway through the session. She had decided on filing for a divorce.

After getting back from Alibaug on a motorboat, Sameer drove Tania to her family home. He looked at her for a moment and realized that she wasn't the same Tania any more. The girl sitting next to him was worn down by the stress of her crumbling marriage and the pressure society was putting on her. He felt responsible at some level for her misery.

'I've been meaning to talk to you since I got back Tania...' he said, mustering courage.

'Tell me,' she said, signalling to the girl at the traffic signal to bring her a copy of *Home Design*.

'When I look back now, the moments when I have felt truly happy and felt good about myself are moments when you were with me. The moments we spent together—the trips to Alibaug, the night before I left to London, studying together for exams, the evenings we spent at India Tea Centre, Christmas and New Year in Goa, you picking me up from the airport when I landed after eighteen months... how did I leave you alone for eighteen months? I still cannot fathom that. The times I spent with my parents and Rajveer. I neglected all that for a course and a gruelling job to earn more money, to go out there, to rise and achieve. I wanted to maximize my potential and all the corporate fluff that comes with it at the cost of my relationships. During all those highs in college, at work and now with SFA, Mexikhana and this resort, I feel empty. I feel I've lost what's most important to me,' he said with emotion. She turned her gaze to him and saw loss and regret in his eyes.

'It's all right, Sameer! Both of us have made mistakes...'

'No Tania, I made the biggest mistake! I realized how foolish I had been, how shallow my life had become, when I was sitting in a park alone and betrayed after Simone told me about her affair during her Middle East trip. I mean, I trusted her and she cheated on me with someone she just met. Ironically, I doubted you all through our long-distance relationship, which was so wrong. I'm sorry, Tania,' he said, gazing in her eyes which were filled with regret. He pulled up a short distance from her house and she cupped his cheeks in her hands.

'Okay, please stop kicking yourself about it! What happened with us is our fate. You have done many good things in life too. You are a great guy, Sameer, and I have realized that the reason why things never worked with Ankur is because I never stopped loving you...'

If anything, he felt reassured. He knew this, remembering their conversation on Vicky's balcony many months ago. They sat in his car for a while, looking at each other. She put her hand on his cheek and patted it. 'I'll call you later, all right?' He nodded to and said goodbye.

He drove back in a contemplative mood. He wondered about the decisions he had taken and where they had led him. 'What If' by Coldplay played in the background as he drove back to his office. He tried hard to get thoughts of her out of his head. It was a futile exercise, trying to ease her out of his life. She had been too much a part of him and what he wanted in life, for him to let go of.

A while later, she called Sameer and said she could not make it with him on the work trip up north as there were issues she had to sort out in Mumbai. She said she would work with the pictures he brought her. She needed time and space to figure out where her life was headed, having decided to divorce Ankur. She didn't want to rush into something and face problems.

~

31
Nostalgia

'Today is the tomorrow we were so concerned about yesterday.'
—CARLOS MARTINEZ VAZQUEZ

20 APRIL 2009
Tania's home, Cuffe Parade and India Tea Centre, near Churchgate Station, Mumbai

Tania had just returned from Hong Kong with her parents where she had been for the past three months to get away from all that had happened around her. She had left a few days after her divorce papers had been filed. While she had been away, Sameer had kept himself extremely busy at work. They had opened their first Mexikhana restaurant in Bandra to much fanfare and had got a huge response. People had thronged to the place and it was impossible to book tables after 8 p.m. on weekends. The newspapers and leading magazines had written positive and encouraging reviews, and a number of celebrities and businessmen made it their favourite haunt. Sameer had sent Tania pictures and articles about the restaurant that lauded her for the contemporary look she had given the place. He was also putting in long hours on the resorts project to complete the Alibaug Sunsets and More Heritage Resort before Vicky's wedding in a couple of months. He had been spending a great deal of his time at work and the free time with the family.

Tanveer had been busy managing his now five-month-old marriage and Vicky spent most of his time outside of work with Sarah, planning their upcoming engagement and wedding. Sarah was on a sabbatical from Indus Air. Six weeks ago she had decided to go back and spend a few weeks with her parents before the wedding. Vicky, who missed her a lot, made his second expedition to Mussoorie and spent four days with her.

Tanveer and Tanaz walked in and greeted Tania with an embrace. Tanveer tried to cheer her up and kept her in splits telling her stories of how Mrs Rustomjee interrupted their love-making all the time by knocking on their door and bringing them knick knacks and sweets to eat.

'Shut up. My mother is only being considerate,' Tanaz said affectionately, to which Tania laughed even more thinking, *this is a lady who would ration him a bucket of hot water each day for his shower till a couple of years ago.*

Naina walked in with a welcome back gift and gave Tania a hug. Tania was happy to see her old friends welcome her back. She had relaxed in the last few months in Hong Kong, spending time with her brother and his family. Her thoughts were homeward bound and she thought about Sameer a lot. She put on a tough exterior to please her parents and make them feel better about the whole situation. Seeing them busy and happy with the grandchildren, she readily agreed to extend their stay in Hong Kong for a few more days.

They decided to go over to India Tea Centre like the old times. On the way to the Tea Centre she talked to them about the days after she had filed for divorce and how she had felt uneasy about the relationship in the early days of their marriage. She said she possibly never had feelings for Ankur. She had gone ahead as society had expected her to get married and settle down. She regretted having ended her relationship with Sameer.

'You did what you thought was best in those circumstances. I wish you were together today, but at that point of time there was no guarantee that he was moving back,' Tanaz said, to which Tanveer nodded along in agreement as they parked outside the Tea Centre and walked in.

'Where is Sameer these days? He used to drop a line now and then saying he is busy with the restaurant and getting the resort operational for Vicky's wedding. I hear Vicky and he have been working till 2 or 3 a.m.!' she said with surprise.

'You're better informed than I am! I don't get permission to see my friends so much now that I am married,' he said jokingly, looking at Tanaz.

'Sshhh, I'm not that bad! Yes, these guys have been working overtime for the past few months. You included, mister. Start coming home on time,' she chided Tanveer, at which Tania laughed.

Vicky and Sarah walked in and were delighted to see Tania back in town. Vicky excitedly told to her about their trip to Mussoorie. He said their wedding in Alibaug, eight weeks later, was to be a two-day event. They were having a small Punjabi wedding followed by one in the Muslim tradition. The soon-to-be-wed couple was excited, each busy with their trousseau shopping.

'Yeah, you guys please help her out with the wedding shopping. For the honeymoon shopping, I'll be there with her 100 per cent,' Vicky said to the girls. 'Why that irritated look? Come on, you know how swamped I am with work. I have loads to get done before we leave for the honeymoon.'

Naina spoke about a wedding she had attended a couple of days ago—of Shania Singh, who was a few years junior to them in college. Vicky in a reflective tone said, 'Shania, the name rings a bell. Oh yes, I remember now,' and broke into a laugh, giving

Tanveer a slap on his back. Tanveer almost spit out the coffee he had just sipped. Sarah, eager to know what the connection was, said, 'Tell me, it sounds like a funny story.'

'Yes, tell us. Seems like my man has something to do with it too,' Tanaz said with a glitter in her eye while Tania smiled along, shaking her head.

Vicky egged Tanveer on, 'At the end of the day it is about you, brother. Let's hear it from the horse's mouth.'

Looking uncomfortably at the women who grinned at him in anticipation, Tanveer began, 'Well uh, her papaji came to college one day, a big bulky guy—Hanspreet Singh—and pulled me out of the canteen for a chat. "Oye! Tu Tanveer hai?" he asked me in a gruff voice to which I nodded. "Oye, if I see you jumping out of my daughter's balcony again, I will bury you alive in my warehouse," he warned me with a grimace and added, "My daughter is from a traditional, cultured and value-driven family and I do not want her mixing with you." I had half a mind to tell him, "Papaji, Shania is dating no less than two or three guys at the same time." She was the female equivalent of Vicky in college. Seeing his size, I nodded to everything he said, apologized profusely and walked away. I hadn't spoken to his daughter in my life, leave alone jump from her balcony.'

He looked baffled and smiled while the rest of them laughed. As the realization dawned on him, he looked at Vicky and added, 'I am sure it was you who set that up. You were dating her before the burly Sardarji caught my collar and took me outside the canteen. You probably told Shania to tell him my name as he hadn't seen your face when you jumped out.' The girls laughed, while Vicky tried to control his laughter.

'Sorry, dude! I had to save my skin. If he had known it was me, he would have gone straight to my dad.' He shifted his gaze to Tanaz who was trying to stop laughing. 'It was a hilarious scene when Shania came in to the canteen to explain the whole issue to him. Tanveer watched her smile and walk up to him turned around and ran out from the kitchen entrance.'

'That was mean, Vicky! Poor Tanveer was petrified,' Tania said with mock anger and then smiled at Tanaz.

Running his fingers through his hair, Tanveer interrupted, 'Yaar, my wife thinks I am a clown. Keep a lid on it.'

Winking at Naina and Tania, Vicky said, 'Come on, dude, Tanveer. After such a long time man! That incident helped you too. No one in college had heard about you till you became known for jumping out of Shania's building. All the geeks and nerds in college made him their hero. Okay, just one more of your stories. Tell them about your trip to the thana to meet the cops.'

Tanveer nodded, smiling, looked at Tanaz and started animatedly, 'On this one, I did not speak to Vicky for a week. Sam and he got drunk at Leopold's on his birthday after which we went over to his place. He called Suman Sharma, the ex-Miss World, claiming to be leading actor Sahil Khan. He had found the number in his mother's diary. Sameer kept telling him not to do it but he refused to listen. He even got me to imitate Sahil Khan, hamming in style with lines from *Don Ban Gaya Gentleman* and *Fauji Hoon Na*. The actress got his mobile number on her phone and she gave it to the police the next day.'

'Boy oh boy, you didn't! What was wrong with you?' Sarah asked.

'Sshhh, listen to Tanveer. This is where the fun starts,' he said with a smirk.

'Vicky was invited to the police station by Inspector Shinde. He told the cops it was me who had called her from his phone and that I had gone to Sholapur for the holidays. He then used his connections and walked free, with the inspector requesting him to send me in when I returned. I went in there after a week. I was very scared. "Come, aaiye sir, arey Pandey bring a chair for Sahil Khan. How are you, sir? Shooting kaise chal rahi hai? Will you sign an autograph for my son?" he asked, looking half-amused, with a wicked grin. "Mazak kar rahe hain sir! There must be a mistake…" I said smiling at him uncomfortably, looking at the other policemen standing around me. "Mazak? Main? Pandey, am I joking?" he asked, at which the constable shook his head. "Sir…" I said, but he cut me off. "Chup, Saala Sholapur ka Sahil Khan!" He pushed his chair and came towards me, looking outraged. I had to listen to a lecture from Shinde on moral values and respecting women and was warned not to call and disturb any models or actresses.'

Looking at Sarah, who stared at him with her mouth open, he continued, 'He asked my father's name and where he worked and then told me, "Your father is a retired LIC officer and his son gets drunk and calls women to trouble them at night. You crazy young fellow! You will get into a lot of trouble.' I told him it was not me but another friend who did this but he did not want to listen and said, "Aye bas kya. Chup rehne ka! Don't lie or else you will be behind bars over the weekend. Last warning hai. Chal kat le abhi!"'

The women were in splits listening to Tanveer imitate the inspector. Sarah laughed and punched Vicky on his arm, saying, 'You guys are horrible.'

Looking at Tanaz who was coughing after laughing too much Vicky said, 'Arey, nothing happened to him. I had paid off the inspector, told him about my connections. His eyes popped out seeing a few bills with Mahatma Gandhi on them and he let me go. I told him to take it easy with Tanveer and let him go with a warning. The funny part was Tanveer freaking out for a week thinking they would go to the Principal's office or call his parents in Sholapur. We scared him a couple of times telling him there were constables standing around outside college. Sam once told him the Principal was looking for him because of which he skipped college for a couple of days.'

The girls laughed with a crackle, with Tania coming to Tanveer's defence, 'It is funny, but anyone would be scared.'

Vicky stretched out, slapping Tanveer's back while Sameer walked in, greeting and hugging each of the beautiful women. Vicky turned to Sam and said, 'Tanveer was telling them about getting drunk and calling Suman Sharma.' Both of them laughed and gave each other a high five.

'Stop, my tummy is hurting from laughing so much,' Sarah said and Tanaz pulled Tanveer's cheek and affectionately said, 'I'm married to a stand-up comedian.'

Sameer brought a chair from the next table and sat next to Tania, remembering that he had last come here with her over six years ago. He gazed at her, noticing she looked cheerful and at peace compared to the days before she left. He interrupted, 'Well, Tanveer has indirectly gotten back at Vicky. Remember SY BMS?' he asked, looking at Tania and starting his own story while everyone looked at him with interest.

While Vicky covered his face with a tissue, he explained, 'Now Tanveer was a big fan of Vicky—he was in awe of what he wore, what he ate, how he spoke, the women he dated. Back then, his one wish in life was to be like him. He often would go around building brand Vicky in college, telling everyone how stylish and sophisticated he was. Once it went too far. He sat with these three girls for chai and samosas and told them Vicky was a 10/10, admiring his physique, his eyes, charm, good looks and so on. From that day on, Tania and me would get asked if Vicky and Tanveer were gay, as it was always Tania and I and these two supposed lovers who were together. We told them we didn't know, but they were pretty close.'

Tania and Sameer looked at each other and laughed. The girls joined in too, while Tanveer grinned, shaking his head. Vicky nodded, looking at Tanveer who smiled sheepishly.

'You had to go overboard, right? For the next one month I got hit on by guys in college. Sunny, who is a fashion designer now, used to ask me to come over and study together. That Mohit asked me to come and do yoga with him and the girls would ask me hesitatingly on the first date, "You're not gay, right?" It was really weird. Thanks Tanveer!' Sarah laughed with tears in her eyes and the rest joined in.

'Yeah, some friends told me of those rumours too. They would say, "You're dating him? Is he straight?" and I would be like, "No baba, he's quite normal",' Naina added.

Sameer shifted his gaze from Naina to Sarah, 'Yeah, Vicky was a gay icon. I told a couple of guys he was a part of a society called "Breathe". Many women avoided him for a while thinking he was dating them just to create a façade. This Antara you were seeing then dumped you, right?'

Tania added, 'Your dad asked you too, right Vicky? He questioned you about your preferences and about "Breathe". One of his associate's daughters had told her dad who had passed on the good news.'

Shaking his head and laughing a little, Vicky said, 'Very funny, guys. My mum got a lot of pujas done. My dad, who hardly spoke to me then, left a stack of his old collection of *Playboy* on my table—half of which Tanveer borrowed and never returned. I had to stop bringing Tanveer home. Dad thought he was my partner or something. I dated two to three flavours in a week and even took one home to my room while my parents were around. My dad sat and had Scotch with me for the first time, proud of my alleged turnaround in preferences.' Everyone was in splits after this.

'Dude, the inappropriate things you used to do during those early days in college! You were really crazy, man,' Vicky said and added, 'He walked up to this girl Vidhi who I dated briefly. Now she was someone he didn't know personally. He told her, "I know you very well. I've heard a lot about you. Did you have fun with Vicky last night?" That resulted in her throwing a book at me and calling me an insensitive jerk for discussing what I did on a date with her with Mr Tanveer.'

'Thanks, Tanveer,' Sarah and Naina said in chorus and gave each other a knowing smile, which made Vicky shake his head.

'I remember in the first month of college when Sam and I started dating… he would keep giving us these thumbs up signs with a big smirk, which would make me feel very odd. I had to tell Sameer to request him not to do that,' Tania said, turning her gaze from Sarah to Sameer and smiling at him with warmth.

'It was quite a picture in class, the two of you sitting at the desk in front of us and writing notes to each other all the time, while I paid attention to lectures and Vicky slept soundly all day… that is, if he was not thrown out for sleeping or imitating one of the lecturers,' Tanveer said, feeling nostalgic.

'Yes dude, you were nuts! All your assignments were done by Tanveer. You would just sit there and keep texting women,' Tania added before giving him a whack on his arm.

'He would come and sit in my class half the time. It was weird and it made me very conscious. A guy two years senior in our class, sitting next to me and not letting me focus on what's going on! Even after these people passed out, he would just walk in and sit next to me. The lecturers thought he had flunked or something,' Naina said, looking at Sarah.

'You never had the guts to do that for me,' Tanaz said to Tanveer, feigning disappointment.

'You went to an all-girls college, yaar!' Tanveer replied

defensively, to which Sameer and Vicky laughed. He added, 'Besides, I was working when we met and started getting to know each other.'

Sam cleared his throat and said, 'Man, I miss those college days. We didn't have a care in the world and it was so much fun. I remember being so gutted and depressed when I moved to Oxford. Let's meet like this more often. Life gets crazy with work, traffic… it's chaos, guys!'

'Yeah, it was like the best time of my life!' Tania said ecstatically, turning her gaze from Vicky to Tanveer then Naina, to finally rest on Sameer.

'Yes, I miss those afternoon power naps,' Vicky said with a chuckle and continued, 'You take a break, after my wedding, man. Go up to the mountains or something.'

Tania agreed with a smile, 'You're right, take a break Sam. Go slow on work for a couple of weeks. What are everyone's dinner plans? I feel like having paani puri, in fact I am craving for it.'

'I feel like going to Jazz and Blues. It's karaoke night today,' Sameer said, looking at the rest of them.

Vicky and Sarah had to leave as they had been invited by one of Mr Khanna's closest friends for a dinner party to celebrate their upcoming wedding. Vicky hated these parties but Sarah had convinced him to go to please his parents. Naina decided to leave too as she had a colleague's birthday to make an appearance at with Nitin. Tanveer and Tanaz wanted to go but explained that Mrs Rustomjee was waiting for them at home.

'Let's go, Tania. I'll take you for paani puri followed by Jazz and Blues. Should be fun,' Sam said to her in high spirits.

Tania nodded coyly and giggled, remembering something and looked in the direction of Tanaz who was getting up to leave, 'It's fun seeing him go red and sweat a lot when eating paani puri. It gets too spicy for him.'

'Yeah yeah, let's go,' he said cheerfully, taking her hand and walking out of the Tea Centre along with the others. Tania called her mother, telling her that she was heading out for dinner with Sameer. Her mother smiled at the other end. It felt nice to hear Tania sound cheerful.

The girls talked about shopping for Vicky and Sarah's engagement with the soft breeze from the Arabian Sea blowing through their hair, while they waited for the guys who were pulling their cars out of the parking lot.

Vicky and Sarah were the first to leave from the Tea Centre. He drove towards the hotel the reception party was at and turned to look at Sarah with a smile. He remembered how the last six years had been since finishing college. He had found love in college only to lose it a few years later. He realized how special Sarah was and felt optimistic about their future as she gazed at him with her dreamy eyes and said, 'I wish I met you in college itself. Imagine being together through all those fun years.'

'I don't,' he said and added, 'I'm glad I met you after I grew up,' to which both of them smiled.

Tanveer and Tanaz drove home, remembering how they would meet for a cup of tea or coffee after Tanveer's day at work and go back home separately. 'Pretending not to know each other at home was really difficult,' Tanaz said, ruffling his hair as he waited for a signal to turn green. 'That's life. It's ironic sometimes, the way things pan out eventually. Who would have thought when we first met that we would get married and stay together in the same place I moved into as a PG! Those first few months I had no hope of you going out with me…'

'Yes, it has been a roller coaster ride for us! Well, I had no hope after we broke up. I thought this is it. But it's great the way things turned out,' she said jovially.

He smiled at her, feeling grateful for his good fate but also knew that there would be other challenges to face in life as well and hoped that both of them could stay happy together come what may. He realized he had come a long way—from being a Sholapur boy who made inappropriate jokes, to Tanaz's husband with a successful career. He hoped to keep her smiling as much as possible.

Meanwhile, at Marine Drive, Sam asked the paani puri vendor to make it extra spicy to lighten things up for Tania who stopped him from eating it and said, 'Stop doing that, Sam. It doesn't agree with you, you'll fall sick!'

A cool breeze blew over by the promenade where they stood watching the rough sea crash against the rocks. They spent a few quiet moments gazing at the crescent moon and the stars, thanks to the clear skies, before they left for Jazz and Blues. Sameer and Tania enjoyed a nice long drive after a couple of hours at Jazz and Blues where he sang 'Baby can I hold you…' for her. Tania looked at him with warmth when he dropped her outside her door and walked her to her porch. They both sat there for a while talking about the years gone by and the years they spent apart. They remembered the time spent in Goa and the night before he first left for London for his MBA.

'So, am I going to see you at the restaurant on Saturday?' he asked while getting up to leave. He was organizing a dinner for the group at Mexikhana.

'I'll definitely be there,' she said. He turned around and looked at her intently. 'Why don't you pick me up on Saturday? We could go together,' she continued.

'Yeah, sure I will. Goodnight, Tania,' he said with a tired smile and leaned in to give her a hug.

She sent him a text message a while later. He saw it before he went to sleep and felt the hope of a better tomorrow. He lay back in bed looking at her message. 'Thanks, tonight felt like the old times! The fresh air really helped… see you soon. Goodnight and hugs,' it read.

Thank You

'A person is a success if he gets up in the morning and gets to bed at night and in between does what he wants to do.'

—BOB DYLAN

This novel would not have been possible without the love and support of a number of people who have stood by me through different phases of my life. Thanks to Mum and Nanima for your unconditional love, blessings and support every single day.

Thanks to my wife, Minaz, for your support, encouragement and patience throughout this endeavour.

Thank you, Rikin Khamar, for sharing your publishing experiences, inspiring me and giving me sound advice on getting the book out to its readers. The final result wouldn't be as good without your support.

Thanks to Ali, my uncles, aunts, cousins, nephews and nieces. It's a blessing to have a family so well knit and supportive.

Thank you Mayur Motwani, Vikram Mirchandani and Saugata Sen—my first readers—for your friendship, your faith in my abilities and for pushing me towards finishing the book. The brainstorming after the first draft really helped.

Thanks Manoj, Manish, Asher, Ms Meera Seth, Sapna, Nikhil, Varun, Shweta and Pranav, Nibha, Pratibha, Nazia, Ashwin, Dhiren, Deepa, Anisha, Naveen, Mr Maru, Dr Peyvand Khaleghian and

Seema for your friendship, through good times and challenging ones.

Thank you to my friends, colleagues and mentors through school, college and at work, now and in the past—I've learned more about life through the experiences we have shared.

Thank you, Mr Ruskin Bond and Mr Gregory David Roberts for the words of encouragement. It was an honour to meet you. I hope you enjoy reading this book. Thanks to Omair Ahmed and Karan Bajaj, my talented and successful contemporaries, for their support and for sharing their experiences. A portion of my royalties from the sale of this book will be allocated to support www.cpaaindia.org (Cancer Patients Aid Association India).

I request you to please consider supporting the above organization in its various projects and initiatives. It supports the less privileged and its efforts bring social equity and justice, and aids sustainable human development.

Live your dreams and make your life a wonderful journey.

Good luck and God bless!

—AHMED FAIYAZ